FIGHTING KUDZU

TABLE OF CONTENTS

Prologue

The game was on the line. The entire season, the championship was on the line. For that matter, my career was right there on the line. All of these things depended on this one play. The remaining three seconds of the game would decide it all. My heart stopped briefly as Bob called my name in the huddle. "Thorvald, get open in the end zone. This one's yours."

The roar of the crowd echoed inside my head as I lined up at wide out. I knew all eyes were on me. I had spent the whole season proving myself. First female player in the NFL. Now I was playing in the Super Bowl with only the second team in history to have an undefeated season. They were watching me, all right.

I wiped my sweaty palms on my pants. Across from me was the Viking cornerback who had covered me closely all day, practically shutting me down. He sneered at me and mouthed something ugly.

I saw movement out of the corner of my eye as the ball was snapped. I set off in my pass route. Viking number 26 was covering me more closely than the plastic covered my grandmother's living-room sofa.

Then I gave old number 26 what Daddy always called "the juke." I faked a cut toward the sideline and left that Viking in the dust. Within a split second I was wide open at the end zone. Suddenly I could taste victory and super-stardom.

I raised my left hand toward the sky so Bob would not miss my wide-openness. He pump-faked right, then looked me dead in the eyes from downfield. He saw me. He pumped toward me, releasing the ball, leather rolling off the tips of his fingers. The ball spiraled perfectly in my direction. My feet left the ground, my hands creating a perfect basket in front of my numbers for the ball. I was watching the spiral right into my hands—soft hands, had to keep soft hands so the ball would stay in them.

Just as the ball was entering my basket, I heard Mama's voice. "Noble! Noble, what on earth have you been up to?"

Her voice distracted me momentarily and I lost all concentration. The ball slipped past my soft fingertips and conked me right in the head. It bounced straight up. Up high. Up for grabs. I looked up at it, ready to pull it into me as it came back down. This situation could still be salvaged.

As the ball came back to earth, my entire field of vision was blurred with purple and yellow. The colors of Vikings. Before the ball could touch my soft hands, a purple, yellow-horned helmet was spearing me in the right side.

I flew backward, landing solidly against the ground on my back. My lungs emptied of all air. I gasped for breath as the leather object I'd risked my life for rolled past my head and into the end zone all by its lonesome. Incomplete pass. Game over. I lose.

The cheers and jeers of the crowd reverberated inside my helmet. I looked through my orange facemask at a blue sky dotted with puffy white clouds.

"Noble, you get in here this minute and explain to me what you've done with my eye liner." Mama again. Eye liner? What was she talking about? "Noble Lee, I mean now!"

Oh. It had just occurred to me. I stuck my fingers under the facemask and wiped at the black semicircles painted under my eyes. My fingers came back smeared with black grease. That must have been eyeliner.

"Noble Lee Thorvald!" I'd run out of names for her to add on.

That meant it was time to face the music.

I got up and trotted off the field toward my back door. The purple and yellow players faded first. My team stuck around a little longer. They surrounded me with our orange and aquamarine. I felt a pat on my butt, then looked into the eyes of Larry Csonka. "You're getting there, Thorvald. Next time. Don't sweat it." Then, Larry and the rest of my Dolphins faded, too, as the back door slammed behind me.

Chapter 1
Spring 1973

I'd turned five in December and was now enjoying my final months of freedom before the onset of endless years of schooling. I'd spent these early, formative years in an average blue-collar, middle-class household. In the early seventies, most of America was doing the same. It was the age of the middle-class suburban family, and mine fit the mold perfectly.

We were living the American Dream in a quiet suburb of Atlanta. The house was a brick three-bedroom ranch-style house on a very large corner lot. The neighborhood was an active one, children on bicycles, women tending flower gardens, men mowing lawns. We knew all of our neighbors, and everyone was very friendly.

My family, too, seemed to fit the description of the ideal. We had both a mom *and* a dad, which was becoming less and less common. Dave and Mel Thorvald were my parents. My mom's real name was Melanie, but people called her Mel for short. I always thought it was really neat that she was a girl with a boy's name. When we told people our parents were Dave and Mel, they thought we had two dads. We always found that amusing.

There were three of us kids. First, there was my sister Rachel, who was five years older than me. We sometimes just called her Rache. Next, a year younger than Rachel, was my brother Chad. And of course there was me, Noble Lee Thorvald. I go by Noble.

We're all named after someone. My parents apparently lacked the creativity to think up brand new names, so they just recycled old ones. Rache got a name from each of my grandmothers. Chad got his first name from my dad's father. It was my opinion that I got the best name of all. My first name came from my great-grandmother, Noble Clarice Maclachlan. Now *that* was a very cool name. My middle name came from my mom's father. People always asked about my name because it was so unusual. I didn't mind. I was real proud to have that name.

My grandmother, who we all called Mamateen, once told me all about my name. Noble Clarice Maclachlan was her mother. According to Mamateen, she was a very fine woman, a real hard worker who raised a whole bunch of real good children. Her parents had named her Noble because they knew right away that she would do good things. According to Mamateen, noble means proud and upstanding. To be noble is to believe in good, and to do the right thing and never be ashamed. She'd said it was a name that I should be real pleased to have. She'd said it carried a lot of responsibility, because noble was a hard thing to be. She'd said she believed that I was up to the challenge.

Now this was the spring before I was to start school. Rachel was already in fourth grade, and Chad was in third. So, counting kindergarten, I'd spent the last four years at home alone all day with Mama. We usually had a pretty nice time together during the day, and sometimes we'd joke about hating to see Rachel and Chad get off the bus, coming home to spoil our perfect day.

These were the years when Mama dispensed to me all of her wisdom. She thoroughly enjoyed philosophizing for my benefit. She opened my young eyes to the ways of the world. I don't think she really meant to do that. I think she just liked to hear herself talk. I never thought that she believed that I was listening. Well, I was listening all right, and she was scaring me half to death.

***

Today was a day on which Mama decided that I needed a life lesson. We were working in one of her flowerbeds. She wore her floppy straw hat and a pair of sunglasses with lenses so big they covered half her face. In fact, the top of her sunglasses touched the brim of her hat. While she was busy weeding, I sat on the ground outside of the flowerbed boring a deep hole into the ground with a stick.

Mama had been talking on and on about her flowers and I wasn't paying much attention. Suddenly she stopped talking and fell from her kneeling position back onto her rear end. She let out a deep sigh and said, "Let's take a cigarette break. Shall we?"

"I don't smoke," I answered.

She removed her gardening gloves. "Well then, you'll just take a plain old break. How 'bout that?" She threw her gloves onto the ground and tilted her head as she smiled at me.

"Okay."

"Good, then." She took her cigarettes and lighter from her shirt pocket. Her long, slender fingers held the cigarette to her mouth as she lit it. She blew out the first puff of smoke with a sigh. As she replaced her cigarettes in her shirt pocket she said, "You know, we're getting close to the end here." I could tell that beneath her sunglasses she was raising her eyebrows at me.

"End of what?" I asked, not sure what to say.

"The end of this." She made a sweeping gesture with both hands, indicating everything around us. "The end of us and our time together." She paused. "You'll be off to school before you know it." She took a long drag off her cigarette. She released the smoke. "What do you think about that?"

I didn't know how to answer her. I loved spending my days with her, having her all to myself, but I was also looking forward to going to school. I stared at the dirt, making swirlies in it with my stick, and I remained quiet.

After a few moments I looked up at her. She was studying me as if horns had just sprouted from my ears. I smiled at her and then looked back toward the ground.

"What if we could find a way to keep you from ever growing up? What if you could stay my same little cuddly Pooh Bear forever and ever? Wouldn't that be great?"

She paused briefly. Thank goodness I didn't have time to respond. "Let's see . . . what could we possibly do to make that happen? Hmmm." She appeared to be in deep thought. I was getting scared and thought I *had* to do something before she said something crazy.

I said softly, "Maybe I would like to grow up."

Her jaw dropped open in mock terror. "You can't possibly be serious. Why in the world would you *want* to grow up? Why would you *want* to give up your beautiful innocence?" She appeared to be disappointed as she shook her head at me. She stopped shaking her head and looked down her nose at me. She pulled her sunglasses down so she could see over them. "You do *know* what innocence is, don't you?"

I struggled. I vaguely remembered something from a TV program. Daddy had let me stay up with him one night watching this show about a guy in a wheelchair. He was a policeman or something like that. I learned that if you were innocent, you didn't go to jail. With this as my only reference, I attempted to answer her. "It's when you didn't do the bad thing that the police think you did."

She threw her head back and laughed a short but loud laugh. Still smiling, she tilted her head toward me and said, "Well, that's a start." She stretched her long legs out in front of her, careful not to damage her flowers. She ground her cigarette butt in the dirt and then threw it into the hedges by the front porch.

Leaning back on her hands she said, "Let me explain innocence to you."

I looked directly at her, nodding my head but rolling my eyes at the same time. I filled one cheek with air and then released it with a "pffft" sound. I was trying desperately to let her know that I was not interested in hearing about innocence. She obviously didn't get the message.

"You see, dear, you're thinking of innocence in a very specific way. Sure, if someone didn't commit a crime, or do a bad thing, for which he is being accused, then that person is innocent of that specific bad thing. So, he didn't have anything to do with that *one* bad thing. The innocence I'm talking about is the *general* innocence people are born with. You're born innocent because you haven't had anything to do with *anything* that's bad. As you grow up, and you're exposed to bad things, you lose your innocence." She leaned forward. "You see?"

Now I was interested because I was confused. I hesitated, then responded. "But I *have* been exposed to bad things."

She took off her glasses and raised her eyebrows in a curious way. "Such as?"

"Well, Chad."

"Chad?"

"Yeah. Like how he won't share the Legos. He calls me names and tries to kiss me when he knows I hate that." I stopped to search for another example. "He locks me outta the basement when he's in there." I pointed toward the house for emphasis.

She smiled and shook her head. Replacing her glasses she said, "Lord, Lord, child. You don't even know the meaning of 'bad things'. See what I mean? You are *definitely* innocent. Only way to

17

hold onto that is to stay young."

I looked back down at the ground in frustration. Now we were back where we started.

The flowerbed was bordered by red bricks lined up in a row at an angle and buried halfway into the ground. Mama struggled with one of the bricks, digging around its edges and wiggling it back and forth loosening it from the dirt. She finally pulled it from the ground. "You see this brick?"

"Yes?" I said it as if it were a question.

"This brick is our solution. This brick is going to keep you young." She smiled proudly.

Terrified to ask, but driven by my curiosity, I had to. "How?"

"We'll put this brick on your head. You'll keep it on your head all the time. At least until you've past your growth spurt. The weight of the brick on your head will keep you from growing. Forever young, forever innocent!" She raised her hands to the sky triumphantly. "Now, come on over here and let's get this thing on that head of yours."

I stared at her, waiting for the laughter followed by the "Just joking." It never came. Surely she wasn't serious about me wearing this brick until I passed my spurt.

"What's the hold up? Come on. The sooner we start, the easier it will be." She motioned for me to move in her direction with her hand.

Slowly, I crawled on all fours toward her. When I reached her, I sat back on my heels.

"Here we go." She carefully held the brick on top of my head. "Sit up straight and hold still. It won't be easy, but just keep thinking of eternal innocence." She slowly removed her hands from the brick and it teetered on top of my head. "That's it! You got it!" She smiled proudly.

I could feel some dirt from the brick grinding into the top of my head. I felt the brick sliding to one side. I closed my eyes tight. I didn't want to look at Mama. I was suddenly very hot, and my stomach felt queasy. I hated this brick. I couldn't do it. I didn't want to do it.

Without warning, I burst into tears. With my body shuddering from the crying, the brick fell from my head and landed on my finger. I screamed, "Ouch!"

Once I opened my mouth I couldn't stop the words from flowing. Through my tears I continued to scream. "Please don't make me wear that brick. It hurts and it's hard to hold it there. I don't want to stay little. I want to grow up. And who cares about innocence? It's stupid. Innocence is stupid. I don't need it!" I stopped to take a breath. A little calmer now, I quietly repeated, "I just don't need it."

I didn't want to look at her, so I stared at my pinky, which had just been squashed by the brick. It seemed like forever and she didn't say anything. Finally I looked up at her. She'd removed her glasses and hat. She smiled at me—a real motherly smile. "Are you okay?"

"I broke my pinky."

"Let me see that." She reached for my injured hand. She massaged the pinky. "I think you're gonna live." She held my hand tightly. "Honey, I am soooo sorry. I was only playing around. I didn't mean to hurt you. I thought you knew it was a joke. That silly ol' brick can't keep you from growing. Nothing can."

She let go of my hand and reached over to wipe tears from my cheeks. "Whether we like it or not, you'll grow up. The clock keeps ticking, things keep changing, and life keeps coming at you full speed ahead. No brick'll change that. I can't stop you from growing up, but hopefully I can get you ready for it. The best I can tell you is to get your armor ready, because life is on its way."

She rubbed me on the top of the head and stood slowly,

holding her back as she did. "Come on. Let's blow this pop stand. We need a change of scenery. How about some Kool-Aid?"

"Okay." I followed her inside, still unsure of exactly what had just happened.

After we had a glass of purple Kool-Aid, Mama wanted me to go back out to the garden with her. I told her that I had some other things I wanted to do. Without questioning me, she said that'd be all right. She told me she'd be in the front yard if I needed her. She apologized to me again and then walked out the door as she donned her straw hat and glasses.

Once she was out the door, I went back into my bedroom. I shared a room with Rachel. Because I was the youngest, I had no say in the décor. The curtains and bedspreads matched one another with a floral print of huge red and purple flowers. The walls were decorated with random black-light posters and pictures torn from the pages of *Teen Beat* magazine. Rachel was ten years old, but looked and acted like a teenager already. Mama said she was mature for her age. She was taller and had bigger boobs than any of her friends. She had to start wearing a training bra in the third grade. She'd decided that this was just fine with her. Not me! While I did want to grow up without that brick, I also knew that I didn't want to be mature for my age.

Rachel hated sharing a room with me and would not let me put any posters on the walls. I did have one poster. It was a poster of the dolphin that's the emblem for the Miami Dolphins. That little smiling dolphin wearing a Miami football helmet. My dad got the poster for me, but Rachel had said no dice—no stupid football stuff in *her* room. So I had to hang my poster on the inside of my closet door. I only got to look at it when my closet was open. Rachel made sure that wasn't very often.

I opened my closet and stared at the poster. I was the number-one fan of the Dolphins. They'd always been my favorite team. It was mostly because of their colors, but this year had been an especially good year for the Dolphins. They'd been undefeated and won the Super Bowl. Daddy and I watched football together every Sunday. I always looked forward to football season, and couldn't wait until I was old enough to play on a real team. I hadn't ever told anyone, but I planned to be the first female Miami Dolphin when I grew up. I was already practicing.

In a box in the floor of my closet was my most prized possession. I generally only got it out during football season, but today I really felt as if I needed it. I slid the box across the floor out of the closet. I removed its contents.

The miniature Dolphins uniform was as small as they came, but it was still a little big for me. It had been a football season present for me at the beginning of the '72 season. For the past two years my dad had gotten me a present for the first game. Football season was our special time together. When it came to birthdays and anniversaries and other special occasions, Daddy wasn't always real thoughtful. But boy was he thoughtful when it came to football season. The poster had been last year's present and the uniform was this year's. Daddy said it would bring good luck. And, as you know from the Dolphin's undefeated season, it worked like a charm.

I took off the shorts and T-shirt I was wearing and began to put on the uniform. It didn't come with pads. It was really just a pair of stretchy white pants with an orange stripe down the legs, and a miniature version of the real jersey. The best part was the helmet. It was a real helmet. It only had one bar for a facemask, like a kicker, but it was still a real helmet. I wished that the jersey had number "39" on it. That was Larry Csonka's number and he was the greatest. My jersey had number "1" on it. I saw these same uniforms in the Sears' catalog, and "1" was the only available number. So I didn't really have a choice, but "39" would have been

21

much better.

All decked out in my Dolphins gear, I took my football and went to the backyard. I went through the backdoor so Mama wouldn't see me. Once in the yard, I took the helmet off and placed it on the ground. I knelt down beside it with my hand on top of it, football-style.

"Okay, guys—what's our next move?" Even though I was alone, I was talking to all the players, but only I could see them. I know—strange. But it had been happening ever since Daddy gave me the uniform. As soon as I put it on, all the *real* Miami Dolphins appeared to help me out with different things. Usually they just helped me with football practice, but they'd really do anything I wanted. It was pretty neat. The only person who knew about this was Daddy. He didn't make fun of me. He was actually pretty proud. He said most people's kids have an imaginary friend, but his kid has an imaginary football team. I didn't like his use of the term "imaginary," because these were *real* people. I didn't mention that to him, though. I figured as long as he was proud I didn't want to rock the boat.

Bob Griese was the first to respond to my question. He was, after all, the team leader. "I get the feeling we're not talking about football. Am I right, Noble?"

"Yeah, that's right, Bob. It's really about life. I'm worried about what Mama just told me. She says I need armor and to get ready for life coming at me full speed ahead."

Jim Kiick was the next to speak. "Well Noble, do you know what armor is?"

I thought about it. Once I had compiled what I thought was a legitimate answer, I shared it. "Armor is a suit you wear so you don't get hurt."

Larry spoke next. "What's that you're wearing?"

"Football uniform."

"What's it for?" he continued.

"To look like the rest of your team."

"What else? What about that helmet?"

I stared at the helmet searching for the right answer. I didn't want to look stupid in front of the greatest football team in the world. I suddenly got his meaning. With great joy I shouted, "It's to keep me from getting hurt! It's like armor!"

In unison they all belted out, "BINGO!"

"Thanks guys. You've been a big help."

Thank goodness—finally everything made sense. Maybe Mama somehow knew that I was going to grow up and be a football player and she was just worried. That whole crazy thing with the brick was just her way of telling me to wear my helmet. I had to protect myself from life. It just seemed like a real round-a-bout way of telling me that. Oh well, Mama wasn't always easy to understand.

I spent the rest of the afternoon in the backyard playing football with the guys. It was a little hot for football. My head was sweating so badly inside the helmet that I felt like I had dunked my head in the creek. Droplets of water were sliding down my forehead and the back of my neck. It wasn't too bad, though. The dripping sweat felt pretty good. It felt like ghost fingers tickling my face and neck. Besides, I had to be prepared to wear my armor. I never heard Larry Csonka complain about having a sweaty head.

Rachel and Chad came home from school at the usual time. I hardly noticed until Chad stuck his head out the backdoor long enough to ask, "Whatcha doin', doofus?" Then he shoved an entire Oreo cookie into his mouth.

I gave him my well-honed look of annoyance and responded, "You're the doofus, and I'm playing football."

With his mouth full of chewed-up Oreo, he calmly replied, "No . . . *you're* the doofus, because you can't play football alone."

He bared his black cookie teeth. "Weirdo!" With that he went back into the house, letting the screen door slam behind him.

He always got the last word. It used to bother me, but I'd come to understand that part of being the youngest meant never getting the last word. Except of course when there was an adult around. Then the "baby" always got the last word. That was one of the few perks of being the "baby."

I continued to play alone for another couple of hours. Sometimes I practiced football and sometimes I just sat and rested and talked technique with the Dolphins. The time went quickly. Soon Mama came to the kitchen window and yelled through the screen, "Pooh Bear, it's time for your Daddy."

"Thanks, Mama," I yelled back as I ran toward the end of the driveway.

Pooh Bear was the nickname my family had plastered me with upon my arrival home from the hospital as a newborn. Chad, apparently already upset because he was getting a new baby sister instead of a litter of puppies, had taken one look at me and said, "She has fur, like Winnie the Pooh." As the story goes, Mama and Daddy thought this was so cute that they decided to call me Pooh Bear. They said I actually did have fur. Daddy said it was more like peach fuzz all over my body. Anyway, I'd gotten used to being called Pooh Bear, but thank God the fur had gone away.

Still wearing the Dolphin uniform, I reached the end of the driveway and plopped myself down on the curb. I did this every day. At the young age of five, I was already a creature of habit, and this was one of my favorite rituals. I would wait here for Daddy's return home from work. When I saw the green Jeep Wagoneer with wood-panel siding turn from the main road onto our neighborhood road, the excitement began to build and I would stand in anxious anticipation. When his car reached our driveway, that was when the real fun began.

I sat patiently, passing the minutes until his arrival. Daddy was a big fan of fifties' rock-and-roll. He said it reminded him of his glory days when he had a duck-tail hairdo and a black T-Bird. He said he used to be a good-looking, rebel troublemaker. I believed him. His stories from back then were all really exciting. I loved to listen to him talk about his glory days

Mama preferred current rock-and-roll. She said she'd rather not be reminded of her glory days. Either way, our house was always filled with some type of fun music. We liked to sing and dance and have fun with music on the radio and records. Funny thing was, none of us were really musical. We didn't play instruments or sing or anything like that, but we still loved music.

Anytime I really just wanted to pass some time, I'd sing a song. So, that's what I was doing now. From underneath my too-large football helmet I belted it out: "You can slander my name all over the place . . . Do anything you wanna do . . . But uh-uh Honey lay offa them shoes . . . Now don't—you step on my blue suede shoes . . ."

At that moment I saw the Wagoneer round the corner. I stood up and bounced up and down—the way kids do when the excitement is more than they can handle. Like a boiling pot whose lid can't contain the steam, and the lid begins to wiggle and rattle. I was like that lid, wiggling and rattling until Daddy would pull up and release my steam.

As he slowly pulled to the curb, his head was already out the window. "Hey, hey, Kiddo. What's with the uniform?"

I stood in the customary position, facing the driver's side window, hands above my head grasping the lip of the open window. As I looked up at my dad, the helmet slipped back on my head giving it a quick unexpected yank backwards. The chinstrap caught before it fell to the ground.

"Mama wants me to wear this for protection."

25

"Protection from what?"

"Protection from life. It's my armor."

"Well all right then." He stuck his fully extended arm through the window. "Jump up." I jumped and pulled up with my arms while Daddy grabbed me around the waist. "I guess for the time being it can protect you from busting your thick noggin on the pavement, in case I accidentally drop you."

Oh my God! It had never occurred to me that he might drop me. This was only supposed to be fun, not dangerous. I had never had to wear armor to do this before. How come all of a sudden everything was so scary?

He held me tight around my middle while I death-gripped his shirt collar. I had never before used the death grip. In light of recent events, I thought it necessary. I just always trusted him to hold me up.

He inched the Wagoneer up the driveway. This was the tradition he and I had been taking part in for about the past six months. We discovered it by accident one day when I met Daddy at the end of the driveway because I was so anxious to share with him the news that our cat, Buttons, had had a litter of kittens behind the couch. After I gave him the message, he just reached out and grabbed me and drove up the driveway with me hanging out the window. It was so much fun that I decided I wanted to do it again everyday from now on. In traditional fashion, he was covering the 50 feet of driveway with me dangling from the window and, despite my newfound fear, I could not help but giggle.

By the time Daddy changed into cool, comfortable clothes, Mama had supper on the table. She called us all to the kitchen. We tried to have a sit down family supper every night, each in our designated chair. We were in our assigned seats looking down at one of Mama's famous suppers. There was fried pork chops. She always kind of burnt the crust on them. We also had mashed potatoes, the kind that come in a box. Having something green at supper was a "mama must." Today's entry in that category was green beans—from a can of course.

To take my first bite of pork chop I was forced to pull my helmet down by the facemask in order to make my mouth accessible. This called for great coordination. Mama watched me struggle with the bite, then she very politely asked, "Don't you think it would be easier to eat if you took off the hat?"

"It's not a *hat,* it's a helmet."

"Either way, why don't you take it off?"

"She said you told her to wear it," Daddy said through a mouthful of potatoes.

Mama pulled her head into her neck the way a turtle pulls into its shell. "I never told you to wear that silly thing." She relaxed and paused in thought. "Did I?"

"Yes you did. You told me I need to wear some armor to protect myself from life. This is my armor."

"Oh, that." Relief covered her face. "That was a figure of speech. I didn't mean you *literally* need armor."

I unsnapped the chinstrap, took the helmet off, and let it drop to the floor. I took my fork and stirred my potatoes. I didn't feel like eating anymore. I was proud that I had figured out what Mama meant, but in reality I hadn't figured out anything.

"Honey, you need to be careful what you say to her." Daddy had apparently noticed my sudden change in mood. "She doesn't even know what a 'figure of speech' is. You have to remember she's only five."

"I know how old she is, Dave. But she *is* very smart for her age. She already understands a lot of things that Rachel and Chad didn't understand at five."

This caught the attention of everyone at the table, and I felt my mood starting to change again, back toward the proud end of the spectrum.

Chad spoke first, "She's not that smart. I mean she didn't even know what a 'figure of speech' is. At least I'm not stupid enough to wear a football helmet around, believing it'll protect me from life."

Mama continued defending my intellect. "You're older than she is Chad. I'm sure by the time she's nine, she'll know a lot more, too."

"She's just a little weirdo."

"I'd say the weirdo in this family is the one who builds people out of his mashed potatoes and green beans." Rachel was usually above taking part in childish name calling, but there was always the exception.

Chad looked at his plate and studied the three small piles of mashed potatoes, each with two green bean legs and two green bean arms. "They're not people, they're robots. Good thing Mama's not claiming you're the smart one." He crossed his eyes and stuck the tip of his tongue out of the corner of his mouth.

"Okay, that's enough. What it boils down to is that we're all weirdoes. We are also all very smart. So there is no contest here. Understood?" We all nodded at our dad. "Furthermore," he continued, "we're all pretty damn good-looking, too." He flashed a huge smile full of perfectly straight white teeth. Everyone, including Mama, laughed with him. The tension was eased, and the rest of dinner went off without a hitch.

Later that same evening, Chad and I were in the basement building a tent city out of bed sheets and window fans. The way it worked was, you took the sheets and tied them together. Then you weighted them down around the edges with things like flowerpots and encyclopedias. When that was done, you put a fan under the sheets and turned it on. That thing would blow up like a bullfrog's neck. The problem was that the sheets would eventually pull out from under the encyclopedias, and the whole thing would deflate.

28

This was all Chad's idea, and he was not thrilled about having my assistance. He actually blamed the failure of the entire venture on me, if you can believe that.

He was beginning to get frustrated when I made a suggestion: "Why don't we slide the chairs over here and sit them on top of the sheets and see if that will hold them down?" I pointed out the four old wooden dining room chairs that Mama kept stored downstairs in our playroom.

He turned on me instantly. When he spoke I felt like he was spitting at me. "Because *we* aren't the ones building this tent, *I* am. It's *my* tent, and all you are is a little pissant pestering the shit outta me. Why don't you get lost and let me think?"

Chad wasn't aware of the fact that I idolized him. Nothing in the world meant more to me than having him allow me to take part in his creations. I wanted nothing more than to stay there and help him finish the project, but I couldn't let him know that.

"Fine. This is a stupid idea anyway, and it'll never work."

I stormed out of the playroom, through the laundry room, and bounded up the stairs. By the time I reached the top step I realized I was crying. I stopped long enough to dry my eyes and calm down, then I went through the door. I looked up and down the hallway. I knew that Rache was in the bedroom, probably doing homework or looking at a magazine. Daddy had to be watching TV, and Mama was most likely in her sewing room. I had to decide which one I would most like to bother. I picked Mama.

The sewing room door was open so I just walked right in. I sat on the floor beside her where she was looking through a stack of fabric. "What are you doing?"

"Trying to decide which fabric I'm going to use to make you a new sundress. Which do you like?" She held up two different fabrics, one was white with tiny pink polka dots, and the other was red, white, and blue striped.

"I hate sundresses."

"Well, I'm making one for you, so you might as well choose a fabric." She held them higher.

"I like the striped one better." With the bicentennial just around the corner, patriotic colors were all the rage.

"Good. Then stripes it is." She lowered the fabrics. "Now that you know what I'm doing, what are you doing?"

"Nothing."

"Just nothing, huh?"

"Yeah. I was helping Chad, but he made me mad and I left."

"How did he make you mad?"

"He just calls me names and makes fun of me all the time. I can't stand it."

"What you need to do is to take control of it."

"How?"

"What do you think the Rolling Stones do when someone's getting on their nerves?"

I groaned. "I'm not real sure." Mama often used some sort of a musical reference to make a point, and I didn't always get them.

"Of course they'd say, 'Hey, hey, you, you, get off'a my cloud.'"

"That's what I should say?"

"You bet. We all have our own little personal cloud, and if we don't invite another person to join us on it, then they have no business there. Your cloud is your own special place to be safe and happy. If someone is keeping you from being safe and happy there, then you just tell them to get off."

"Where is my cloud?"

"Everywhere you go."

"So, all the time, no matter where I am or who I'm with, if I don't feel safe and happy I can tell people to get off my cloud?"

"Sure, unless of course you're on their cloud."

"How do I know?"

"You just figure it out along the way."

"So when Chad is bothering me, I should just say 'Get off my cloud.'"

"Yes. And make sure he knows you didn't invite him on your cloud. That'll surely get him."

"I'll try it next time."

"Let me know how it goes." She looked at her watch. "Would you look at the time. We need to get you bathed and ready for bed."

"That sounds good. I really need a bath."

She leaned toward me and took a deep sniff of my head. She grabbed her throat and made noises that sounded a lot like the noises I made the time I tried to swallow a Brussels sprout whole. Rolling her head around on her shoulders as if she were dizzy, she said, "You *do* need a bath. Let's go before it's too late." She grabbed me by the hand and we ran down the hall to the bathroom. "You start stripping and I'll get all of the makings for the perfect bath."

By the time I was naked, Mama had the tub filling with lukewarm water. She put in a squirt of Mr. Bubble, and as the water ran bubbles blossomed under the faucet and then spread throughout the tub. She pulled a clean towel and wash cloth from the linen closet. As she closed the closet door she said, "Jump in."

I stepped easily into the tub. The water felt nice. It was just the right temperature. I lowered myself into the fluffy bubbles. As the water continued to rise, the bubbles climbed higher up my body, slowly inching their way to my chin. With the bubbles chin high, Mama turned the water off. For a moment it was quiet and all I could hear was the crackling and popping of the bubbles as they continued to grow and change.

Mama knelt beside the tub and dunked the washcloth into the

water. She was humming as she took the bar of Ivory soap and lathered the cloth. She held it out. "Where shall we start?"

"Feet," I answered as I poked my left foot through the bubbles.

"Feet it is," she said grabbing the foot and scrubbing it. The humming continued.

"Whatcha humming?"

She stopped the humming and the scrubbing and thought for a second. "I'm not real sure." She recommenced the scrubbing. "Would you like to sing?"

"Yes!"

"What should we sing?"

"You decide."

"How about a little Simon and Garfunkel?"

"Okay."

She began. "Cecelia, you're breaking my heart . . . you're shakin' my confidence daily." I joined in. "Oh Cecelia, I'm down on my knees . . . I'm beggin' you please to come home . . . come on home."

Cecelia was one of my favorite songs to sing with Mama because I had my own parts in it. For instance, the "Come on home" part was all mine. I did that in kind of a deep voice. We kept going. "Makin' love in the afternoon with Cecelia up in my bedroom . . . makin' love." The "Makin' love" part, again all mine. "I got up to wash my face, when I come back to bed someone's takin' my place."

We sang until every inch of my body was thoroughly scrubbed and all that was left was my head. By this time the bubbles had all deflated and all that remained was a white film covering the top of the water. Without the bubbles, the water wasn't very deep. Mama turned the water on again and instructed me to slide up and stick my head underneath. I did as I was told and then she turned the water off and lathered up my head with Johnson's Baby Shampoo.

We didn't sing while she was washing my hair. Fingernails scratched at my scalp as my head bobbed up and down from the pressure. I was thinking about Cecelia. We sang that song pretty regularly, but I never thought too much about the words.

"Mama?"

"Yes."

"What is 'Makin' love in the afternoon'?"

Mama stopped the scratching and my head stopped bobbing. She was definitely thinking. "Okay." She thought a little more. "Okay, here we go." She stuck her hands down in the water to rinse them and sat back on the floor. My head was still soapy, but I didn't say anything.

"You know how it feels to love somebody?" She didn't wait for a response. "Well that's only a *feeling*. When you love someone, sometimes it's nice to actually *show* them how you feel. You can express that feeling through hugging, kissing, saying nice things, and so on. And making love is just another way of showing someone that you love 'em." She smiled, obviously quite proud of her explanation.

I wanted to make sure I had it right. "So, Simon and Garfunkel are singing about how they were just showing Cecelia that they love her, then they left to wash their face, and then someone else comes in and starts showing Cecelia how *they* love her?"

"That's it. Now let's rinse your head." She seemed in an awful hurry to change the subject.

I pulled my head away from her, still not clear on this Cecelia business. "But why was Simon and Garfunkel so upset that someone was taking their place?"

She let out a deep sigh and sat back again. "It's pretty complicated, Pooh. Basically, I think what it means is that everybody *can* be replaced, but nobody *wants* to be replaced."

"How can people be replaced?"

She sighed again. I got the distinct feeling that she was not enjoying this conversation. It felt good though, to finally turn the tables. "When people stop doing the things that they are needed to do for people in their life, the people in their life might find another person who *will* do the things that are needed. Then, that new person will replace the old one." With a look of doubt she asked, "Do you understand?"

"No." I was only being honest.

"Okay, let's take that football player guy that you like so much. What's his name?"

"Larry Csonka." Now she was talking my language. I sat up straighter.

"Let's say that Larry started messing up on football things. Let's say he starts dropping the ball every time he has it, and he keeps getting tackled before he goes anywhere, and he surely isn't scoring any points . . ."

"That would never happen." I interrupted.

"Well, just say it did. What do you think would happen to your old pal Larry?" I didn't answer because I didn't even want to consider it. "I'll tell ya. Larry would be replaced by some fresh young buck who never makes mistakes." She nodded her head in total self-satisfaction.

I really wanted to leave this particular subject, so I refocused the conversation. "But, what about Cecelia? Why did she need to replace Simon and Garfunkel?"

"I can only assume that he wasn't doing a real good job of showing her how he loved her." She shrugged her shoulders.

"So he wasn't real good at makin' love."

A smile slowly spread across her face and a quiet laugh escaped her. "I'm sure that's it." She leaned in toward the tub. "Now let's rinse that head before it sets up like that."

34

That night I lay in bed just letting it all sink in. The world was dark except for a night-light that was strategically placed in the hallway. I was afraid of the pitch dark. Rachel refused to let me have the nightlight in the bedroom, so the hallway combined with a slight opening in the bedroom door was the best compromise we could reach.

The faint sound of voices and the flickering white television light that occasionally peeked through the open door let me know that Mama and Daddy were still up. We always went to bed a lot earlier than they did. They stayed in the den at the opposite end of the house, so they generally didn't bother us. We were usually asleep well before they went to bed.

I could hear Rache breathing deeply, in and out, in and out. She was apparently already in deep sleep lying about five feet away from me in her own twin bed. I was overcome with the desire to join her and leave my own vast bed behind. I knew if I did that she would have a fit and push me out onto the red shag carpet. I didn't want to take that chance. I stayed where I was.

I don't know if Mama had molded me into a worrywart, or if I had been born one. Either way, I worried more than any five-year-old had any business worrying. It didn't take a whole lot for me to lose countless hours of sleep to worry. One time I heard Mama and Daddy discussing money. Since then, I've always been worried that one day there wouldn't be any more money for food. Chad told me a story once about how dinosaurs still roam the Earth in the deep jungles of South Georgia and that they are slowly migrating north. Since that story I had been terrified that I would be awakened one night by earthquake footsteps on their way to crushing our house.

Given all of the excitement of this day, it seemed only fitting that I'd be awake and fitfully worrying. I still struggled to understand all that I had learned today, and the more I struggled

35

the more frightened I became. I wondered when I would lose my innocence. Would it be painful? How long would it take? Did I really want to lose it?

Was life really coming full-speed ahead? Would it run over me? What kind of armor would help? These questions filled my head the way a movie fills the screen in a theater. That was only the beginning. Next, I found myself wondering about my cloud. I wasn't sure how big it was and how I'd know if someone was on it. I wondered if I'd be able to tell when I was on someone else's cloud without being invited. Oh Lord! And what about being replaced? If I didn't love people just right, would they find someone new? If I didn't love Daddy the way he needed, would he find a new girl to carry down the driveway? What about Chad? If I told him to get off my cloud, would he get a new girl to be his little sister?

OH GOD! STOP! STOP! STOP! I had to stop thinking about all of this. I put my fingers in my ears and hummed the theme song from *Petticoat Junction*. It was a frail attempt to cover the voices that were inside my head.

It didn't work. The worry voices screamed from within. I decided that quiet humming wasn't sufficient. I took it to the next level. At the top of my lungs I sang, "There's a little train that is coming down the track at the junction . . . Petticoat Junction!"

"What in the world are you doing?" Rachel was now sitting straight up in bed.

In my most pathetic voice, "I can't sleep, Rache."

"So you think singing as loud as you can will help you sleep? What ever happened to counting sheep?" She paused and let her anger slip away. "Why can't you sleep?"

"I'm afraid."

"Of what?"

"I don't know."

"Want to come over here with me."

Oh, yes! Thank you God! I sat up quickly and didn't even try to contain my joy. "Yes!" I pulled the covers back, but before I could put my foot on the floor Rachel said, "You better jump."

"Why?"

"I'd hate for that thing under your bed to reach out and grab your foot."

"Shut up! I hate you Rachel!"

"Jump," she giggled.

I stood up and leapt from my bed to hers. When I landed and fell across her she made an "oommph" noise. "Ow—you mashed my innards!"

"Sorry. Move over."

"You do know that I'm doing you a favor."

"Yes I know. Thank you, thank you, thank you. Now please move over." I was still thinking about the beast under my bed and anxious to be under the safety of covers. She reluctantly slid over and I crawled in beside her. She reached down and held my hand.

"Good night, Noble. You're safe."

"Thank you, Rache. I love you."

"Love you, too." Her voice trailed off.

Not long after, I fell asleep.

Chapter 2
January 1974

Worrying was a constant in my life. Much had happened in the last few months. There had been many new causes for worry. I started kindergarten. Mama was sick a lot lately. Daddy worked late a lot of nights and most of the time he didn't even have supper with us. Mama had been so sick that she would go directly to her room after supper and wouldn't want to be bothered. She didn't bathe me anymore, and we seldom had a chance to talk the way we used to.

I guessed that this was what she meant by losing my innocence. Things weren't as simple as they had been. But I still had no regrets about the brick. I was enjoying school. My teachers really liked me. They agreed with Mama that I was really bright for my age. I had also made some new friends. I figured losing my innocence was a small price to pay for everything I was getting from going to school.

Worry still managed to consume a large chunk of my time. On top of all the old worries, I now also worried about Mama being so sick, and about Daddy having to work so much.

I worried because Rachel argued with Mama a lot and had become downright mean to her. Rache said it was because Mama wasn't being nice to Daddy and that's why he never came home anymore. She said that Mama was running Daddy off and she wasn't going to stand around and watch her do that to her Daddy.

I couldn't figure out how Mama could be running Daddy anywhere. She was so sick all the time that she didn't have too much time to be mean to him. But, I did hear them arguing occasionally late at night after we were in bed. One night I actually heard Daddy leave and slam the door. I heard Mama in her bedroom crying softly.

I went to Mama that night. I wanted to help her feel better the way she had made me feel better so many times. I walked quietly across the dark hallway and into her dimly lit room. She was sitting on the edge of her bed with her back to me.

"Mama?"

She slowly turned. She had a tissue in her hand and her eyes were red circles in the middle of black smudgy makeup pits.

"Mama, are you all right?"

She laughed oddly as she wiped her nose with the tissue. "Oh, I'm just terrific. Can't you see that?" Her words were slurred and angry.

"Where's Daddy?"

"Oh, he's out for the night. He won't be home until tomorrow."

I felt heat rising from the pit of my stomach into my throat. "Where's he sleeping?"

"A motel is what he told me." She blew her nose as a new tear slid from her eye.

"Why?" It's all I could say.

"That's a question I suppose he's going to have to answer."

She looked so sad and frail. Her typically tall, lanky frame was hunched at the waist; her shoulders sagged forward. Her chest almost touched her knees. I approached her slowly. I wanted so much just to be able to do something. I sat beside her on the bed

40

and put my small arm around her shoulders. "You're not alone, Mama. We're here."

Her body began to jerk with sobs. She moaned as she pressed her head into my shoulder. I wrapped both arms around her to try and calm her. Her body merged with mine and her jerks and shudders became mine. We sat on the bed rocking and shaking together. I prayed that God would make the motion and the noise stop. As I prayed I felt my own eyes burn with tears. I could only wonder what was happening to my Mama. What was happening to my family?

One of the things Mama warned me about back when we were still having regular discussions was heartbreak. This explanation came about after I demonstrated for her the Elvis impersonation I'd been working on. I wet my hair and slicked it back, put on a pair of black pants and one of Chad's silky pink church shirts with the collar turned up and unbuttoned to the middle of my chest, and the show began.

It started with my left hand raised, microphone in the right hand (really a hairbrush), and my right leg bent at the knee toward my left leg. As I got the beat in my head, I began swiveling my right leg in and out at the hip. Then, in my very best Elvis voice, came the singing: "Since my baby left me . . ." a pause to curl my lip . . . "I found a new place to dwell . . . down at the end of lonely street, at Heartbeat Hotel."

From her front-row seat on the couch, Mama screamed, "Bravo, Bravo," as she clapped her hands wildly.

With a bow I said, "Thank ya. . . . Thank ya ver much."

"But Elvis, I believe you messed up on the words."

"Where?"

"It's not Heart*beat* Hotel, it's Heart*break* Hotel."

And of course what followed was Mama's explanation to me of what heartbreak actually is. In a nutshell, she said that

41

heartbreak is when someone you really care for, really love, does something horrible to you. When this happens, it hurts your heart so badly that your heart will break, and things between you and that person will never ever be the same.

With everything that had been happening between Mama and Daddy, I assumed that somebody, maybe both of them, was experiencing heartbreak. It seemed to be really bad. Mama cried a lot and was spending more and more time alone in her room, or in her sewing room with the door closed. Daddy was home less and less, and when he was home, he wasn't his usual fun-loving self. He seemed tired and angry all of the time. He didn't want to be bothered by me.

Once me and Rache and Chad sat down to talk about what we thought was happening. We were all very scared. We met in the basement playroom for some privacy. This was unusual for Rachel. She hardly ever came down there. She said it was damp and it smelled like two little dirty kids. That day she had made an exception.

We all sat close together on the floor amid Legos and Lincoln Logs and Playskool Little People. Rachel started everything; "Mama and Daddy are going to get a divorce."

I knew some kids at school who had divorced parents. Their parents didn't live together anymore. "How do you know?" I asked, suddenly panicked.

"It's obvious, dimwit," Chad couldn't say anything without calling me a name in the middle of it all. "Daddy's having an affair. He's never here. He's probably got some young pretty girlfriend on the side and it's tearing Mama apart."

"Daddy has a girlfriend besides Mama?" This news devastated me.

"No way!" Rachel was in obvious disagreement with Chad on this particular point. "Daddy just can't stand to be around Mama anymore because she's a drunk."

"What are you talking about?" I didn't understand how they both seemed to know what was going on and I had no clue at all. They had to be making this up. They were probably playing a joke on me.

"Do you really think that Mama's sick all the time? Of course not. She's layin' in her room as drunk as Cooter Brown. I found all her empty liquor bottles. She puts 'em in a special trash bag in her bathroom so we won't see 'em. But I caught on and I checked it out, and sure 'nuff. there they were." My sister had become so angry that her ears were red and her eyes were wet. With each word, her voice and her anger rose. "Mama's a drunk and she doesn't give a shit about any of us anymore, especially Daddy. This family is going to break up because she's only thinking about herself, and I for one hate her. I hate her!"

I couldn't believe that Rachel was talking so hatefully about Mama. I loved Mama and that would never change. She wouldn't try to hurt us. She wouldn't stop caring about us. She was our Mama. Rachel's tears had started flowing freely. Chad stared down at the floor pushing a toy car across the carpet. The emotion welled in me as I watched my brother and sister. Anger and fear mixed in my chest creating a reaction that forced them to spew from me.

I stood and kicked a block at Rachel. "You're a liar!" I kicked another object, which flew across the room. "You're both liars! Mama is not a drunk. And Daddy is not with a girlfriend. And this family is fine as long as you both keep your stupid, lying mouths shut."

I ran from the room feeling as if I had no place to go. Every place in the house seemed to belong to someone else. When I reached the top of the stairs, I ran down the hall and banged out the kitchen door. Outside the air was cold. I didn't care. The yard sloped down and ended where it reached the woods line. I kept

43

running even after the yard stopped.

About thirty yards into the woods was a creek. There was a small clearing on the opposite side where I loved to play on the rare occasion that Mama would let me leave the yard. I stomped through the shallow water oblivious to the cold. Finally I came to a stop.

The ground was covered with moss that provided a soft, squishy place to rest. The moss was so thick it was as if there was nothing solid beneath my feet. I sat, sinking several inches into the pillow of moss. I pressed my forehead into my hands. I jammed the heels of my hands into my eye sockets. I tried to fill my head with thoughts other than the newly exposed secrets of my parents.

This place was my favorite place in the world. Even in the summer this little mossy area was snuggled in its own personal pocket of cool air. I'm not sure where the cool air came from. I made up stories about how it might have come to exist. Maybe a spirit inhabited this small area. Maybe sometime a long time ago, before there were any houses around here, something really horrible happened in this very same spot. Or, it could have been that this is where all of the fairies in the woods lived and they needed for it to be a little cooler to survive, so they used their magic to make cool air. I don't know, but the summer air in this spot just didn't feel the same as any other Georgia summertime air I had ever felt.

There were also ferns out here. They got huge in the summer. I loved lying down on the moss watching the ferns lean over me and meet each other in the middle, creating a canopy above me. Glints of sunlight, like swords, shot through the ferns and came down stabbing me in the chest. Moisture bled through my clothing. Surrounded by the smell of damp dirt floating in the cool light air, I was sure that this was what Heaven must be like.

But this was not summertime. The air was not cool but

freezing. The ferns were small and there was no canopy. The sun hid somewhere in a gray sky. My feet and lower legs were soaked and numb from the cold. My thoughts could not stay away from my family and I was the furthest place on earth from Heaven.

I couldn't believe that Daddy might be having an affair. I couldn't believe that Mama was a drunk. Or maybe it was just that I didn't *want* to believe. I suppose it was possible, but why? Why would they do those things to us? It just couldn't be true. Rachel and Chad were just mad because I was better in school than they were. They were just trying to get me back for that. It was jealousy. That's what it had to be. These things just couldn't be true.

As I convinced myself that Rachel and Chad were simply involved in a jealous conspiracy to upset and irritate me, my tears dried and my heartbeat returned to an acceptable level. I did begin to feel relief, but not total relief. I guess I wasn't completely convinced.

I was, however, relieved enough to let my fear recede momentarily. Just as an open hydrant stops the destructive force of a fire, the relief momentarily halted the destructive panic that rose inside me.

My attention was now drawn to my tingling feet. Each time my heart beat, I could feel it in my toes. The cold and wet had caused my feet to begin to thump rhythmically. With each thump, my feet felt as if they grew and then returned to normal size. I watched them closely, sure that I could see their size changing. I never actually saw it, but I could certainly feel it.

As I watched, my entire body shivered and my teeth chattered. Tiny shivers were periodically interrupted by a bigger total body spasm. I quickly realized that I needed to get my cold, damp body out of these woods and into a place that was warm and dry. I tried to stand. The emotion and the cold had almost completely drained my tiny body of its energy. Standing was difficult and I knew that returning home would be even more difficult. I willed my body to generate enough energy to get me home. I secretly cursed Rachel and Chad for putting me in this predicament in the first place. My anger at least served a purpose. It warmed and energized me enough to force my way back through the woods and up the hill to the back door.

I slowly entered the door afraid, for some unknown reason, of what I might find on the other side. I found the kitchen and living room dark. I could see that the light in the hallway was on and the television was on in the den. I quietly moved my aching body through the darkened rooms and into the hallway. I peered around the doorjamb into the den and saw Rachel and Chad sitting on the couch facing the TV. I eased past the door and to the bathroom at the end of the hall. I closed and locked the door behind me and ran myself a warm bath. No sooner had the water begun to run than the knob of the door jiggled, followed by a knock.

"Who is it?" Anger was still evident in my voice.

"It's me, Noble." I recognized Rache's voice. "Are you okay?"

"I'm fine."

"Can I come in?"

"Why?"

"To talk."

A little company, even if supplied by a lying conspirator, would actually be welcome at this moment. I stepped to the door and opened it just a crack, and then I stepped away. Rachel opened the door the rest of the way and came in.

I was peeling wet socks from my red feet. Rachel dropped the toilet lid and had a seat. She studied my feet as I pulled down my pants, which were also wet from the knee down. "Where in the world have you been?"

"At the creek."

"Aren't you freezing?"

46

"That's why I'm taking a bath." I leaned over the tub and turned off the water.

I pulled the sweatshirt over my head, threw it to the floor, and stepped into the tub. The warm water sent needles of pain throughout my frozen feet. I screamed. I alternately removed each foot from the water and shook them as I gritted my teeth. Eventually they began to thaw and the pain diminished. As I submerged the rest of my body, the needles of pain shot into my legs and butt. I tightened my jaw and waited for the pain to subside.

I leaned back in the tub stretching my legs out. I was small enough to be able to straighten completely out. I let the warm water penetrate my frozen muscles, and I became heavier as my body relaxed.

"Do you want to talk?" Rachel had given me all the quiet she was going to.

"I let you in, didn't I?"

Rachel knew that this was a "yes," so she began to talk. "We weren't just being mean, Noble. Something is definitely going on with Mama and Daddy. And, no matter what it is, we have to be ready."

"I don't believe it." I had apparently subconsciously decided that denial was the least painful way to go.

"Well, you better believe it. I *know* that Mama is drinking a lot. I noticed back over the summer she was drinking a lot more Pabst Blue Ribbon than usual. Now she's drinking other stuff because I've seen the bottles. I've even seen the full ones. She keeps 'em hidden in her makeup drawers in her bathroom. I'll show you if you still don't believe me."

Despite my efforts to relax, I once again felt the anger beginning to build in the pit of my stomach. "Rachel! Who cares? Why is it important what Mama has hidden and what she does

47

when she's in her room? Who's she hurting?"

Rachel's jaw dropped in utter disbelief of what I had said. "It's hurting us all. Daddy may leave for good. Then what's going to happen to us? Don't you think that's gonna hurt?"

She stood, simultaneously shaking her head. "We shouldn't be mad at each other. We should stick together. This isn't gonna be easy, Noble. It's already getting harder each day. We gotta stick together." She left the bathroom and closed the door behind her.

The room became eerily quiet and I felt as if I was the only person in the world. I fought the urge to cry. I already felt as if my head was swollen to twice its normal size and full of thick, gooey liquid. I knew that more crying would only make this feeling worse.

A song seemed to be the appropriate prescription here. I started "Cecelia." ". . . you're breaking my heart, you're shaking my confidence daily." As I continued, the words became obscured by a quaking voice: "I'm begging you please to come home . . . Come on home." By this point I was completely overtaken by the tears and couldn't continue.

This had been mine and Mama's song to sing together. She had her parts and I had mine. It wasn't the same alone. It also brought back memories of our conversation about being replaced. I wondered now if we were all in the process of being replaced because we had failed to do what needed to be done in the lives of the people we loved.

Chapter 3
February 1974

It was the first Valentine's Day I'd ever had at school. We were set to have a huge valentine exchange. I told Mama about it well in advance and she purchased a cellophane package of Disney character valentine cards for me.

My teacher, Mrs. Jancowitz—who we kindergartners just called Mrs. J. because her name was so tough—gave each student a list of all the other kids in our class. We were told that we didn't *have* to give one to everyone, but it was strongly suggested.

The night before, I sat down in the middle of the den floor with my list and Disney valentine's scattered all around me. I set to work, carefully selecting which valentine to give to which classmate. It was a really special night because Daddy was home early. He was leaned back with his feet up on the footrest of his recliner chair. Mama was working in her sewing room, and Rachel and Chad were in their rooms doing homework. It was a pretty peaceful evening by recent standards.

"How you doing?" Daddy's voice boomed down from his chair.

I surveyed all that was around me before I responded. "Well,

I'm having a hard time with Ricky Taylor. I don't like him at all. He always has snot in his nose that sucks in and out when he breathes. I don't know which one to give him." I looked at Daddy with a slight shrug.

"Isn't there a card in there with a picture of Goofy with a nice long-string booger hanging from his nostril? Maybe it could say 'No goofin', I *picked* you to be my Valentine.'" He laughed at his own joke. I joined in.

Still laughing, I said, "I wish. That would be perfect for him."

After a few more moments of laughter Daddy spoke again. "What I meant is, how are *you* doing? You know? In general, how's everything going?"

"Fine."

"Things have been a little tough around here lately, huh?"

"Yeah, I s'pose so."

"It's gonna be all right, Pooh. I promise. I'm working on getting everything taken care of."

"Everything like what?"

"Mama's been pretty sick lately. She may have to go to a hospital soon. Or somethin' like that."

This news excited me. I knew that everything would be okay. Mama would get better, and our family would go back to normal. "Will she be okay?"

"I don't know. All we can do is wait and see. But we'll do everything we can." He reached down and roughed up my hair. "Meanwhile, you'd better get back to those cards. It's tricky *pickin'* just the right one." We laughed some more as I got back to work.

The following day, Valentine's Day, started off the same as all other days. We got ready for school and ate breakfast of cold cereal off of TV trays while watching *The Little Rascals*. Rachel and Chad headed for school on the bus and Mama and I climbed into the big blue Ford LTD. Mama drove me to school because there was no bus. My kindergarten was at Mount Pisgah Baptist Church. Skyview Elementary School only started with first grade.

She pulled up to the front steps. She seemed a bit odd today, really sad. She hadn't said much all morning. I climbed out of the car with my sack of valentines in one hand and my tan nap-mat under my arm. My book satchel with paper and all other important school material was in the other hand.

Before I closed the car door I stuck my head back inside. "Happy Valentine's Day, Mama."

She smiled a half-hearted smile and said, "Thank you, Baby. Have a nice day."

I dropped my goods on the pavement and slid in and across the wide bench seat close to her. I grabbed her by the head and gave her a forceful kiss on the side of the face. "Love you, Mama. You're my best valentine."

She grabbed me and pulled me to her. Her voice quivered, "You're my best valentine, too." Without releasing me she suggested, "Why don't you just skip school today and come back home with me?"

I pried myself away from her and looked into her eyes. They were watering and made me really just want to stay close to her. I turned and looked out the open door at my sack of valentines. So much work had gone into those. This was a special day at school and I didn't really want to miss it. "But we're exchanging valentines today, Mama, 'member?"

"Yes, I remember, Honey. You're right. You go. Go and have a great day with your friends."

She smiled, but I watched a droplet of water forming in the corner of her eye. I was torn. I looked from her to the open car door. A horn sounded from behind us. We were blocking traffic in the circular drive. "Go on, Pooh. It's okay. I'll see you this afternoon."

"Okay." I kissed her again quickly, then slid from the car. I picked up my belongings from the ground and waved to her with my valentine sack as she drove away.

The day had gone great. It was a fun day. Mrs. J. and Miss Peterson, her assistant, brought refreshments and we had a party. We ate cookies and drank Kool-Aid and passed out valentine cards.

Before we passed out cards, we each made our own valentine holder. Most of the kids used construction paper to make giant envelopes. I decided to take three of the paper plates that Miss Peterson brought for refreshments and make a heart. It was a heart with a face, and two of the plates made a mouth that opened up like a fish mouth. The mouth was where the cards went. It was like a heart mailbox. Mrs. J said it was very creative.

Everyone had to attach their cardholder to their chair. Then we all went around the room, placing the cards for each of the kids in their cardholder. When it was all over and we'd returned to our seats, I found that my heart's mouth was stuffed full of tiny white envelopes. I was so excited to open them all and see what nice things my classmates had chosen to give to me, but that would have to wait. Mrs. J said we had to rest a little before we opened them.

We had to rest each day at the same time. I usually didn't mind because it gave me a chance to think about things. Today I wasn't really in a restful mood. Nevertheless, I took my usual resting position. I spread my nap-mat in the corner behind my seat. I lay down on my stomach so that my face was on top of the bold black magic-markered letters that spelled N-O-B-L-E T. We all had our last initial after our name. I felt in my case it wasn't really necessary, but Miss Peterson had done it anyway.

I was going over the details of exactly what procedure I would use to open my millions of envelopes when I heard Mrs. J ring her little bell that signaled the end of rest time. I could barely contain myself. I jumped up immediately, folded my nap-mat, and placed it neatly in the bin beside my chair. I quickly took my seat. I slid my chair so far under the table that my chest was pressed against its edge. I reached across and pulled the heart with a mouth over to me so that it too was touching my chest.

I looked around the room and all of the other kids appeared to be as anxious as I was. Laura Kramer sat in the chair right next to me, and when I made eye contact with her she showed me her best anxious look and clenched her fists in front of her chin. She was a picture of how I felt.

Finally Mrs. J gave us all the go ahead, and the fun began. Some of the kids ripped into their envelopes with little bits of white paper flying everywhere, taking only enough time to see who had sent that one before moving to the next. I had a carefully planned system for the opening of my valentines.

I pulled the list of all the kids in my class from my book satchel, along with a pencil. I removed the first envelope from the heart's mouth. On the outside of the card in the thick-penciled scrawl of a kindergartner was written NOBLE T. Again with that unnecessary last initial. There were no other Nobles anywhere around here that I knew of.

I carefully opened the card. It was a picture of a clown with something about a funny valentine and it was signed Eric B. Eric Burton was the biggest boy in class. He picked on everybody. I hated him because he was so mean. I often found myself wishing I were big enough to punch him in the nose because he was so awful to kids like Willy Simpson and Gene Goza. Willy and Gene were always crying because of some nasty something that Eric had done.

I was very disappointed that my first dive into the heart mouth had produced such a card. The only one worse would be Ricky

53

Taylor. As I reached into the mouth and pulled out a second card, I was silently praying that it wouldn't be from Ricky.

I worked diligently through the majority of the cards, marking off the names of the senders as I went. I was down to the last few and still had not opened the one I was hoping for. Finally I hit pay dirt. I opened the envelope, which looked amazingly like all of the others. Inside was a card containing a picture of a cartoon chicken wearing sunglasses. The words said "Cool Chick," and it was signed Jill B. I smiled as I stared down at the card.

Jill Brasil was my favorite friend. She had long dark hair that reflected the light. Her eyes were jet black, like the black marbles from my Chinese Checkers game. Sometimes I could see myself in her eyes when I was close enough. Her skin was always tanned and her cheeks were pink. She thought I was funny and she would laugh at anything I said. Jill was definitely my favorite friend.

I took the card from her and stuck it in the front pocket of my satchel. I didn't want to put it in the bag with the rest; it was too special for that. I finished the task of opening. I was the last person in the whole class to finish. Everyone was giving me a hard time about that, but Mrs. J said I was just being thorough. We didn't really know what that meant, but I was taking it as a compliment.

At the end of the day we all took our loot and headed out to the driveway. I saw Jill at the coat rack. She was pulling a blue furry coat over her arms.

"Hey, Jill."

She swung around, her long hair flying over one of her shoulders. I was very aware of my own short, blonde, shaggy hair. Mama said I got too dirty to have long hair. She said we could never keep it clean. Jill must've been very clean because her hair was really long.

"Hey, Noble."

"Thanks for the card. It was really nice."

54

"Yeah. Thank you, too."

"Okay. See ya tomorrow."

"See ya."

I didn't take time to put on my coat. I bounded down the stairs, coat dragging behind me, anxious to see Mama and tell her all about my cards. When I reached the sidewalk, I looked up and down but didn't see Mama's car anywhere. I kept looking, sure that she was simply running late.

"Noble Thorvald!"

I turned toward my name.

"Over here, Noble." It was Mrs. Rogers. She was our next-door neighbor. Margaret Rogers was her daughter. Margaret was a skinny little redhead with a ponytail and a million freckles. Her head was sticking out of the passenger window of the Toyota, "Come here, Noble."

I ran over and looked in the window at Margaret. Mrs. Rogers looked over at me and said, "Your mother called and asked if I could give you a ride home today. Says she's not feeling well. Didn't sound too good either. Come on, get in."

As Mrs. Rogers dropped me off at my driveway she said, "Y'all need anything be sure and call."

"Yes, Ma'am. Bye Margaret." I slammed the door and ran to the house.

The house was quiet and dark. I removed all of my cards from the bag as well as the heart with a mouth and the special valentine from Jill. I quietly walked down the hallway. "Mama?" No response. "Mama, where are you?" I stopped at her closed door and leaned into it to see if I heard anything. Nothing. I slowly turned the knob and opened the door.

Mama was lying in the bed, still and quiet. "Mama?" I whispered. I went to the edge of the bed and sat beside her. "Mama?" Another whisper.

She opened her eyes and stared blankly at me as if she didn't recognize me. I smiled down at her. "I want to show you something. What I got at school today." I pulled the cards out onto her bed.

She sat up partially. "What the hell are you doing?"

"I wanted to show . . ."

She cut me off in mid-sentence. "Get the hell outta here."

With that she flung her arm across the bed and my cards scattered on the floor. I felt the heat of tears beginning to sting my eyes. I crouched on the floor and began to neatly collect the cards.

"I said get out!!"

"I'm getting my things." The tears were flowing now and I had to gasp to be able to speak.

"I want you out now! NOW! NOW! NOW!"

I grabbed what I could hold in my arms and I ran from the door while she continued to scream, "NOW! NOW! NOW!" I slammed the door behind me and leaned against the wall in the hall. I slid down the wall until I was sitting on the floor. I looked at what I was able to salvage of my valentines. There weren't many, and the one from Jill was not there.

I tried to stop crying, but I couldn't. I managed to get the heart with a mouth, but now it was torn and crumpled and one of its eyes had been torn off. I cried softly as I tried to smooth it. The house was dark and quiet. The only sound was of me trying to stifle my sobs as I attempted to organize the remnants of my valentine jackpot.

The heart was lying on the floor looking up at me with a small tear down the center of its forehead. It was now a broken heart. It made me think of Mama's description of what heartbreak was. She said when someone breaks your heart, things between you and that person will never be the same. She had struggled to describe what a broken heart actually felt like.

At this moment, I understood why she had struggled so. I knew that I was feeling heartbreak, and it was hard to describe. Once I was watching Mutual of Omaha's *Wild Kingdom* with Marlin Perkins. This show had been about python snakes. Marlin explained that pythons didn't kill by biting, because they have no venom. The python kills its prey by wrapping around its torso and squeezing. Every time the poor trapped animal exhales, the snake tightens. For the prey, breathing gets more and more shallow until it eventually can't breathe at all. It dies a very slow, painful death by suffocation.

This is what I thought heartbreak felt like. I could barely breathe, and I felt that any minute the struggle would end and death would come—slow and painful. Mama had just broken my heart, which meant things between she and I would never be the same. The python tightened its grip again and I fell to the floor. I lay crying among my torn valentines, struggling to breathe.

Chapter 4
August 1974-November 1974

Our lives had been incredibly chaotic and unstable over the past several months. Daddy did as promised, sending Mama away for help. I didn't quite understand all of the details of her sickness, but Daddy sat us all down and tried to explain it to us.

Mama was an alcoholic. This was a disease; therefore, there was treatment for it. Apparently, treatment for this disease was just starting to be commonly practiced, and treatment facilities were not very common. Daddy spoke to some expert and made arrangements to have Mama admitted into one of these treatment facilities.

He explained to us that Mama had no control over her alcohol consumption. He apologized for her and said that he knew she wasn't trying to hurt any of us. For some reason she had just gradually sunk into a depression and this led to her inability to control her drinking. Daddy said it was just her way of easing the pain in her own life, and she just didn't realize the pain it was causing in other lives. He said we'd all support her and do everything we could to try and help her get better.

About six months after the valentine episode, Mama went

away. She was going to be in a hospital in Milledgeville for a few months, and we wouldn't be able to see her at all.

The day she left was a bittersweet day. We were sad to see her go, but anxious for her to be returned to us all better. Daddy carried her big blue Samsonite to the car and threw it into the trunk of the LTD. We all gathered around the car, not quite sure what to do. Mama gave each of us a long and gripping hug. She smiled a plastic smile that wasn't fooling anybody. Even though she kept telling us that everything was going to be okay, I could tell that she was sad and afraid. I wanted to be strong for her.

The only one who cried was Chad. He had confessed to me the night before while we sat in the darkness of his bedroom floor that he was terrified of Mama leaving. He said he wasn't real sure why, but I knew exactly why. Chad was becoming a serious troublemaker. He was in trouble all the time at school, and he was quite destructive of all property at home that belonged to anyone other but himself. Daddy would come down on him hard, and then Mama would take up for him and keep him out of trouble. Chad was simply afraid to think of how he might cope without Mama as his defender. I disregarded his tears as tears of selfishness. He wasn't crying for Mama. He was crying for himself.

Rachel didn't cry but smiled a very believable smile. I think she really was happy to see Mama go. Rache had always been very accusatory toward Mama. She accused Mama of ruining Daddy's life as well as all of ours. Anything that went wrong automatically the fault of our mother in Rachel's mind. She was very hard on Mama, never giving her the benefit of the doubt. I shuddered at the thought that Rachel might, underneath those smiling green eyes, be hoping that Mama would never return.

I kept my face as stiff as possible. I didn't want anyone to know what I was feeling. I was happy that Mama was taking the first steps toward getting better, but I was also very frightened. The

60

worry-wart trait of my personality became more dominant with each day of my life. It was not, as I had hoped, a passing phase. This episode seemed to provide me with plenty of worry fodder. I was afraid that this new treatment wouldn't work and she wouldn't get better. I was afraid that she would decide she liked it there and wouldn't come back. I was afraid that Daddy would like her not being here so he wouldn't want her to come back. I was afraid of what would happen to our home without Mama. The gardens, the cooking, the laundry—who would tend to all of that? I had so many fears that they tumbled through my head like a rockslide, clanging against one another, drowning out any other thoughts. As Mama and Daddy pulled away from the house on that day, waving goodbye, the terror settled into my bones, preparing for a lengthy stay.

One of my worries was quickly laid to rest. Mamateen came over that first day to get us off to school, and she was waiting when we arrived home from school. However, she made it clear that she couldn't stay at our house full-time as she had a home of her own to tend to. She invited us to come and stay with her, but Daddy said we needed to maintain our routine as best as possible.

My dad solved this problem right away. By the next day, we had a full-time housekeeper/babysitter. Deeanna Hawkins was her name, but she preferred to be called Dee. She was apparently a friend of a friend of Daddy's and was currently out of work. Since Dee needed a job and Daddy needed a housekeeper, it was a perfect match.

We had to get ourselves ready and off to school on the first day of Dee's employment in our household. Daddy was always gone to work already by the time we left, and Dee wouldn't be able to begin until the afternoon. It seemed a fairly simple task to get ourselves onto the bus without incident.

Daddy woke us all before he left. Rachel and I quickly jumped

61

from bed to begin with our newly acquired responsibility. Daddy was dressed and ready to go, coffee mug in hand. "Now, y'all sure you'll do all right?" He seemed nervous.

Rachel, obviously feeling very grown up, said, "Of course we'll do all right. We're fine. We've been going to school for years now. We could do it with our eyes shut."

"Not her." My dad waved his coffee mug at me. I hoped he was only referring to my inexperience at school because I was only in my second week of first grade, and not to my inexperience in general.

"She's fine. Right, Noble?"

"Yes, Daddy, I'm fine. This is a piece of cake."

"All right then." He gave us both a goodbye kiss. "Make sure your brother gets up."

"Aye, aye!" Rachel saluted him.

He walked out the door with a smile and a wink.

Rachel prepared breakfast while I attempted to rouse Chad. Despite the fact that Daddy had already awakened him, he was still sleeping soundly. I shook him gently. "Chad, get up. We gotta get ready for school." He moaned and rolled over. I shook him harder. "Chad! Get up now. You'll miss the bus."

In a groggy voice he replied, "Get out, brat."

"Fine." I left him sleeping.

When I entered the kitchen, Rache had three plates, each with a Pop-Tart, accompanied by three glasses of milk.

"Chad won't get up."

"I'll get him up in a minute. Eat your breakfast."

Rachel and I were dressed, fed, and ready to go with five minutes until bus arrival. Still no sign of Chad. Rachel had tried unsuccessfully numerous times to get him out of that bed. With everything else done, Rache went into the kitchen and emerged with a glass of water. "He's gonna get up." She marched to his room and I couldn't help but follow.

She stood over him with the water. "Chad, you know if you don't go to school, Daddy will kill you."

"I'm going. Give me five more minutes."

"You don't have five more minutes." With that she turned the glass upside-down, dumping the water all over him and his bed.

He jumped out of the bed immediately, wearing only his white Fruit-O-The-Loom briefs. "Holy shit! You're an idiot!" His face was the color of strawberries.

Rachel remained very calm. "You have two minutes before the bus gets here." She turned on her heel and left the room. I was not far behind.

We gathered our things and walked to the end of our street where the bus picked us up. A small group of neighborhood children were already waiting for the bus. We joined the group and Adam Lagerberg, Chad's best friend, asked, "Where's Chad?"

Rachel hated Adam. "Not here, you geek." Adam responded with a disgusting noise and Rachel just turned her back on him.

"He's coming." I said this more out of hope than out of a need to answer Adam.

Conversations were taking place amongst the group. Margaret Rogers kept trying to get me to talk to her about my teacher and the other kids in my class, but I wasn't interested. I nodded to her politely but my attention was focused on the front door of my house, hoping that Chad would soon emerge.

Eventually, we saw the bus rolling down the street toward us, and still no sign of Chad. The bright yellow bus stopped in front of us and the door opened. I waited until last to get on. Rachel was one of the first on and took her customary older-kid seat toward the back. She seemed unconcerned about Chad.

Everyone else had boarded, and I was still standing on the pavement looking at my house. "Come on, kid. Gotta get y'all to school." Mrs. Cochran was our big greasy bus driver. She looked and smelled like she needed to bathe a little more regularly. Chad called her Mrs. Cockroach.

"Mrs. Cochran, I'm waiting for my brother."

"Don't got time to wait."

"He's on his way. Really he is."

She wasn't convinced. "I got me twenty more of you young'uns whose already here and needin' to go to school. So you either get on here and go with us, or you get left behind like your brother." She snarled when she said "brother," and I was under the distinct impression that his strong dislike of her was a mutual feeling.

It appeared that I had little choice, so I slowly climbed the two steps into the bus. As she was pushing in the handle to close the doors I saw Chad burst through the front door. His wet hair had been slicked to his head. Several papers fell from a notebook, and a Pop-Tart was clenched between his teeth. He ran hard toward the bus. I turned quickly and grabbed Mrs. Cochran's hand on the door handle.

"Child, you best let go of me." Mrs. Cochran jerked her hand from mine.

"See. He *is* coming. Don't close the door yet."

She sighed and gave me an angry look with her puffy cheeked, acne-scarred face. But, at least she waited.

Chad jumped onto the bus in a storm of noise with his arms raised above his head in triumph. "I made it! Yeah! And the crowd goes wild!"

Mrs. Cochran closed the door behind him and he flashed her a charming smile. "Beautiful mornin', huh Mrs. Cockroach?"

"You take a seat now, young fella—and watch your mouth."

As he began his slow, steady strut to the back of the bus, he paused long enough to give a second grader in the front seat a scare. "What are you lookin' at, moron?"

The kid looked down at the floor and whispered, "Nothin'."

Chad continued toward the back with a constant raucous around him. I sat alone in my third-row seat, breathing a sigh of relief. We had successfully completed our first mission as children who were getting by without a mother.

For about the next three months, Mama was at the hospital. Dee was there every day, taking care of all the things that needed to be taken care of. The first day we came home from school after the bus incident, Dee was right there waiting for us.

I was shocked at the sight of her. She was the most beautiful woman I had ever seen. She reminded me of my Barbie doll. At least the way she was before I cut her hair and painted her face blue.

She had long thick blonde hair. Daddy once made a wooden bench at work and said it had a natural pine finish. Dee's hair was the color of that bench. Her blue eyes were so pale that they were almost white, and her smile made me think of a row of white books, all the same size, with deep dimples as bookends.

She met us at the door bouncing like a cheerleader, wearing cut off jeans and a tube top. "Hey, y'all."

We were all southern around here, but when her mouth opened and words came out, all I could think was, *Boy, is she southern.* When she said "hey," she stretched it into at least a three-syllable word.

"Hey." My response was accompanied by a smile because I was still in awe of her appearance.

"I'm Dee. I'll be takin' care a y'all while yore Mama's gone." I believed that her accent would eventually grow on me. "You must be Rachel, and Chad, and yore Noble." She pointed at each of us as she said our names.

"Wow. Your smarter than you look." Rachel said this as she

65

brushed past Dee and went into the house.

Chad followed her, laughing as if he had just heard the funniest joke on earth. I stayed put and watched Dee's face transform from a picture of joy to a picture of confusion. The white books were now hidden behind full pink lips, and the bookends had disappeared completely. I felt sorry for her and wanted to make her feel better.

"They're mean to me, too." That was all I could think of. "They'll warm up to ya." I smiled but her face didn't change.

"I think you're real pretty." I gave her this as a consolation.

It apparently worked. Her smile returned right away. "Aren't you just the sweetest little thang?" She grabbed me and pulled me to her and gave me a tight squeeze.

From that moment on, Dee and I became very close. Having her around made Mama's absence less obvious and less painful. She was very good at keeping the house neat and orderly. She was even better at cooking than Mama. She didn't use any of those cans and boxes. Everything that she cooked was fresh and from scratch. Once, I asked her how she learned to cook like that. She told me that where she came from, up in Ellijay, Georgia, didn't nobody cook from cans and boxes. She said that one of the greatest prides of the mountain women was their cooking. It was something that all women passed on to their girls.

My mama wasn't from the mountains. She was from a small town in East Georgia where everybody made their living at the shirt factory. My grandmother MeeMee used to sew at that factory. I guess she didn't have time to teach my mama about cooking. I guess that meant that my mama wouldn't teach Rachel and me about cooking either. Thank goodness for cans and boxes.

In addition to the cooking and cleaning, Dee was also a lot of fun. She was young for an adult. She told me that she was twenty-four. That sounded kind of old, but compared to Mama and Daddy, who were each thirty-six, that seemed awful young. She would play games with me. We'd play hide-n-seek in the yard, or chase. One of my favorite things was when she'd make up some biscuit dough and let me build things out of it, then bake it to see how it'd turn out.

Rachel and Chad never really warmed up to Dee like I thought they would. They were mean to her and tried to make trouble. I asked them once why they were acting that way. They said that Dee was trying to replace Mama and they weren't gonna let it happen. Chad said he thought that Dee was Daddy's young girlfriend. Rache didn't agree with that, but she did agree that Dee was overstepping her boundaries.

After my brother and sister had planted that "replacing Mama" seed in my head, the worrying commenced. I thought that Dee would be a really fine mama, but that worried me. Was I starting to wish that Dee was my mama? Did I want her to take Mama's place? If so, did that mean that Mama had stopped loving me the way that I needed?

After that, I was a little different toward Dee. I still played with her, but I tried not to spend so much time with her. I knew Mama would be home soon, and I wanted her to come back and love me the way I needed. I didn't want to replace her. I didn't want to give Dee the wrong idea and make her think that she was going to be my new mama.

In November, Mama finally came home just in time for the holidays. Her homecoming was a huge affair for us all. It was on a school day and Daddy made us go ahead and go to school. Dee was there in the morning to see us off. I was very sad to say goodbye to her. She didn't seem sad at all. She wore her usual bookshelf smile that turned to a frown at the sight of my tears.

"Honey, don't you go getting all mushy on me now."

"But I'm gonna miss you."

"Oh, don't you go to worrying about that. You'll be seeing me." Her smile returned and I believed her without even giving it a second thought.

We kissed each other on the cheek and I ran off to catch the bus. I stopped at the end of the driveway and turned to wave at her. She stood waving back at me in a turquoise ribbed turtleneck sweater and hip-hugger jeans. She looked like a TV commercial. Rachel and Chad hadn't even looked back. I didn't care what they thought—I was glad that Dee had come.

When we got off the bus that afternoon, both cars were in the driveway. Daddy had already returned with Mama. We all ran up the street and to the house. Since I was so much smaller, keeping up was out of the question. But I ran as fast as my Keds sneakers would carry me just the same.

By the time I made it to the door, Rachel and Chad were already inside. I burst in to find Mama on the sofa with Rache on one side and Chad in her lap. I stopped and tried to catch my breath. Mama looked over Chad's shoulder. "My God, if it's not my little Pooh Bear." She smiled and her face looked so fresh and rested. "Get your tiny little butt over here." She slid Chad off of her lap.

I was so thrilled that I could barely move. I was smiling so hard that the little muscles in front of my ears were aching. I walked to her and she swept me up and pulled me into her lap. She leaned over me covering my face and neck with little chicken-peck kisses. It tickled and I laughed until I couldn't breathe. I was thankful that I had not had anything to drink since lunch, because if I had I surely would've peed all over Mama.

Chapter 5
November 1974-May 1977

Things quickly went back to their old selves. Mama busied herself preparing for the holidays. In the evenings she cooked supper and helped us with homework. She didn't spend time in her room anymore. She always wanted to be with us and we loved it. Daddy still had to work late occasionally, but most of the time he was home, too. We were right back to living that American Dream.

We had Thanksgiving dinner at Mamateen's house with innumerable aunts, uncles, and cousins. There was a lot of delicious food. I mostly filled up on Mamateen's cornbread dressing. I couldn't really stomach that giblet gravy though. There were way too many unidentifiable objects floating around in it. When I asked what they were, Mamateen only answered, "Well, genius, they're giblets, of course." Since she made me feel so stupid, I didn't pursue the topic. But, until I knew what giblets were, I wasn't about to eat any.

Mama's contribution to the dinner was sweet potato casserole. She spent a lot of time making it without the help of boxes and cans, but I still didn't want to eat it. I felt strange about eating something that was the exact same color as the mud at the little league field. I wouldn't mind scraping off some of those marshmallows melted on top, but that would be rude, so I stayed away from it altogether.

After dinner, all the men unbuckled their pants and sat and watched football while the women cleaned. I chose to join the men while the other kids played in the yard. Thanksgiving was a great family day. I could feel my family coming back. I was happy.

Christmas was equally successful. We went on our annual shopping trip to Downtown Rich's. We rode the Pink Pig, which was a miniature monorail train that went in a big circle on the roof of Rich's. It circled the Great Tree. What a tree!! The ornaments on it were bigger than my head!

Santa was very generous. My favorite gift was a red, white, and blue guitar. It was just like Buck Owens guitar from Hee Haw. I didn't really know how to play, but I pretended very well. I would play and sing Donny Osmond songs.

Chad mostly got building equipment. He loved Legos, Lincoln Logs, Erector Sets, Tinker Toys, etc. He was always building something.

Rachel got a new turntable and a bunch of 45 RPM records. It was really neat. We would turn it up loud and sing, "I'm on top of the world lookin' down on creation and the only explanation I can find . . ." with the Carpenters.

Yes, Mama was back, and life was good. Those Carpenters really knew what they were singing about. We *were* on top of the world.

Things went real well for an entire year. Life was moving on real smooth in the Thorvald household. One day, out of the blue, everything changed.

It was right before Christmas in 1975. Thanksgiving had been another nice family time, except this year we had gone to my Aunt Pearl's house instead of Mamateen's. There were no indications of

70

trouble, but trouble was coming.

It was December 15, three days before my birthday, and a little over a week before Christmas. We came home from school that day and when we entered the house we knew something was wrong. Usually there were lights and music and Mama was busy sewing or cleaning or reading. But on this day none of those things were present.

As we entered the still, dark house, the three of us just stopped and looked at one another hoping for someone to tell us what was happening. "Where's Mama?" I spoke first.

"How should we know," Chad responded.

"Let's find out. Come on." Rachel led the way down the darkened hallway. We stayed close together and eased slowly toward Mama's bedroom door. We proceeded with such caution you would think that we expected to find a monster behind the door.

We stopped outside the door. I could hear my heart beating rapidly. My mouth was dry and my palms wet. We looked at one another.

"Open it." Chad instructed Rachel.

Rachel simply nodded and reached for the knob. She turned it in slow motion and pushed it gently. We didn't enter, but peered into the room.

The two drawers to the nightstand were open and their contents all over the floor. Mama was lying face down on the bed, buck naked, and there were two empty liquor bottles lying on the bed beside her. There was a card or note by her hand as if it had fallen from her grasp.

"Jesus Christ," was all Chad could mutter.

"Is she okay?" I was afraid that she was dead because she was so still.

"We have to call Daddy." Rachel decided to take charge and

she started to close the door.

"No." I grabbed the door before it closed. "We have to make sure she's okay."

"Be my guest." Rachel gestured toward the open door with her hand.

Reluctantly, I passed through the door and to Mama's bedside. As I approached, I heard her breathing. Her nose was making scratchy noises as she breathed in and out. At least she was alive. I reached for the paper by her hand. It was a Christmas card. It hadn't been mailed because there was no address on the envelope, just the name Dave. I opened the card that was obviously meant for my dad. For a second grader, I read very well, so I knew exactly what it said. "Merry Christmas, Dear. Hopefully next year we'll be able to spend the holidays together. I'm counting the days. All my love, Dee."

Holy cow! No wonder Mama was upset. She had found a love letter/Christmas card for Daddy. Chad was right. Daddy was having an affair. And, oh my God, it was with our babysitter.

I couldn't move. Anger welled in me and it tossed and splashed and caused butterflies to move into my stomach. I wanted to hit my dad. I wanted to pull Dee's blonde hair out by the roots. I wanted Mama to wake up and go kick Daddy's ass. How could he do this?

I stared down at my naked mother. She gurgled and drool ran from her mouth to her pillow. I tickled her face with my fingertips. She was a mess. Nude, unconscious, slobbering, hurting. "How could he do this to you?" I didn't expect an answer, but I really wanted one.

I cleaned up the mess on the floor, threw away the empty bottles, and covered Mama after washing her face. I left her alone to regain consciousness.

Rachel and Chad were sitting together on the living room sofa.

72

"I called Daddy," Rachel said. I was shocked that the first thing out of her mouth was not "How's Mama?"

"What did he say?" I wondered to myself, *Could he possibly have said, "Oh, she must have found my secret love note."*

"He wasn't there. His secretary said he was at a site. She said she'd tell him to call if he checked in."

I didn't even want to think about Daddy right now. I was too mad. I didn't want to see him. Why did we need to let him know what had happened? What could he do? It was his fault anyway. Mama had been doing great. We were all doing great and Daddy had messed up. He couldn't come home and make things better.

I didn't want to talk about it, so I left the living room. I wanted to be somewhere where I knew I wouldn't be bothered. I got a drawing pad and some crayons and went back to Mama's room. I sat beside her on the bed, listening to her congested breathing and drew. The picture was of a white sandy beach under a blue sky and blue ocean, the beach dotted with green palm trees. The only people on the beach were my family and me, except Daddy. He wasn't in this picture.

I waited with Mama until Daddy finally came home. The door opened and Daddy quietly came through. His face looked the way Chad's face looks when I'm starting to get on his nerves. Like he was just fed up.

He studied the scene before him and let out a deep sigh. "Good God, Mel, what are you doing?" He knew Mama wouldn't answer. He just had to say something.

He sat beside me on the bed. "What's happening, Pooh?" He smiled in a concerned way and I held back the urge to spit in his face.

Instead, I picked up the secret love card and threw it at him. "*This* is what's happening."

He looked at it only for a moment. He apparently recognized it

73

immediately. He closed his eyes and took a deep breath. "Oh, shit." He whispered.

He finally looked up into my red eyes. Eyes that hadn't left him since he'd entered the room. I had to struggle to contain my emotion. "This is your fault." I spoke each word clearly to ensure that he understood what I was saying.

He didn't seem to want to accept any responsibility and instantly began to defend himself. "It was a brief thing with Dee. Your mother was in the hospital. She wasn't here for me. I needed . . ." He paused and thought about how to continue. "I needed someone. Dee was here. I made a mistake. But we've all made mistakes." He nodded toward Mama's unconscious form as he said this last part.

"No!" I felt the tears pooling behind my eyelids. "No! This is different. Mama is sick. That's not the same kind of mistake." I thought for a moment. There was so much I wanted to say to him, but I wanted to make sure he understood. "You replaced her. That's a really huge mistake."

By this time the tears were rolling freely down my cheeks and snot was running from my nose. I had to continue. "People need second chances. You can't just replace people so easy. You should've waited for Mama to get better. Cecelia should've waited for Simon and Garfunkel to wash his face." I had to take a second to breathe. Daddy just stared at me, unable to understand my outburst.

A little more quietly now, I finished my speech. "Dee would be a real good mama. But do ya see me making her my new mama? I have a mama, and I'm not gonna replace her just 'cause it's easy. You did the easy thing. Now Mama's sick again, and it's not easy no more." With this I threw my picture at him and left him alone with his wife.

For the next year-and-a-half, my life was like riding the

Scrambler at the county fair. That ride whips you back and forth from one side of the car to the other. Sometimes you slam into the side so hard it rattles your teeth. It'll sling you right out if your not hanging on for dear life.

The constant whipping around in my own existence caused my body to ache. I was hanging on to anything I could grab because I was so afraid of being slung right out of my existence.

Mama recovered from that one day of slippage, but it was not her last. She began to slide further and further backwards into a dark place, and it was becoming harder and harder for us to pull her back. Every entrance into our home became an entrance into the unknown. There was no telling what would happen next, and nothing surprised us anymore.

During Mama's weeks of sobriety, she said she just couldn't take Daddy's "cattin' around." Daddy spent more and more time away from home and said that he just couldn't take Mama's drunkenness. From this circular passing of the buck, the end of my family was born. Neither parent was willing to assume their responsibility in the downfall of their marriage. Therefore, neither was willing to attempt to make necessary adjustments. This meant that there was absolutely no going back. The foundation on which my family was built was rotting and crumbling away.

Chapter 6
May 1977

On a warm Saturday afternoon in May 1977, the end would finally arrive. Daddy had been gone for several days and Mama had been drunk since before he left. We'd reached a point of fending for ourselves, eating peanut butter sandwiches and making our own decisions about when to go to bed and whether or not to bathe.

A spring rain shower interrupted this warm afternoon. I was outside playing with a tie-dye colored rubber kickball. Kicking it on the roof of the house and then catching it before it could hit the ground. Then the rain came.

One heavy drop plopped on my head. Soon that one was joined by many others. They were large and spaced far apart. I started to go inside, but decided I'd just stay out and enjoy the rain. This was an action that at one time in the not-so-distant past, would have been unacceptable. Now, nobody seemed to care where I was or what I was doing, so I stayed.

I walked to the creek in the woods. I wanted to enjoy this rain alone. I sat on the bank with beads of water crawling down by face and body. I watched the drops hit the surface of the creek and send ripples toward me. Not long after, the rain ended as quickly as it had begun.

I listened to the frogs and insects play their symphony of noise as the sun got busy drying things out. I wished I was a frog with nothing to do but sit in the woods, loving the sun and the rain and singing with the other animals.

I sat there envisioning myself as a happy frog until I was almost completely dry. I looked back up the hill, back toward my reality, and was reminded that I was not a frog.

When I entered the house I was greeted by a chorus of screaming voices. Daddy had apparently come home while I was at the creek and he and Mama were fighting. They were in the living room standing in the middle of the floor. Rachel and Chad cowered together on the sofa, crying and screaming for them to stop.

"You're a cheatin' sonofabitch and I don't want you anywhere near me or my kids." Mama's words were slurred, and her nightgown-clad body swayed from side to side.

"I'll gladly stay away from you, you stinkin' drunk. But they're my kids too and I will *not* leave them."

Mama lunged toward him and began to flail her arms at his face. "I hate you and your little whore girlfriend. I hate you, Dave Thorvald. I hate what you've done." She kept swinging as he attempted to avoid her punches. I watched them, completely stunned, but I could watch no more.

"Stop it!! Stop it!!" I screamed and ran toward them. I positioned myself between them. I could feel Mama's blows catching me in the top of the head, but I persisted at separating her from Daddy.

Daddy grabbed Mama's arms and pinned them to her sides. She struggled to free herself but was no match for his strength. I stood by them crying and still pleading for them to stop fighting.

"Mel. For God's sake, you hit Noble. Calm down." Daddy's

voice was loud. Mama became still and her glazed eyes tried to stay focused on him.

"Get out."

"Believe me, you couldn't make me stay if you tied me down." He briefly looked into her sad eyes. "You make me sick." He shoved her to the floor.

"Kids, I want you to pack a bag. We're leaving." He walked away from my mother, who was still lying on the floor. Rachel and Chad got up, still crying, and went to do as instructed.

I squatted down beside Mama. She stared at the ceiling. Her face was made of stone. All of the emotion had just drained away. The muscles around her mouth were slack and dark, and puffy crescent moons were perched beneath her eyes. She tried to push herself up, but her arms gave beneath her like strings of spaghetti.

"Are you okay?" She responded to this question by looking at me with empty eyes.

"Go with your father." Her words were soft and difficult to understand.

I helped her move herself into a sitting position leaning her back against the sofa. "I love you, Mama. I'm afraid to leave you."

Her empty eyes momentarily filled with a sweet sadness. She put great effort into forming her words. "I love you, too my Pooh. I don't want you to leave either." She stretched her hand out toward my face, but it never made it. It fell limp and her eyes went empty again.

Sometimes I thought that Mama's soul only sometimes lived in this body that used to belong to her, but now more often than not the soul retreated to some safe haven while the body simply existed. I knew that her soul had just retreated to that safe place, and I was left staring at the empty shell that used to be home to a very good spirit.

***

79

Daddy and my siblings appeared in the doorway, each with a small suitcase.

"Noble, do you have your things?"

Without looking at Daddy I answered, "I'm not going anywhere."

"Yes you are. Now go and pack a bag or you'll go without one."

I looked at him, shooting my anger into him like arrows from a bow. "I'm not going. She needs somebody. I'll stay with my mama."

He took a step toward me and I prepared myself to be yanked up, but he stopped before he reached me. With a shrug of his shoulders he said, "Fine. You wanna stay here with *her*, in the Hell *she's* created, and be angry at *me* about it, I'm gonna let you." He turned toward Rachel and Chad. "Let's go."

They all walked away. They went through the door and I heard the car start and pull away from the house. I listened to the sound of the engine fading in the distance as they drove away from us, leaving us alone together in our Hell.

The house was quiet except for Mama's rhythmic breathing. I had never in my life felt so alone, and the fear of not knowing the right thing to do, the fear of making an irreversible mistake, began to weigh on me and press me hard against the floor like Mamateen's heaviest quilt. I could barely move under the weight of that quilt. It kept me pinned in place. I just lay there and cried my helpless self to sleep beside my helpless mother.

***

I awakened shortly thereafter with the certain knowledge that we couldn't just lay here forever. I managed to rouse Mama long enough to get her moved to her bed. I believed that this was at least a start, and all that I was currently able to do. So, I crawled in bed beside her and curled up against her belly.

80

With each breath she released, I was bathed by the stench of cigarette smoke and alcohol. I ate it in and it filled my lungs, my belly, my head, and my heart becoming a permanent part of my cells. I realized that it wasn't just her breath that stank, but her skin, and her hair, and her clothes, and everything around her. A place that used to emit the clean fragrance of freshly laundered sheets and Ivory soap was now soiled with an odor that made me think of burning rotten fruit.

I then realized that I was not swallowing the smell, but the smell was swallowing me. I knew I had to accept this horrible air that became my cocoon. This was the stink of Hell, and Hell was where I was. This gagging odor was the least of concerns when one was in Hell. The emotion was a concoction of fear, anger, and confusion flecked with a sadness that I felt all the way into my bones.

***

These exact same emotions would visit me again in my future. Twenty years later on a rural road in a sparsely populated area of Carroll County. I approached what appeared to be a dead possum on the side of the road. As I drew closer, I slowed a little and thought I noticed some movement on the dead animal. Curiosity forced me to stop.

I stepped from the car to closer examine the country roadkill. Grasping and pulling at the chest of the possum was a baby possum crawling from its mother's pouch. I saw fear and confusion in that baby's eyes as its head bobbed from side to side and its mouth opened and closed.

At that moment in my adulthood, on the side of a country road, I recognized my own fear of twenty years earlier. The fear of a dead baby clinging to a dead mother. I know I should have rescued that lonely, motherless animal. Instead, I drove away as quickly as I could, trying once again to outrun a terror that had been right behind me for two decades.

***

In the middle of the night while my mother and I slept in that dark and foul room, I was awakened by a sudden thump. I sat up in bed while Mama's soul continued its vacation from her body. A light came on somewhere down the hall and I heard footsteps approaching slowly.

"Mama," I half cried, half whispered, hoping that my voice would reach my mother wherever she was. Mama never answered, and the footsteps drew nearer.

In an instant the door was pushed to its full openness and the light was flipped on. I couldn't contain the scream that had been perched on the edge of my lips. I also had closed my eyes tightly because I didn't want to see this beast that had been sent to take us deeper into Hell.

"Good God Almighty! Jesus Christ bless this child's soul." I recognized the voice, but before I could even open my eyes I was being pulled into a soft but firm hug.

When I finally managed to unsqueeze my eyelids, my face was pressed into Mamateen's neck and she was rocking me gently. "That Daddy of yours is one hardheaded idiot of a man, and he is right this minute sittin' in my doghouse for leavin' your precious little heart in this place all alone."

She continued to rock me and I was still getting over the shock of the fact that she was not a beast from Hell come to collect my mother and me.

"Lordy, Lordy, help us all." She said this quietly as she shook her head at my mother's unmoving body. She turned her attention to me. "How's my sweet mama's namesake gettin' along?"

She often called me her sweet mama's namesake instead of just Noble. She said that my existence was a tribute to her mama, and if anybody deserved a tribute, her sweet mama surely did.

"I'm fine, Mamateen, but why are you here?"

"I've come to take you away from this mess, girl. You're going with me."

"I can't leave her, Mamateen. She needs me. She can't be here alone. What if something happens to her?"

She pulled me into the soft powdery smell of the folds of skin just below her chin. "Sweet, sweet, angel sweet baby girl. You can't do nothing for her now. If you stay here, y'all both gonna suffer. Might as well you get out and come on home with me where you can be safe."

I pushed myself away from her even though the most secure I'd felt in months was right here, fitting comfortably into the flesh of her body. "Who's gonna make sure my mama's safe?"

"Tryin' to make sure she's safe is like chasing the moon and tryin' to catch it. You'll wear yourself out doin' all that tryin', and you'll never be any closer." She gave me a nice squeeze and a little shake.

"Your mama has put herself in this place, and only she can get herself out. Best thing for us now is just step back and give her some time and some room to figure that out."

I wanted desperately to let Mamateen pick me up and prop me on one of her generous "Maclachlan hips," and carry me out the door surrounded by the glorious aroma of grandma. As much as I wanted that, I knew that I couldn't leave Mama alone here. She might die here and I would be to blame.

Mamateen seemed to know that I was struggling. "Why don't you think on this real hard for a second. Think about what's gonna happen to you if you stay here. Will ya just lay up in this bed with her? What will you eat? Lot to think about." She gave me some time to ponder.

I remember battling with this decision. I looked at my grandmother. Everything about her was comfort. She was a girl who had grown up on a cotton farm as a member of a very large Irish immigrant family. They had overcome many hardships. She struggled through great trials, and came through with flying colors.

Mamateen's once-thick, flame-red hair was now gray and tightly curled. Her blue eyes were clear and deep. They were the color of seawater in the Gulf of Mexico. I sometimes thought that if I looked into them deeply enough, I'd be able to see the inside of her head, the way you can see the fish swimming in the Gulf waters.

Her real name was Christine Elizabeth Maclachlan Thorvald. The Mamateen came from Rachel, who'd attempted to call her Mama Christine but was unable to get it exact. The other grandkids were all just introduced to her as Mamateen. That would come to be her grandmamma name for the rest of her life.

Despite her hard life, she'd wound up with a great sense of humor. She would tell funny stories of her childhood. She made faces and played silly games with us kids. But underneath that silliness was a sweet and serious woman full of worldly wisdom.

I liked to think of Mamateen as music. There were times when she'd enter a room and I'd feel a deep vibration while watching her move with grace and assurance. It was as if her movements sent out sound waves that only my soul could hear, and they caused it to rattle around inside of my chest. She was the deep, moaning sadness of a cello accompanied by strong, solid notes of a piano. She was sprinkled with the Irish plunking of a harp. The piano was her strength and wisdom, the harp her fun, and the cello was an underlying pain. This was the comforting tune of Mamateen.

I wanted her to whisk me away and we could float along together on the music she made. But, I kept asking myself, *What about Mama?* I knew that she needed comfort and strength and fun and music. I wanted to help her get them. Despite Mamateen's pull, I decided I had to stay.

"I'm just gonna stay here and do what I can for her." I said it matter-of-factly, as if there would be no argument. I had underestimated Mamateen.

"The Hell you will. You might as well get it through that thick skull you inherited from that buzzard I call my son." As she said this, she knocked on my head. "You are going with me, like it or not."

I had to stand my ground, "No, Mamateen. I have no choice in this matter."

"You damn right you have no choice." She grabbed me in a tight bear hug and scooped me off the bed. "I'll send your daddy back for your things."

I realized immediately that she was kidnapping me. I wriggled in her arms and screamed, "Put me down! Put me down, now! No, no, no! I'm not going!"

I kicked my legs as her grip on me loosened a little. Next my arms thrashed and I could feel Mamateen's strength with each blow of my small fist.

As we started through the bedroom door, I acted instinctively. I grabbed tightly onto the doorjamb. I pressed against the inside of the door with my legs, using all of the force I could muster.

Mamateen pulled on me gently. "Child, you need to calm yourself. I will *not* let you stay. Calm yourself and we'll get outta here without anybody getting hurt." She managed to stay remarkably calm.

I tightened every muscle in my body and tried to become a stationary extension of the door jam. Tears were streaming down my cheeks and blurring my vision. "Please, please don't take me." I looked back over my shoulder at Mama.

Sometime during all of this commotion, she had awakened. Her eyes were staring blankly toward me. Her body was still empty of its soul. I felt Mamateen pry at my fingers and peel them loose from my grip on the door. This gave me a new sense of urgency.

"NO!!" I screamed as loudly as I could. "I have to stay."

Mamateen had loosened my grip and was now hugging me to her so tightly that I could barely breathe. "You cannot stay," was all she said as she turned.

Over her shoulder I got one last look at Mama. She was still lying there slack-faced and motionless. In a futile effort to change the subject I yelled, "I love you, Mama."

She didn't respond. I saw a tear pool in the corner of her eye and then glide down her hollow cheek as Mamateen pulled my spent body through the door. At that moment I knew that she was aware that I wanted to be with her but couldn't. At least she knew that.

Chapter 7
May 1977-May 1978

After stripping me away from my mother, Mamateen took me back to her house where Daddy, Rachel, and Chad were waiting. We ended up living there with our grandmother for a number of months while the details of the destruction of our family were finalized.

In the meanwhile, Daddy spent a lot of time with Dee and it became even clearer to me that Dee was his replacement for Mama. I overheard them talk of marriage, but they had to wait until the divorce was final. I only assumed that that meant Mama had to be out of the picture for good before Daddy could get married again.

We stayed with Mamateen until the end of the summer. Living with her was pretty nice. I got to sleep with her and she comforted me when I was awakened by nightmares. I dreamt of Mama being dragged into dead hollow tree trunks by unseen animals with blazing eyes. She screamed as she was pulled into the hole and I reached for her. Our fingertips touched but I could never get a grip on her. She was sucked into the opening, her screams being replaced by my own.

Mamateen was a warm and constant presence that supplied me with firm-ground footing, the likes of which I had not felt in some time. She had our breakfast ready for us in the mornings, complete with vitamin supplement. She provided me with a daily lunch of peanut butter and jelly sandwiches cut into two triangles, accompanied by Fritos and grape juice. We had made-from-scratch Southern suppers every night. She bathed me in warm lilac-scented baths and powdered my "John Henry" before shrouding me in a gown that smelled like sunshine from having been dried outside on the line. We finished every day with stories she created about a mischievous boy named Rusty Stob.

This steady routine made me forget at times the haze of uncertainty that had surrounded me only months earlier. I felt stable. I knew what to expect. In some situations, predictability is the greatest comfort.

Just before school started, Daddy announced that we would be moving back into our old house. We had not seen Mama since we left the house. Mamateen told me it was because she was trying to take care of herself. When Daddy broke the news that we'd be going back, I was elated. I remembered Mama being there the last time I was there, so I simply assumed that she would still be there.

We packed our things and went home. Upon entering the house the first thing I noticed was that it was very clean. Mama had been awful busy getting it clean for us to come home to. This was cleaner than I ever remembered it being before. After throwing my suitcase onto my bed, I made a beeline to Mama's room. She was not there, and all of the things that belonged to her were gone also. I ran back to the living room where Daddy was still standing.

"Where's Mama?"

Daddy squatted down to be eye to eye with me. "Pooh, I thought you understood that she wouldn't be here."

"Where is she?"

"She went back to Winder to be near her family. She's close to MeeMee and Aunt Louise now."

"When'll she be back?"

He stood, taking away the eye-to-eye. "She's not coming back. We'll be living here now without her."

I was terribly confused. If Mama wasn't going to be here, I wasn't sure that I wanted to be here. All I could manage to say was, "How? Why?"

Daddy picked me up, giving me back the eye-to-eye, but now at his level. "I know it's hard to understand. But, your mother and I are getting divorced. We won't be married anymore. We'll do fine without her."

I wrinkled my nose and squinched my eyebrows. "I don't want to be without her. I want to see her."

"Honey, y'all can see her soon. Right now we're waiting for a judge to tell us when you can see her."

I continued to look at him as if he were speaking to me in Pig Latin, which I had yet to figure out how to decipher. He read my look. "I know it doesn't make sense to you. It doesn't make much sense to me. You're just gonna have to trust me."

Trust was a commodity that I had very little of. I was not certain that I could believe anything that anyone told me. My situation reminded me of the summertime heat rising off the blacktop. When the heat is visible and it blurs everything within sight. Things would appear one way one instant, and then another the next. You couldn't trust anything you saw in that heat, same as I couldn't trust anything in my life right now.

Rather than argue or protest or demand explanation, I simply put my head down and pushed myself out of Daddy's arms. I was becoming accustomed to disappointment, and I had lost the will to try and keep it away.

Only a few weeks after we moved home, Dee moved in.

Daddy said that they were going to get married soon. He said that until they did, Dee would be here to take care of the house and us. As much as I tried to hate her presence, I just couldn't. Like Mamateen, she provided a stable routine that I could hold onto. She talked to me and played with me and laughed with me. She told me scary ghost stories at bedtime. These were true ghost stories that she had actually experienced, and they would scare me half to death. Then she would make a blanket pallet in the den floor, and she would sleep with me there, like a slumber party. I slowly became very attached to Dee. The longer I went without seeing or hearing from Mama, the less I thought about her, and the less I missed her. Life was getting back up to speed.

Chad and Rachel both felt differently about Dee. They were angry with Daddy for being able to divert his attention so easily. They thought his attention should be with us at the time, and not on some new young bride-to-be. They weren't interested in having a new mama; they simply wanted more of Daddy. They also thought that Dee was just too young and stylish to be a proper mama.

While I was getting on with life and trying to reestablish firm footing, my siblings became intolerable at home. They were both skipping school on a regular basis and staying in trouble when they actually did go. Rachel had started smoking cigarettes and getting in trouble for smoking at school and for selling pot. Chad was just disappearing with his friends and staying gone for days at a time.

Daddy yelled at them and punished them, but it only made things worse. Chad would sneak from his bedroom window and do as he pleased. Rachel would simply break rules right in front of Daddy's face and gladly accept the next round of punishment. Their behavior made it difficult for me to adjust to our new family. They teased me about being a "goody-goody" and a tattle. I just didn't want to be in trouble. I didn't want anyone to rock our boat.

Daddy and Dee finally got married. Daddy told us that the

divorce was settled and Mama was staying in Winder. He didn't know when we'd be able to see her. He said that he had been awarded full custody of us and Mama was not granted visitation rights. The judge said she had to go through rehabilitation before we could see her. At the time I only understood this to mean that I still would not be able to see Mama.

As time passed, distance grew between all of us. Rachel and Chad were each so preoccupied with themselves that they had no time for me. I was afraid to get any closer to Dee because I felt as if I was betraying Mama and Rache and Chad. When Daddy wasn't at work, he and Dee were busy talking and laughing with each other. He barely paid any attention to me at all. I was lonely and I wanted my mama.

I was in my fourth-grade year at school. Despite the unrest I felt at home, I still managed to do well in school. School was my sanctuary. I had friends who enjoyed being with me. My teachers thought I was smart and funny and they gave me a lot of attention. I was always saddest when school was out.

It was Thanksgiving break from school and, even though it was only a five-day break, I dreaded the time at home and away from my sanctuary.

The day before Thanksgiving I was at home alone with Dee. Daddy was working and Chad and Rachel were God knows where. I was watching TV while Dee began preparations for Thanksgiving dinner in the kitchen. The phone rang. I ignored it. Dee answered it.

I heard bits of her conversation. "Dave's not here . . . kids are gone . . . only Noble." After hearing my name I strained to hear her conversation.

"I'm not sure if I should. Maybe you should call back later, when Dave's home." She listened to the other end. "Yes. I know it's a holiday. I'm not sure." She listened again. I moved into the kitchen doorway. I could tell she was nervous. She stepped back and forth from one foot to the other as she twirled the phone chord in her fingers.

"Okay. Okay. Just hold on a minute." She saw me in the doorway and took the phone from her ear. She pressed her palm over the receiver. "Noble. This is for you." She raised her eyebrows and said, "Now if you don't want to talk I can . . ."

I interrupted her. "Give it to me." I held my hand out. I felt butterflies flapping around inside my stomach, tickling. The tickle made me feel a bit nauseous.

Hesitantly she handed me the phone. I pressed the receiver tightly against my head. The plastic was warm. I listened for a moment before speaking. "Hello?"

"Hello my little Pooh Bear." Mama's voice was practically a squeal.

I had not heard her voice in over six months. The sound of her deep Southern drawl, unaffected by alcohol, pierced me. She said the word bear as if it were spelled b-a-y-a-h. It had been an eternity since I had been called Pooh Bayah.

These words from her touched me somewhere deep inside, in a place that I had almost forgotten even existed. This long-missed touch stirred heat in my belly that radiated out to my limbs and my head. Dizziness and a wave of nausea hit me. I could taste metal in the back of my throat. I wanted to speak, but I knew the second I opened my mouth tears would flow.

"Mama," was all I managed to say before, as predicted, tears streamed from my eyes and my body was racked by quiet sobs.

"Oh no, no, no child. Don't start cryin'." As she said this I could tell that her own voice was shaking with emotion. "This is a happy time. I'm talking to my baby. Don't cry, Honey. Stop your cryin'."

We were both silent for a few moments as we struggled to

regain our composure. I wiped my tears and took deep breaths. Dee knelt beside me and rubbed my back.

"How ya been doin, Mama?" My voice still cracked, but at least I got the words out.

"Oh, Babydoll, I been doin' just great. Just great I tell ya. How *you* been doin?"

"School is good. Rachel and Chad are never home. I miss you a lot of times." There was so much I wanted to say that I didn't even know how to start.

"Pooh, I *know* your doing well in school. I would expect no less from my baby genius. And goodness gracious alive how I miss you, too. I worry myself sick wonderin' how y'all kids are doing. I want to see y'all so bad that I just ache for you."

With all of her talking, the first shock of hearing her voice had passed. My sadness was now being replaced by joy. My voice was steadier. "I want to see you real bad, too."

"I'm gonna call and talk to your Daddy real soon. See what we can arrange. I need you kids in my life. I need y'all somethin' ferocious."

"I need you too, Mama."

"Well, you just be patient. How's that hussy Tweedle Dee treatin' y'all?" She laughed a short laugh.

"Who?" I didn't know a hussy named Tweedle Dee.

"I mean Dee. How's your stepmother treatin' y'all?"

"She's nice." I was afraid to say too much. I was afraid of betrayal.

"Well, all is well here in Winder. Winder up and let'r go!" She laughed again. She always said that when she spoke of her girlhood home. "MeeMee and Aunt Louise and Uncle Oliver and the boys all send their love."

"Okay."

"Tell your brother and sister I love them and miss them to beat

93

the band."

"I will."

"Now y'all take care and have a nice Turkey Day. Be patient and I'll talk to you soon."

"Okay Mama. I love you." Tears began to rise again. I didn't want to let her go.

"I love you too my little Pooh Bayah. Be good now. Bye-bye."

"Bye, Mama." I held the phone tight against my ear until I heard the dial tone.

Dee took the phone from me. "You all right, Honey?" I nodded and went back to my place in front of the TV.

Mama told the truth about talking to Daddy. Over the next six months she called regularly. They were still trying to work out the details of us seeing her.

On the phone she told us of her new life. She had rented a nice big house with her "divorce settlement." She had gone through rehabilitation and was no longer drinking. She had gotten a really good job as a teller at the People's Bank. She was spending time with her mama and sister. She seemed to be doing very well. She seemed happy.

Finally the time came for us to see her. It was arranged for us to spend a long weekend with her at the end of May, 1978. We were out of school and Daddy and Dee were planning a short getaway to the mountains. They said it was because they never got a honeymoon. Mama would keep us from a Thursday afternoon to a Monday morning while Daddy and Dee were gone.

I was very excited. Chad and Rachel were both excited as well. I wanted to see Mama. I think that they just wanted to get away from Daddy and Dee. We packed our bags and Daddy drove us to Winder.

Daddy pulled into the driveway of a fancy old white house right in downtown Winder. It was across the street from the First

Baptist Church. It was a spectacular house. The front porch wrapped all the way around both sides. There was a huge side yard with a row of tall magnolia trees. There was a front walk that led from the sidewalk to the front porch steps. In the front yard was one giant oak tree. Its branches stretched out wide and up high. Its old roots were causing the sidewalk to buck up around them. It was beautiful. It looked like a home right out of a story. I fell in love with that house at first sight.

Mama emerged through the front door, screen slamming behind her. "Hey y'all!" She ran down the steps to greet us. "Hey my children. Come on over here and give ya ol' mama a hug." She knelt down and threw her arms wide open. We all ran to her and were engulfed in a group hug. There were tears whose sharpness was dulled by the giggles of three children thrilled to see their long-lost mother.

Daddy stood back while Dee waited in the car. He sat three small suitcases on the walkway. "Here's their things. We'll be back Monday mornin'."

Mama looked up at him. "Won't y'all have a glass of lemonade?"

"We need to hit the road."

"Suit yourself."

Daddy got in the car. As they pulled away he honked the horn and waved. Dee looked the other way.

"Hit the road, Jack and don'tcha come back no more no more no more no more," Mama sang with glee. We all joined in and sang two more choruses of "Hit the Road, Jack" as loudly as we could in the front yard of that storybook house.

The inside of the house was just as beautiful. All of the rooms had slick, shiny hardwood floors. The windows stretched all the way from the floor to the high ceilings. Mama had the whole house decorated in bright colors. It was gorgeous.

95

"I have a room for each of you. This one's yours Rachel." She opened the door to a room right off the living room. It was decorated in red and purple floral prints. Rache gasped and stepped into the room with its full-sized bed.

"This is so groovy, Mama. Thanks a million."

"Now let's see yours, Mr. Chad." We walked down the long hallway and opened the door at the end. The room was done in blues and greens. It was very modern.

"Cool," Chad said as he threw his suitcase onto the bed.

Mama put her hands on her knees and bent to face me. "Best for last." She gave a little shudder of excitement, then grabbed me by the hand. "Come on." We ran two doors down from Chad's room and she threw the door open. "Voila."

My mouth fell open at the sight. I was looking right into Miami Dolphin Wonderland. The room was decorated in colors of aquamarine and orange. She had even painted the walls aquamarine. The curtains and bedspread were covered in the Dolphins logo. Posters were on the walls and a helmet sat on a top shelf in the bookcase that was built right into the wall. I had never had my own room before. I was thrilled.

"Gosh, Mama. Thank you. I love it."

"Look at this." She walked to a door in the side wall beside the bookcase. She pushed it open. "Right into my room. In case you need anything."

"All right!" This was a perfect room. This was a perfect place.

The weekend was great. Mama spoiled us with movies and eating out and toys. When Sunday night rolled around we were all sad that we'd have to leave in the morning. We were having supper at Hawg Wild Bar-B-Q.

"I don't want to leave tomorrow, Mama," Rachel said.

"Maybe if we're lucky, your daddy'll let y'all come back for good." Mama smiled before sticking a fork-full of pork into her mouth.

"You mean it?" Rachel asked.

"I'm gonna do my best, Babies. I'm gonna do my best." She smiled again and raised her plastic cup full of sweet iced tea. "Here's to us. Together forever." We all clinked our cups together and laughed. We each took a turn at repeating "Together forever" before taking a swig of tea.

Chapter 8
July 1978

Mama did talk to Daddy about letting us come to live with her for good. He didn't really like the idea, but everyone did their part to convince him. We three kids told him that Mama was doing great and we liked it with her. We practically begged.

Mama told him that she was sorry for all of the heartache she had caused, but she deserved another chance. She told him she didn't want us to think that our mama had abandoned us. She wanted us to know that she wanted us.

Even with all of this persuasion, I believe it was Dee that was the clincher. One morning early, Daddy and Dee were sitting at the kitchen table drinking coffee and discussing our potential move to Mama's. We kids were supposedly still sleeping. In actuality, all three of us were crouched down by the kitchen door, listening intently to their conversation, ready to bolt at the first sign of being discovered.

Dee was giving her perspective on the matter. "I know you're worried about the kids, but Mel has a point. She does deserve a second chance. And, they wanna go."

"It's just so risky," Daddy responded.

"She seems to be doin' great. It could be a good thang for everbody." She paused and I could hear the smile in her voice when she continued. "Just thank, we could finally live like newlyweds."

We heard someone slide a chair back from the table so we stealthily ran back down the hallway into Chad's room. With the door shut we began our discussion. Rachel's face beamed with a huge grin, "That's the first time I agreed with anything that woman has ever said."

"Yeah, can you believe that witch is on our side?" Chad added.

I couldn't believe they were happy. "Don't you think she's just trying to get rid of us? Don't you think all she cares about is acting like 'newlyweds'?" I said this last part in my best impersonation of Dee, with my hand on my cocked hip and a bat of my eyelashes.

"No shit, Sherlock," Rachel said this with a grunt. "Who cares if she wants to get rid of us? We want to get rid of her too. As long as we get to go live with Mama, I could care less what she says."

Not long after that discussion, Daddy gave us his verdict. He said that he was going to allow us to go and live with Mama on a trial basis for a month. If all went well, then he would consider letting us stay for good.

We were going to spend the month of July with her. That way, if we ended up staying we'd have time to get registered for the new school year. I was so excited that I felt like small currents of electricity were constantly jolting through by body. My skin tingled in anticipation and I was unable to sit still at all.

We were going to have a new life in a new place. It was like being an explorer in search of something that no one else had ever seen. I thought that this must have been how Columbus felt as he set out to prove the world was round. Better yet, I felt more like Alvar Nunez Cabeza de Vaca. My fourth grade teacher, Mrs. Usher, called Cabeza de Vaca the "compassionate conquistador."

She said that as he made his way across the southern part of North America, he befriended the natives and eventually saved them from slavery. This made him my favorite of all of the North American explorers that we studied. Also, I really liked to say his name.

When July rolled around, we were all packed and ready to go. Mamateen once told me that, while her side of the family was Irish, my father's father's family was Norwegian. Mamateen said we were related to some Vikings. This bit of information had almost converted me from a Dolphins fan to a Vikings fan, only I hated purple.

Anyway, Mamateen said that some of our Viking relatives were some pretty rough characters who sailed around raping and pillaging and conquering helpless people. She said that having that blood in his veins is what had made my grandfather, Lester, so intolerable, and that I should pray that my easygoing Irish blood would drown out my Viking meanness.

Something about setting out on our adventure seemed to have brought my Viking blood to the surface. I was on a conquest. I felt like nothing could stop me, not even Irish blood. I made a Viking hat out of cardboard for the occasion.

As we loaded our things in the car, my beautiful hat caught Daddy's eye. "What's this all about, Noble?"

"I am not Noble. I am Alvar Nunez Cabeza de Vaca."

Daddy furrowed his brow and bit his lip. "What exactly does that mean?"

"I am a Viking on a conquest adventure and my name is Alvar Nunez Cabeza de Vaca."

Daddy squatted beside me and pulled me in close to him by the waist. He whispered in my ear. "Just between you and me, I don't think that Cabeza de Vaca is a Viking name."

I poked out my bottom lip, disappointed at Daddy's attempt to

101

burst my bubble. "But I *really* like that name."

Daddy nodded. "Okay then. Cabeza de Vaca it is. I'm sure there's some Viking somewhere named Cabeza de Vaca. If not, then you can be the first." He put his arm around my shoulder. "Will you make me a promise, Alvar?"

"Sure," I answered without hesitation. I loved to make promises. I took pride in the fact that I almost never broke them.

"Well, promise that if this adventure becomes too much for you, you'll call me for help."

"What do you mean?"

"Well, every great conquistador had his problems. If you start having problems on this adventure, it's okay to ask for help. Promise you'll call if you need help."

"I promise."

Several hours later we were dropped off at our new temporary home. Mama was anxiously awaiting our arrival. Daddy dropped us off with little more than a kiss on the cheek and a "Be good," and then he was gone and our adventure began.

Mama said that she was determined to make it the best month of our lives. When July was over, nobody was gonna be able to take her babies away from her ever again. We couldn't wait to get started.

She was absolutely right. The month of July was one of the best times I ever remember having. Mama still had to work, but she let us do most anything we wanted to do. Since our house was in the downtown area of Winder, we were close to everything. The Winder City Public Pool for swimming, the cinema for movie watching, the Dairy Delite for ice cream, and even the public library for Chad to get science-fiction books; all within walking distance of our house. Mama would just leave us money every morning and tell us to have a good, safe day.

Even with all of those things to do, the yard of that house was my favorite place on earth. In the side yard there was the row of four magnolia trees. They were so close to each other that their limbs were entwined and you couldn't tell where one stopped and the next began.

The limbs of those trees were thick and they twisted and turned. The ones close to the bottom stooped right down to the ground, like they were bending over to pick me up. Then they shot right back up toward the sky. Those magnolias were perfect for climbing.

I'd climb up in them and move from one to the other, back and forth, and never touch the ground. I'd play up there for hours. Pull those thick plastic-like leaves off and tear them into fun shapes. Break off the heavy buds and blooms and drop them to the ground. magnolia bombs.

In the backyard there was a big old pecan tree. It was a beautiful tree. It had leaves that were long and slender, like Mama's fingers, and they bowed toward the ground as if they were sad. Pecan trees reminded me of weeping willows, only not quite *as* sad. Weeping willows look *weak* and sad and the pecan is sad, but still strong. While the leaves look weepy, the limbs are sturdy and can support my weight. Being able to support my weight has always been the most important characteristic of a good tree.

Between that pecan tree and another smaller oak tree was a rope hammock. On the side fence along the edge of the yard was a muscadine vine. I'd lie in that hammock and feast on whatever bounty the yard was currently producing. In late summer, the muscadines were ripe for picking. I'd pull the tail end of my T-shirt up and fill it with fruit. Then I'd lay there in the hammock and bite the tough muscadine skins and suck the sweet goo from the middle. It was certainly the best yard that God ever created.

In late fall and winter, the muscadines were replaced with pecans. I'd repeat the same process with my new crop. I'd dig the meat of the nuts out of their shells, careful not to break the good part, get it out all in one piece.

This yard seemed to give me everything that I needed. It provided me with comfort, pleasure, discoveries, and even food. I felt as if I could have lived totally alone in that yard forever. It was peace and rejuvenation.

Living in this storybook house with the best yard in the world was when I realized that being outside was one of the most pleasurable things in my life. In addition to all of the treasures that I discovered in this one yard, I also realized that outdoors was always involved in the things that brought me the greatest joys.

In the heat of the summer, when everyone else sat in their climate-controlled homes sipping iced tea, I enjoyed feeling my own sweat saturating my cotton clothing and running down my face and neck.

In the coldest part of winter, when everyone else sat in their climate controlled homes sipping hot cocoa, I enjoyed seeing my own breath come from my mouth and feeling the tingling of cold ears and nose.

On rainy spring days, when everyone else sought shelter and carried umbrellas, I enjoyed turning my face to the sky and feeling the heavy drops pop me. I loved the musty smell that the hot pavement had after having been sprinkled with a warm rain.

Mamateen once told me that if it ever rains when the sun is still shining, it means that the devil is beating his wife. The rain is her tears. I always felt so guilty about getting so much enjoyment from someone else's pain. But, those unexpected downpours on a sunny day always left the earth sounding, smelling, and feeling different. Those rains were the simplest way for me to find happiness. They made me feel like anything could happen, and when it does, everything will change. I hated it for the devil's wife, but for me those rains seemed hopeful.

After our perfect month with Mama, it came time for Daddy to decide if we could stay. We let him know what a great time we had been having, and that Mama had been nothing but a model parent. He must have been enjoying his newlywed days, too, because it didn't take much convincing him. He said yes so quickly that I couldn't believe I had heard him right. But I had. He said we could stay, but he reminded me of the promise I had made. I reassured him that if I got lost or scared on this journey, he'd be the first to know.

Chapter 9
August 1978-April 1979

We started school and began the process of settling into our new lives. Things were going smoothly for the most part. Rachel and Chad each fell right into school. They both made friends easily and began to spend more and more time away from home.

Rachel was in tenth grade now and some of her new friends were old enough to drive. She was out a lot. She went to football games and school dances and pizza parties and sleepovers.

Chad quickly found himself a girlfriend named Charlotte Mooney. She lived close to us, so he was always off walking to her house to spend time with her. He somehow managed to charm himself into the very good graces of Charlotte's mama, so he was *always* welcome at their house. He was invited to do everything the Mooneys ever did. When they had dinner, he was invited. When they went to the movie, he was invited. Even when they went to Grandma Mooney's house for the weekend, he was invited. It got to where Chad spent more time with them than he did with his own family.

I was a bit different. I didn't really venture out so much. I had a very difficult time making friends at my new school. I went from a middle-class suburban school where being smart was honorable, to a lower-class rural school where being smart made me an outcast. There was no one beating a path to my door in order to befriend me. After all, who wants to be friends with a snobby, brown-nosing, geek of a white girl?

However, this didn't bother me. I convinced myself that school was no place for socializing anyway. I was in school to learn, and if I planned to be a world-renowned astronaut and rocket scientist (yes, I had given up on football), there was no time for socializing. At school I had to keep my nose to the grindstone and I could socialize at home. The magnolias were my friends. They were perfect friends. I always knew where they were—they would wrap me up and hold me tight, and they always, *always*, laughed at my jokes. Who needs people friends when you can have tree friends?

The days began to look a whole lot like one another. We all rutted ourselves into a stagnant routine. I am not generally bothered by routine. Routine usually makes me feel safe. There's comfort in knowing what comes next. This routine was different. It was a lonely routine. For me, it went like this: school, afternoon homework, dinner with Mama while Rachel and Chad were out, playing in the yard until after dark, then bath and bed. The next morning brought with it a repeat performance.

It was lonely because it really didn't involve other people. I disliked my classmates so much that my time at school was spent hidden within myself and within the books that I could get my hands on. Dinner with Mama was really my favorite time of day, although it too was lonely. The meal generally consisted of Stouffer's Salisbury steak dinners, frozen pizzas, or chicken pot pies. The conversation was limited. Mama was too tired from working all day to share with me her cherished words of wisdom. I liked being there with her, but I wanted her to talk to me. I wanted her to ask me about my day. I wanted her to dance around singing David Bowie songs with me while we cleaned the kitchen together. I wanted her to teach me about life the way she used to do.

It wasn't like that. We ate quietly. She sighed occasionally. Kitchen cleanup involved throwing cardboard containers into the garbage and rinsing two forks. No singing. No dancing. No music in our lives at all anymore.

One night the routine changed slightly. Instead of staying safely embedded in the well-worn rut, Mama poked her head up to get a glance of what it looked like outside the rut.

We were eating our Salisbury steak dinners, Mama chewing each bite slowly, me burying green peas in mashed potatoes and swallowing whole to avoid their taste. Mama swallowed, then looked up from her food directly at me. I shifted uncomfortably in my Naugahyde chair. I felt fairly certain that the predictability was about to be drained from my life.

"Have you ever *really* wanted to grab the brass ring?" She paused, but my senses told me that she wasn't really looking for an answer. And thank goodness because I had no idea what she was talking about. I waited for her to continue.

"I mean have you ever really wanted it so badly that you'd do anything to get it? You reach and stretch and reposition, then on one more pass, BAM!" She slammed both palms against the table for emphasis. I jumped at the noise and inadvertently bit into a mashed-potatoed green pea. I gave her my "I think you're a lunatic" look as I swallowed the mess in my mouth.

She sat up straight and shrugged her shoulders. "You got it. You pull your hand back and there it is." She held out her index finger and thumb as if holding a small item between them. She stared at her hand. "There it is."

She looked at me with a forced smile. She opened her hand and held it high above her head as if whatever had been there had

109

disintegrated and was being blown away by the wind. I smiled back at her, hoping that a response was not expected.

With a frown she said, "It's not really brass. It's not really what you expected at all. All that effort and it's just not what you expected."

She paused and took a short sip of her iced tea. Then she looked back at me with a tilt of her head. I knew what was coming next. "That ever happen to you?" This is where my response was required.

"I don't think so." I stuffed my mouth with a large bite of steak to avoid having to speak further.

"It's happened to me." She rested her chin in the palm of her hand. "Oh yes, it *has* happened to me. See, what happens is that I think I've figured out what I want in order to be happy. Then, I work and work to get it." She shook her head. "It turns out it doesn't make me happy at all. It's just like that brass ring that's not really brass." She put her chin back in her hand and stared into space. "Happiness, that's not really happiness."

I continued to eat, hoping Mama would ditch this conversation and go back into our usual uneventful dinner routine. Much to my disappointment, she was not about to let this one go just yet.

"Like right now," she continued. "I thought this life would make me happy. My own job, own house, my kids living with me." She shook her head again. "No . . . no," head still shaking, "I'm not really happy."

Her head stopped moving and she looked right at me. "Not really happy."

As she looked at me I saw droplets of water in the corner of her eyes, and my stomach tightened. As my mother and I sat gazing at one another over Salisbury steak, I saw her fear. I felt it.

I knew that she was standing on the edge of a bottomless pit, struggling not to step over. My own fear blossomed inside me. I was afraid she was going to take that step. I reached across the small table and grabbed her hand and squeezed it as tightly as I could.

I closed my eyes and said a quick silent prayer. *Dear God, Please, please, please help me hold her. Help me keep her from going over. Help me make her happy so she'll step away.* While my eyes were closed, I felt her other hand come down on top of mine. When I opened my eyes to look at her again, the tears were rolling freely down her face.

The first six months of living in Winder had been pretty uneventful. After the dinner conversation with Mama, she snapped out of it briefly. The turbulence of the holidays kept her busy, and kept her anchored to solid ground. I began to breathe a little more regularly and worry a little less about her slipping.

The excitement that accompanied celebrating Christmas for the first time in her own home surrounded by her own family kept Mama high for months to come. She was positively bubbly through Christmas and New Year's and beyond.

By late February, she'd come down from that high and was back to the gloominess that had leaked from her on the evening of the Salisbury steak conversation. Our routine was back in full force and Rachel and Chad were spending even less time at home. I don't know exactly where they were, with friends or something, I only knew that I hardly ever saw them, and Mama made no attempts to make them spend time with us.

I missed my siblings. I missed my Daddy. I missed Dee. I even missed my Mama now that she had once again hidden herself within. Loneliness and isolation began to creep slowly over my body the way a vine climbs its way up a tree, growing, tightening, strangling.

My refuge from my world was, as always, school. I buried myself in schoolwork to fend off the feeling of isolation. I studied,

I read, I created. When I felt my sanity slipping through my fingers, I would do my homework and sanity would be briefly restored.

By early May, the heat of the southern summer had already settled itself. The two-mile walk home from school left me drenched in salty sweat everyday. I walked slowly to enjoy the unmarked canopy of a royal blue sky and the floral breeze. The colors and the smells and the feel of spring gave me life.

This particular day I was walking and humming and internally planning my strategy for the completion of my social studies project. South American capitals, it was sure to earn an A. I was enjoying my thoughts and the day, happy, for the moment, with my life.

As I turned the corner onto Johnson Street and got the first glimpse of our house, I stopped dead still on an uneven crack in the sidewalk. I knew immediately that something was wrong. Mama's Galaxy 500 was sitting in the driveway. She usually didn't get home until around five. What could she possibly be doing at home so early?

I looked down at the spot on the sidewalk where my foot was resting. "Step on a crack, break your Mama's back." I snatched my foot up as if I'd just been scalded, and I broke off into a full speed run toward home, backpack full of books smacking against my back as I went.

I charged through the door yelling, "Mama!" I dropped my backpack in the foyer floor with a swift dip of my shoulder then I rushed down the hallway. I burst through the closed door to her bedroom calling for her. There was no response. I stood in the open doorway, searching.

The bathroom door was open, and through the doorway I saw what I had most feared. A foot, *her* foot, on the floor, poking into view from behind the toilet. I ran to her.

She was sprawled naked on the bathroom floor. It appeared as if she had been kneeling at the toilet and had fallen over. The room was full of the stench of vomit. Sprays of dried puke were all along the toilet and floor.

I fell down beside her and pulled her head into my arms. As her face neared mine, her breath hit me like a sledgehammer in my chest. I heaved and gagged and swallowed my own puke just before it escaped me. At least I knew she was breathing. I shook her and screamed as loudly as I could, "Mama. Mama, wake up. Are you okay? Wake up. Please wake up. Please!"

Her only response was an involuntary lolling of her head to the side as I lost my grip on it. I was fighting nausea, tears, and panic. I laid her gently back on the floor and thought quickly about what to do next.

I picked up the phone from her bedside table and held the receiver to my ear. Who to call? I couldn't be here alone with her, but I didn't know who to call. I poked my finger in the circle marked 0 on the rotary phone and gave it a spin. Within seconds it was answered. "Operator."

"I need an ambulance fast."

"What's the problem?"

"My mama's very sick."

"Can she talk to me?"

"No. She's out cold."

"What happened?"

"I don't know. Please send somebody. It's 110 Johnson Street. Hurry." Before she could ask any more stupid questions, I hung up. I ran outside and sat on the porch steps waiting for the ambulance. I just couldn't make myself wait inside with her.

Several minutes later I heard a siren screaming from the direction of Broad Street. It was definitely getting closer. Thank God, the operator hadn't just blown me off as a crank.

113

I stood and nervously bounced up and down on my toes, hands jammed tightly in the pockets of my cut off jeans. I watched in the direction from which I heard the siren approaching, anxious for it to come into view.

Finally the ambulance rounded the corner and slowed to a stop in front of my house. I ran to the curb to meet them. Two young, clean-cut, white men in blue uniforms jumped from the van and began to heft large toolboxes full of medical equipment out of the back. The blonde haired one looked at me seriously, "What's the problem?"

"My mama is passed out on the bathroom floor. I don't know what happened."

"Show us." He motioned toward the house with one of his boxes.

I ran ahead of the two men to the bathroom. To my surprise, Mama was sitting up now. Her back was pressed against the pink tile wall and her head was dropped forward, chin against chest.

The dark haired one shoved me to the side and knelt beside Mama. "Ma'am, can you hear me? Ma'am, are you all right?" He took things from the box and unwrapped plastic wrappers.

Mama lifted her head and in a slurred, almost indistinguishable voice asked, "Who the hell are you? What're you doing in my house?"

The serious faced blonde looked into her face and said, "Ma'am, your daughter called us. We're just gonna check you out real quick." He tore a paper wrapper. She reached up and slapped it from his hand.

"Don't need checked out. Go on. Get outta my house."

Blondie persisted, "Ma'am we really just need to . . ."

She interrupted him with a piercing, maniacal scream. I covered my ears and felt the familiar sting of tears pooling in my eyes.

"You're gonna have to calm down." This time the dark-haired one tried to talk to her.

"Get outta my house now! Leave me alone." She screamed the crazy scream again.

"Let's go, Ted, there's nothing we can do for this drunk. She's gonna have to sleep it off." Blondie was now packing his boxes.

Ted looked my way. My hands were still over my ears, and I knew my mouth was hanging open, but I couldn't close it. He looked away quickly and began to help Blondie pack up.

They stood with their toolboxes and brushed past me in the doorway. I stepped after them. "You can't leave." They kept walking. I grabbed Ted's shirt.

"You're s'posed to help me."

Ted turned and looked at me, he gave a slight smile. First smile I had seen from either of these two "angels of mercy." "Is there anybody you can call?"

"I called you." Desperation began to burn through my skin. I wanted to dig my dirty tomboy nails into Ted's arm and force him to stay and help me.

"Look little girl, there's nothing we can do. She's not sick. She's drunk. Just let her sleep it off, she'll sober up eventually."

My desperation was morphing into anger. I wanted to dig my nails into Ted now not to make him stay, but to hurt him. "My name is Noble, not little girl, and she *is* sick. You aren't very smart, are you?"

Ted snorted, "You're wasting our time, *Little Girl.*"

"Let's get going, Ted." Blondie was calling from the front door.

"No problem." Ted spun around and lugged his burden back to the van.

I thought I'd gotten a glimpse of compassion in Ted, but as they drove away in the van, I knew there couldn't possibly have been anything nice in either of those two men.

I crumpled to the floor in the foyer and let my emotion escape. I followed Mama's example and screamed repeatedly like a madwoman until my energy was spent.

I thought that the 0 on the phone would yield help. I had been told that that was the answer to all emergencies. Now I knew that no one would help. As I sat in the floor, daylight slowly turning to darkness beyond the large windows, I realized I was completely alone. I had to help myself, but I knew that I couldn't.

I cried, not for Mama, not for Rachel and Chad, just for me. I cried because I felt sorry for myself. I began to ask, "Why me? Why am I being punished? Why am I being forced to live through things that I just can't handle anymore on my own? Why am I alone? Why is everyone else living beyond this door while I lay here in the floor dying alone, crushed by my own presence in this place? Why?"

After I recovered from the ambulance episode, I knew that there was nothing I could do for Mama. I left her alone in her room to take care of herself. I felt horrible for doing that, but I had reached that point where I *knew* there was nothing more I could do. I retreated to my own room. Surrounded by the comfort of the Dolphins, I buried myself in my social studies project. I escaped from my world into the world of South America. It was the only way I knew to forget what really surrounded me.

Even though I had school the next day, I decided to wait up until I heard Rachel make her typical early-morning entrance for her usual three hours of sleep before making the daily silent exit. I no longer saw Rachel, only traces of her existence. Sometimes I wondered if I had really just made her up. Maybe somewhere in my psyche, a psyche that was currently stretched beyond recognition, I had created a sister who didn't really exist. An imaginary being that made me feel safe, like Larry Csonka had done years earlier. I waited up, hoping desperately that she was real.

I did eventually hear her come into the house and sneak quietly into her room. I released the grip I had on the blanket pulled to my chin, and I silently got out of bed and went to her room.

The hallway was dark. A tiny sliver of light coming from a small opening in Rachel's door was the only thing cracking the darkness. I walked toward it, the light at the end of the tunnel. At the doorway I gently pushed the door open further.

Rachel was sitting in the middle of her bed in tight jeans; shirt unbuttoned enough to expose her impressive cleavage, winged Farrah Fawcett hair, and blue eye shadow. She had changed in the months that she had been absent from my life. She looked like a grown-up, not just another kid like me.

Part of me was afraid to approach her; afraid of what response I might get from the "new Rachel." I had to give it a shot. I stepped into the light of her room. She looked up from a magazine, cigarette in hand.

"Hey, what are you doing here?" She smiled at me. Good, maybe the "new Rachel" wasn't so different from the old one.

"I wanted to see you."

Her smile broadened. "Great! Come on over." She patted the bed beside her.

I ran to her bed, bare feet slapping against hardwood. I jumped up beside her and buried my face in her chest. Instantly I was crying uncontrollably. It was such an incredible relief not to be alone anymore. It felt so nice to be physically close to another human being. My crying intensified as she held me tight against her and rocked me gently.

It seemed like I cried in my big sister's arms for hours, but it still wasn't long enough. She finally pushed away from me and

117

looked down into my face.

"What's going on with you, Pooh?"

"Mama got drunk today and was sick. The ambulance people wouldn't help her and I didn't know what to do." I paused. "I don't know what to do anymore." Tears began to roll again.

Rachel wiped damp strands of hair out of my face. "Honey, it's high time you realize there's nothing you *can* do. It's outta your control. It's outta my control. Hell, I'm starting to believe it's outta Mama's control."

She kissed away a tear from the corner of my eye. "You just have to stop beating yourself up about it. Mama's a lush, and that's not your fault."

"I know." I studied my hands, not wanting to look at her.

"You can't take care of her either. You can't. You need to just concentrate on taking care of yourself."

She put two fingers under my chin and tilted my face up to hers. "Take care of yourself like Chad and I do. Eat, sleep, go to school occasionally, and have fun. Stop wasting so much energy on her." She paused. "You'll be happier."

The cigarette burned in a small ashtray beside her. She smelled stale, a little sour. There was a small burn in her bedspread, probably from a stray cigarette ash.

I placed my bare feet back onto the cold floor. Looking into her blue shadowed eyes, I searched for something. I wasn't sure what it was, but it was something that I really needed. I didn't see it there.

"I don't think I can do that. I don't think I can be like you and Chad." I turned and walked from her room feeling more alone now than I had when I walked in.

Chapter 10
May 1979-December 1979

Over the next few months, Mama declined rapidly. After the ambulance, she was drunk and barricaded in her room for five days straight. This resulted in the loss of her job. Her boss, Mrs. Cannington, called on the third day of her stumble. I told her that Mama was sick and couldn't even come to the phone. She told me that if Mama didn't call or show up with a doctor's note by the end of the following day, she was fired.

I tried banging on Mama's door to rouse her. I yelled at her to let her know that her job was in danger. She never responded. I called the People's Bank the next day and asked for Mrs. Cannington. I was prepared to lie or do whatever I could to save Mama's job. Mrs. Cannington would not take my call.

I rolled myself up in a quilt that Mamateen had made for me when I was only four, and I lay in Rachel's bed, curled in a ball. Somehow, being in Mamateen's quilt, in Rachel's room, in the position I had been in my mother's womb, made me feel less alone. I cried and mourned the loss of Mama's teller position. Without her job I thought that she would never come out of her room again. I wondered how we would survive now.

On the fifth day of her stumble, I decided that I needed to go back to school. My teachers inquired about my four-day absence. I told them that my mother had been very sick. They were all very sorry, glad I was back, and willing to help me with any make-up work. I didn't need help. I knew that I could make up everything with no problem. I was actually anxious to get started.

As soon as I got home from school that day, I set into making up all of my missed schoolwork. I had without a doubt been missing school, and getting back at it revived my saddened spirit.

I worked diligently in the quiet of the sunroom, which was just off the side of the den. Mama still had not emerged. There'd been no sign of Rachel or Chad since the first day. I knew that soon, food and cleanliness would become concerns, but for now I chose not to think about those things. For now I was just a regular sixth grader doing regular sixth-grade homework for the same sixth-grade teachers who other sixth graders did work for.

In these moments it was easy to imagine that I was not myself, but another girl living across town in a new home in a neighborhood surrounded by friends. I was another girl whose father was in his study finishing up some "business," and whose mother was in the kitchen making a delicious and nutritious dinner. The sound of imaginary children playing outside in the street tickled my ears. The smells of my imaginary dinner cooking tempted my empty belly. I worked happily with a smile on my face.

My concentration was interrupted by a loud thump. I looked up at the doorway and waited quietly. Another bump followed and I heard shuffling and scraping in the hallway beyond the door. I was too afraid to move. It had been days since I had heard any noise other than my own inside this huge hollow house. I was glued to my seat, eyes fixed on the doorway.

Momentarily, Mama's narrow frame was in the doorway. She

paused there briefly, swayed, and then grabbed the doorframe with both hands to steady herself. She searched the den. I remained still and quiet.

Her hair was oily and plastered to her head with the exception of a cow-licked strand at the crown. Her thin, green gown was stained around the collar and down the front. Her face was puffy, and crust was dried and cracked around her mouth.

She kept searching, and finally saw me through the opening to the sunroom sitting contentedly in front of open schoolbooks. She started toward me. Still I stayed perfectly still and quiet. I was unable to move. I felt as if I was watching a ghost approach me, a long-lost enemy back to haunt me from the grave. My voice was gone and my muscles weren't receiving the "move" messages from my brain.

As she got closer, her face became darker with hollows under her cheekbones. Her eyes were cloudy and her mouth was so dry there seemed to be scabs on her lips. She opened her mouth and I swore I heard her face crack. At this point I was certain I was seeing an apparition, a return from death.

Her mouth was open for what seemed like hours before a sound finally came forth. "Hey there my Pooh Bayah." Her voice was scratchy and raw. Hearing it made my own throat hurt and I had to reach up and rub away the pain from the outside before I could speak.

"Hey, Mama." I remained in my seat. I expected her to vanish any minute. I thought she wasn't really here with me, she was just my own mind reminding myself that I was not another girl across town. Something inside of me just wouldn't let me forget for very long.

She didn't vanish, but joined me at the table instead. She put her forehead into her hands and began to rub her temples. She followed this with a long deep moan, almost a growl. Head still in her hands, she said, "What's going on?"

I continued to look at her as if she couldn't possibly be for real. I'm sure my face was the picture of disbelief. "Well," I said matter-of-factly, "I'm making up schoolwork that I missed for the past four days, and you got fired."

"Good for you." This is all she could manage to say as she massaged her face and neck. Then she licked and smacked her lips. "God, I need some water. And I'm half starved to death, too."

She said these things as if they were things that people risen from the dead said to other people everyday. I looked at her with the same disbelief, wanting to ask, "Hey, do you realize you've been laid up drunk for five days straight? No shit you're hungry." But I just couldn't say it. I could only stare at her, resisting the urge to reach over and slap the scabs right off her lips.

She sat up straight and took a deep breath. "I think I'll take a shower." She pushed away from the table and began to leave. She turned as she went back through the den. "I'll cook when I'm finished. Are you hungry? Hell, I believe I could eat a horse." Then she was gone as quickly as she had appeared.

I kept watching the empty doorway, waiting for something to acknowledge that none of this was really happening. After she had been gone for a few minutes, I went back to work. I expected her to be gone for another five days.

Chapter 11
January 1980-November 1980

My tolerance for Mama's drinking declined rapidly. It had once again reached the point where her sobriety was momentary. She could only manage to exist without alcohol for brief snippets of time. The abuses I had to endure grew both in frequency and intensity. Rachel and Chad remained elusive, and I was left to endure the brunt of Mama's intoxicated fury.

I attempted to avoid her, staying holed up in my room or hiding amongst the magnolias, often staying late after school and catching a ride with my teacher, a concerned Mrs. Davenport.

I focused even more of my time and energy on my studies as I advanced in school. Studying, reading, writing—these things became my passion. I received perfect grades, awards and honors, and encouragement from members in all areas of my school faculty. Learning became the one thing over which I knew I had control. My knowledge base grew so rapidly that I, in my awkward adolescence, was unsure what to do with it all.

Hiding in the shadows of my soul, withdrawn from everything except what I held inside of my head, was not enough to spare me from my mother's drunken anger. Regardless of my attempts to avoid her, there was always the inevitable run-in.

On one particular cold winter day, during my slow walk home from school, I heard a tiny crying voice coming from a small thicket of brush by the roadside. I squatted beside the thicket and listened carefully. The soft, high- pitched whine came from within once again. It sounded like a baby's cry. A very tiny baby, but a baby nonetheless. Unsure of what I would find, I parted the brush in search of the voice.

Standing in the undergrowth on wobbly legs was a very new baby kitten. His eyes were milky and his mew conveyed terror. I lifted him from the ground and pulled him into my chest. I rubbed his fur. White with gray splotches, his fur had a greasy feel. Snuggled in the warmth of my body, his crying stopped and he began to suck at a loose thread of my sweater. This soft pink nose and soft pink paws had obviously been taken from its mother too early. He had been left in that cold bush all alone. Left to die. I had no choice but to take him with me.

His name was Socrates, and he quickly became my best friend. My only friend really. He was able to lap milk right away, and shortly after began to eat food.

I did the grocery shopping with money I took from Mama's purse. Also, Carlos, who managed the local Golden Pantry Food Store, allowed me to cash child support checks sent to Mama from Daddy. He also gave me a sizeable discount. He was a nice man. He also didn't ask any questions when I started buying cat food.

Socrates thrived despite Mama's dislike of him. The first time she heard him squealing in my room, she stormed in and said, "What the hell is that noise?" She saw him wobbling in the middle of my bed and added, "Where the hell did *that* come from?"

"I found him Mama. He needed me."

"Well, we sure as hell don't need him. You get rid of that damn cat pronto!"

124

I ignored Mama's demand and chose simply to help Socrates maintain a very low profile. He stayed outside during the day, keeping close to the house. At night I kept him in my room. He slept across my chest or in the bend of my knees.

Socrates greeted me at the sidewalk everyday when I got home from school. His purr and rub against my leg let me know that he was glad to see me. He needed me, wanted me. I was filled with emotion that had been absent for so long. The recognition of a previously unobtainable unconditional love caused me to see the world in a completely different way. It was now brighter, more brilliant, not quite as heavy. Socrates gave me hope.

By the spring, life was taking on a whole new sparkle. Nature's awakening always seemed to put a little hop in my step. On one particularly beautiful spring day, I was walking home from school, humming and enjoying the warmth of the sunshine on my cheeks and the backs of my ears. I reached the walkway to the house in anticipation of Socrates' welcome. Socrates didn't emerge from under the porch.

I assumed that the warmth of the spring sun had put him into a nap that couldn't be disturbed. I approached the porch and softly called his name. He still didn't come out. I knelt down and peeked under the porch, still calling his name. Still no sign of Socrates.

I jumped up, feeling my body going into panic mode. I ran around the house screaming Socrates' name. After two complete laps of the yard and a thorough search of every possible hiding place. I gave up and entered the house.

My breathing was labored. My eyelashes were clotted with the wetness of my tears. My face was damp and dirt-stained. I ran directly to my mother's room. Purpose, as well as fear, driving me to confront her.

I burst through her bedroom door and found her sitting up in her bed in a pair of white sweatpants covered in dark stains, and a

T-shirt whose neck was stretched out to the point of barely covering her sagging breasts. A cigarette with a half-inch ash dangled precariously from her lips. Her eyes were squinted to keep the curls of smoke out.

"Mama! Where is Socrates?" This came out of me in a quick burst of air.

"What?" She didn't remove the cigarette, and the ash fell to her bed as it wiggled on her moving lips.

I took a deep breath to calm myself. If I didn't slow down, she would never understand me. "I can't find Socrates. Do you know where he is?"

She finally removed her cigarette and rested it on the edge of an overflowing ashtray. "As a matter of fact, I do know where he is." She paused.

I waited to see if she would continue, but that was all she offered. "So . . . where is he?"

She shifted her weight, readjusting her posture against the headboard of the bed. "I paid my friend Bob five dollars to get rid of him."

I stood silently, feeling the blood rise into my face. A wave of heat washed over me and I momentarily felt dizzy. Once I regained my stability, the heat came from me in a rush of words. "What do you mean, 'get rid of him'? What did you do?" I brought the palms of my hands down hard on the bed, right beside her. "What did you DO?"

She began to laugh a deep, guttural laugh. "What did I DO?" She was mocking me. "I got rid of that little pest. I think Bob threw him in the river." She laughed harder.

Rage consumed me and the tears flowed freely down my face. I squeezed my fists so tightly that my chewed off nail nubs dug into my palms. I screamed as loudly as I could. "I hate you. I hate you. I hate you, you mean bitch." I turned and ran, her laughter

126

chasing me from the room.

I ran all the way through the house and out the front door. I knelt and looked into the darkness under the porch, hoping I'd see two green cat eyes staring back at me. Quietly I called his name, "Socrates. Socrates. Oh . . . Socrates . . . please, please, please."

Tears continued to flow as I laid flat on my belly and slid on the hard-packed dirt into the space under the porch. There was a smoothed out indentation in the solid earth where Socrates had preferred to nap. I curled myself up in the spot in an attempt to absorb the last of his warmth. I cried and grieved the loss of the only unconditional love I had ever known.

I had always been the only person who seemed to remember Mama's beautiful soul. The only person who had patience with her and compassion for her. The only person who knew she needed someone with her, and willing to be that someone. It seemed that the time had finally come that those feelings of mine toward her began to wane. Her drinking had become much more constant and she herself had turned completely evil. Her fun, kind, caring part seemed to have, not just receded, but to have run off completely. As if it had never existed at all.

Her abuses toward me increased on a daily basis. After I lost Socrates, I had very little tolerance for her. She threw a hot chicken pot pie at me because I had failed to make her something to eat. It missed my face by a fraction of an inch and smashed into the wall behind me. I refused to clean it up, so it stayed glued to the wall for months. She came to my room in the middle of the night while I was sleeping and began beating me within an inch of my life with a broom because I had taken her liquor money from her purse to buy food.

During all of these things, the promise that Alvar Nunez Cabeza de Vaca had made to Daddy echoed distantly in my head. I knew I could call him, and he would help me. I also knew that if I did that, I would be admitting to him that I was wrong about Mama. I didn't want to be wrong about her. I also wasn't quite sure I was ready to leave her. I was afraid that without me there to watch over her, she would die. So, every time the conquistador's promise moved to the forefront of my mind, I just pushed it back and suppressed it.

Then one day, I finally reached my breaking point. It was early morning and I was getting ready for school. I was excited because I had a big math test. I felt very well prepared for it and just knew that I was going to ace it. Mama came swaying into my room and plopped down on the bed. I turned from my dresser to face her. For several moments, neither of us said a word. Finally she spoke. "I need you to stay home today. You're not gonna go to school."

I rolled my eyes at her and responded, "I *am* going to school. I have a test and there's no way in hell I'm staying here with you all day." I turned back around and continued dressing myself.

"No, hell no, you're not going. I said you're staying and by God you're staying." She stood and came to me and brought her face to within inches of mine. "If you go to school today . . . I will be dead when you get back."

I leaned away from her. "What are you talking about? You're not going to be dead."

With a look of satisfaction, "I'll kill myself. I need you here and I can't let you go to school today."

"Are you serious?"

"Completely."

"You're threatening to kill yourself if I go to school?"

"It's not a threat. And I'm sure you'd hate to have that on your conscience."

I turned quickly and left the room. My promise to Daddy had just come rushing into my head. I pounded into the kitchen to the only phone in the house and picked up the receiver. I began

128

dialing.

Mama was not far behind. "What are you doing? Who are you calling?"

"Daddy."

Before I could dial the last two numbers, Mama's hand flew to the phone chord and yanked with super human strength. The chord ripped from the wall and my connection to Daddy was never made. I threw the receiver at her and it hit her in the head. She touched her head where she'd been hit, looking for blood. My rage was uncontrollable. "You are a mean, crazy bitch. I hate you. I can't even believe that I've ever loved you. I can't believe you're my mother. It scares me to think you created me. What does that make me? You are insane and I am *terrified.*"

I ran to my room and locked the door behind me. I threw myself on the bed and tried to soothe my anger. Tears didn't come. It was harder and harder for me to cry about anything. I believed that I had used up my lifetime supply of tears in the first ten years of my life. So I just lay on the bed clenching and unclenching my fists, and gritting my teeth until my jaw ached. I felt the anger begin to recede and I realized I needed a plan. In that moment, I acknowledged that I couldn't stay here another day. I would have to go, and let the chips fall where they may.

When I finally emerged from my room, the house was silent. I assumed that Mama had gone back into her room. I tiptoed down the hallway toward the front door in my sock feet. My shoes were in my hand. I quietly opened the front door and stopped on the porch to put my shoes on. Then I walked down the steps and the walkway to the sidewalk. Once at the street, I turned to look back at the house.

I knew this would be the last I saw of this storybook house— this house that had made me believe that anything was possible. I thought I felt tears welling in my eyes as I turned to face the

129

magnolias. Then I remembered that my tears were used up. I waved toward the row of strong, proud trees. I lifted my shoulders, thinking that they were urging me to be strong and proud as well.

With one last little wave, I softly said, "Thank you. You were good friends . . . The best." Then I turned quickly and walked toward the center of town, not allowing myself to turn and look back.

Less than ten minutes later I was standing in front of the Golden Pantry. I realized that this was as far as my plan took me. I was completely empty-handed. The only thing that was certain to me was that I would not return to Mama's house, not for any reason.

There was a pay phone hanging in a rectangular box attached to the front of the store. It cost ten cents to make a call. I didn't even have a dime in the pocket of my worn jeans. I approached the door of the store while composing a story to tell Carlos. I was hoping to convince him to lend me a dime without getting too suspicious.

I entered through the front door only to find that Carlos was not standing behind the counter. There was a very large, black woman there instead. Her nametag read "Sheree." She smiled at me and asked if I needed help. "No thanks." I ran back out the door.

I stood in front of the phone, staring at it, willing it to momentarily allow me a free call. That didn't work. I took two fingers and scooped them into the coin return hoping to discover a forgotten dime. Nothing. Frustrated, I plopped down on the sidewalk in front of the phone. I slowly scanned the pavement in front of me thinking that I might see a coin that had been dropped by a rushed customer. Still nothing. I rested my elbows on knees, chin in hands, thinking. Determined to find a solution that would keep me from having to return to that house, and to Mama.

After I had been sitting for about a half an hour, and no one had come or gone from the store, I was beginning to lose hope. "Hey there, girl."

I looked up to see Sheree standing in the door eyeing me. "Hey. My name is Noble. You can call me Noble." I looked back toward the pavement.

"Well then, hey there Noble." She paused. "You okay?"

"Just fine thanks."

"You waitin' on somebody?"

"Nope."

"Then what you doin?" I shrugged. "You loiterin'. That's what they call what you doin. Loiterin'. And you cain't do it here." She pointed at a sign in the window that said, "No Loitering".

"That's not what I'm doing."

"Then why don't you just tell me what you *are* doin? Maybe I can help." She raised her eyebrows and said, "I don't want to have to call the police. On account of your loiterin'."

I sighed. "I'm just waiting to make a phone call."

"What you waitin' for?"

"A dime."

"Where that dime gone come from?"

I shrugged again. "I don't know yet. I'm still figuring that out."

She looked up at the sky for a moment, then back at me. "Well I doubt it gone be fallin' out the sky."

I looked up at her, getting my first good look. She had smooth round cheeks sitting up high on her face. Below them were the corners of a broad, white smile. Her eyes squinted as she studied me, and her hands rested firmly on large hips. I nodded at her. "Yep. Doubt that's gonna happen." I turned away again.

"How 'bout I just give you a dime? Then you don't have to wait no more for one to miraculously appear."

131

I faced her again. Her smile had grown wider. Her head was tilted to the side and she just seemed to be radiating kindness. I found myself wanting to jump from the curb and run to her. Bury my face in her fleshy waist, and just try to disappear in her shroud of kindness. Instead, I simply muttered, "That would be very kind."

I felt one warm, soft hand rest on the back of my down-turned head. The other appeared in front of me with a thin dime held between thumb and forefinger. "Here you go then, child—I mean Noble. Go ahead and make that call."

I reached out and took the dime from her hand while once again looking into her kind face. "Thank you very much ma'am. I certainly appreciate it."

She roughed the back of my head before removing her hand and said, "It's not a problem at all. Glad I can help." Her smile vanished momentarily. "You need anything else?" I saw concern there in her eyes and I just shook my head. "Well, if you do, I'm just right inside." She pointed to the door and began to back toward it. I nodded at her again and repeated my thanks, and she disappeared into the store.

I slid the dime into the phone and dialed my dad's phone number. Dee answered on the third ring. As soon as I heard her voice the tears that I thought didn't exist anymore began to pour. All I could say was, "I need your help."

"Oh my God! Noble, is that you? What is it, sweet thang?"

I took deep breaths to control myself and began my story. After hearing it all, Dee was also crying. I told her where I was and she said, "I'm calling yore Daddy. Baby, hold on. We're on our way."

After I hung up, I flopped myself back down on the pavement. A wave of relief washed over me. I felt like a million pounds had been taken off my back. I felt so light that I thought I might just float away. I still cried a little, and gasped for air as I enjoyed my new lightness, sprawled on the pavement in front of the Golden Pantry. But I knew it was going to be okay now. I knew everything was going to be fine.

It would take them a couple of hours to arrive, but I wasn't going anywhere. I would wait right here. Lying on this pavement with gravel digging into my back and dirt clinging to me. I would not leave until Daddy lifted me off this ground. I gasped, and snorted, and sighed trying to get the air back into my lungs.

"You doin' alright?"

I turned my head to the side and found Sheree's shoes just beyond my nose. I managed to expel a quick, "Yes."

"Doesn't look like it." She knelt down closer to me. "What do you need?"

"My Daddy's coming. He'll be here before long. That's all I need."

I heard her knees pop as she stood back up. She was shaking her head dramatically. "If you say so, but you got me all worked up in here. I just don't feel right leavin' ya like this, but I s'pose you'll let me know if ya need me."

"Yes. Yes, I will." I closed my eyes hoping it would signal her to go. When I opened them a minute later, her shoes had vanished.

In the next couple of hours, people came and went. Some asked me if I was okay. Some stared at me with extreme interest. Some just ignored me completely. I was bound and determined not to leave this position. I knew Daddy and Dee would be there soon and I just had to wait it out.

The lifted burden, combined with emotional exhaustion, led me to drift into a light sleep. I vaguely heard continued comings and goings while drifting in and out of sleep. I finally felt calloused hands cup my face and squeeze. I opened my eyes, expecting to be looking into Sheree's eyes, "No. Really. I'm not loitering. I'm leaving soon."

As my eyes focused, I realized I wasn't looking at Sheree, but at my Daddy. His eyes were rimmed in red and he squeezed my face harder while pulling me toward him. I pressed my face into his broad chest and he hugged my head. I pressed myself into him so hard I thought I might just merge with him, and I said a little prayer to Jesus. "Thank you Jesus. Thank you for my Daddy. Thank you for Sheree. Thank you for taking care of me. Jesus, please take care of my Mama, too." And Daddy picked me up and carried me to the car.

He placed me in the front seat between him and Dee. Dee wrapped her arms around me and I leaned into her, allowing her to hold me and comfort me. She laid her cheek against my head and whispered warmly, "It's okay, Baby. Everything's okay."

The car seemed to have just started moving when, once again, it was coming to a slow stop. I popped my head up to see where we were. We were sitting in the street in front of Mama's storybook house.

I clamped my fingers around Dee's forearm. "What are we doing? Why are we here?" The panic was evident in my shaking voice. I thought they were going to force me to go back in and to continue living with that horrible woman who had given birth to me. I sat up straighter and tightened my grip on Dee. I repeated, "Why are we here?"

"Ouch." Dee's face was contorted in pain as she tried to pry my fingers from her arm. "It's okay, Noble." She tried to smile through the pain. "You're not gonna stay here." I loosened my grip and her face relaxed.

Daddy turned the car off. "I'm going in to get some of your things. And Rachel and Chad."

"They're not here."

"Where are they?"

"Don't know. They're never here. With friends, I guess."

He sighed and pushed the door open. "You just wait here with Dee. I'll be back." He stepped out and slammed the door behind him.

Dee and I sat in silence and watched Daddy stride purposefully toward the front door. He disappeared through the screen without even knocking. Dee and I continued to sit silently, staring at the front of the house, waiting for something to happen. We sat that way for about fifteen minutes, neither of us speaking.

Finally the door came swinging open with a bang as it slammed the side of the house. Daddy emerged carrying two brown paper grocery sacks, one in each arm. He opened the back door and tossed the two bags onto the backseat. He closed the door hard and then opened his door.

I could see the anger just under his skin, red and puffy, like it was about to bust right out of his face. He slid into the seat and pulled the door shut. He looked at me, breathing hard through flared nostrils. Through gritted teeth, he hissed, "Tell me where I can find your brother and sister."

"I don't know Daddy. I don't know where they are."

"Jesus H. Christ!" He slammed his hands against the steering wheel. "How the hell can two kids be gone from their home and not a damn soul knows where they are?"

He threw the gearshift forward and jammed his foot on the accelerator. We took off fast down Johnson Street. Our first stop was Tatum Middle School. Daddy was inside for about ten minutes before returning in the same storm of anger. He got in the car facing forward. Shaking his head, he said, "Chad hasn't been in school in days."

He let out a sigh and we took off again. Next stop was Barrow High School. Again, he was inside for only a few minutes before returning. He practically threw himself into the front seat, yanking the door shut behind him. "Same bullshit story! She hasn't been to school in days. Hell, apparently, she hardly ever comes at all."

He put his head in his hands and let out a long breath. Rubbing his eyes, he said, "Jesus, Joseph, and Mary. I don't know what to do now. I don't have a clue." He lifted his face from his hands and looked toward me and Dee. "What do we do?"

Dee was absently rubbing my hair. It felt so nice that I wasn't too concerned about the drama that was now taking place in my father's head. I was enjoying a moment of having someone else do all the worrying. "We go home." Dee stated it very matter-of-factly, as if there were no other choice.

"I can't leave those two kids here like this. I need to find 'em. I need to take 'em home with us. Lord knows what'll happen to 'em."

"Dave, they've been living like this for awhile now. I think they like it. You cain't take 'em if you cain't find 'em. And that's their choice."

"Aw, God. But what kind of father am I if I leave 'em?"

"You may not wanna hear this right now, but it's a little late to be thankin' about that. Seems the damage is already done." She continued to gently stroke my hair, refusing to look at my father.

He pushed himself back from the steering wheel. "Are you suggesting this is my fault?" His voice was slowly growing louder. "Please tell me that's not what you're doing. 'Cause if I remember correctly, you were all for letting these kids come live with their mama. Hell, you practically begged me to send 'em."

Dee stopped rubbing and looked up to meet my father's eyes. "I'm not saying it's yore fault. There's plenty a blame to go around. I just thank it may be a little late to try and make it right."

Daddy's shoulders slumped again and he returned his head to his hands. "So we just leave? Leave 'em here? Wherever they are?"

"I think that's our only choice. At least for now. We can hope they'll do like Noble, and call if they need us. That's all we can do." She started rubbing my head again. "Let's just thank the good Lord we got Noble back right now."

Daddy looked over at both of us again. I could tell he was holding back tears. I guessed he didn't want me to see him cry. I thought he was trying to stay strong so that I wouldn't be scared, but I wanted to tell him that it was alright with me if he wanted to cry. I wanted him to know that I thought it was okay for him to be scared too.

He reached out and grabbed my head and pulled it toward him. He leaned over and kissed me on top of the head. "Yeah, least we got this little shit back." He let out a short laugh.

I looked up at him with a smile. "You don't have to laugh, Daddy. It's okay if you want to cry."

He took his hand from the back of my head and wiped his nose as he sniffled. "Nah. I'm good." He turned away, shoved the car in gear, and, once again, we were off.

This time we were leaving Winder behind and heading back to middle-class suburbia. During the couple of hours it took to make the trip, I leaned on Dee, and she held me and rubbed me. I relaxed and drifted into a contented sleep. I was trying not to think of Mama, or Rache, or Chad. I was trying only to think about the fact that I had to do this. I knew that if I wanted to survive this life, I had to make that phone call. I had to be in this car heading toward yet another new life. This time, however, I was not a conquistador on an amazing adventure. This time, I felt more like a wounded animal trapped in the wild, being transported to a zoo, or a park, or some place like that, to be rehabilitated. It was sad, but necessary.

Chapter 12
December 1980-May 1986

Transitioning into a new life with Daddy and Dee was not at all easy for me. I thought it would be this wonderful reentry into a traditional family. I thought I was now going to be like those perfect girls I always imagined in those perfect families with those perfect lives. Since my definition of a normal family had become "a two-parent household in which neither parent is an alcoholic," I thought I would now be cloaked in all of the warmth and comfort that was found in a normal family. That was not really the case.

Daddy and Dee both had very busy lives. Daddy's construction business had been growing and he seemed to work almost all of the time. He even worked a lot on the weekends. Dee was a social butterfly and spent all of her time joining groups and trying out new hobbies. She had a book club, ceramics classes, salon days, catalog parties, cake-decorating classes, belly-dancing classes, and on and on and on.

I still took care of myself for the most part, since Daddy and Dee had gotten used to a routine without kids. In that respect, things were similar to the way they had been at Mama's. But despite this similarity, there were major differences in my old life and my new life. Some of the differences were good, and some were not so good. On the up side, I didn't have to put up with Mama's daily chaos. On the down side, I had no magnolia friends. But for the most part, everything was better.

One of the major bonuses of having a more stable home life was the opportunity it provided me to be involved in school activities. While with Mama, I was always afraid to commit myself to anything at school. I never knew how she would respond to my involvement, and I was never sure if she would follow through on any responsibility it might present her with. Rather than risk embarrassment by getting involved and having no support from home, I just steered clear of any extracurricular involvement.

Once I started the eighth grade at my new school, a world of opportunities seemed to open up to me. I saw sports teams, art and science clubs, performing arts, social activities, and tons of academic opportunities. Before now, I had never paid attention to these types of things. Since they didn't seem to be options for me in my previous life, I had simply ignored them.

While finishing up my final year of middle school, I gradually allowed myself to get involved. I started by joining the school newspaper staff. I enjoyed that so much that I tried out and made the basketball team. In the spring I had a small part in the spring play. This involvement elated me. I made friends and got close to teachers and coaches and learned a lot of new things. I now understood why Dee joined so many clubs and took classes. It gave me a new and different interest in school. I still loved academics and did well in class, but I had found the rewards of being a part of a group.

The best part of all was that if I needed dues or fees, or a ride home after school, I could always count on Daddy and Dee. They even occasionally came and watched some of my games. I never could have expected Mama to do those things. Daddy and Dee still

140

didn't surround me with all of the parental adoration that I longed for, but their simple dependability made the transition come a lot easier.

I completed that year of school and poised myself for high school. I spent that summer carefully planning how I would succeed in high school. I decided that I was simply going to attack it with so much motivation and desire that I was going to dominate every aspect of it. I made the decision that I was going to involve myself in anything that I could, and that everything I became involved in, I would be the absolute best at. I wasn't just going to be the best student. I was going to be the best athlete, the best writer, the most popular, the funniest, the most creative, everything I could be I was going to be. And I wanted to do it in the most memorable way possible. I was going to *own* high school.

I walked through the front doors of Sweetwater High School on the first day of school, in the fall of 1982, as a freshman with a serious attitude. I already had to deal with being one of the smallest kids in my class, so I thought that, in order to get noticed, I had to be bad.

Following with the style of the 1980s, I used mousse and gel and hairspray to mold my hair into a six-inch tall Mohawk. I took a pair of my old jeans (I hadn't grown much in the past few years) and shredded them to within an inch of their lives. I used a drinking straw to blow multi-colored paint onto one of my dad's old T-shirts. I topped it off with a pair of yellow Converse All Stars, and red Wayfarer sunglasses to complete my first day of high school fashion ensemble.

There was no doubt that as I entered I was noticed. Everyone, including kids who knew me from middle school, stopped to gander. In middle-class suburbia, the punk style had not quite taken hold. The vast majority wore Levi's or khaki pants with button-downs or polos in pastel colors. The shoes were loafers or deck

141

shoes, and there wasn't a single collar that was lying flat.

I saw them looking and whispering behind their hands, but I knew I had made the right decision. I was a first-day freshman who was already known by members of every class. They might not know my name, but they knew me. I was now that weird freshman with punk hair and paint on her shirt. Soon they would know my name. It was just a matter of time. I strolled, in the coolest possible way, to my homeroom, with a smile tugging at the corners of my mouth. I knew I was going to be a superstar at Sweetwater High.

Upon entering every class, the teacher would look at me with so much dread. My appearance seemed to insinuate that I was going to be difficult. I felt powerful for that. I spent my entire life trying to *not* be difficult. But now I felt proud that people might even think I had that potential for difficulty. I knew if I smiled, it might ruin my persona. But that smile just kept tugging at my mouth.

As the days and weeks went by and I became settled in a routine, people's perceptions of me began to change. I continued to dress in my unique punk fashion, but as individuals got to know me, they realized that my appearance didn't dictate my personality. Despite my first-day attitude, I chose to assert myself in a pleasant and respectful way. I began immediately acing all of my academics and got involved right away in both newspaper and yearbook. I went on to also be a starting player on both the basketball and softball teams. My peers and my teachers alike began to see me as a hard-working, dedicated student, even though I was a bit strange. I loved this perception. I wanted to be different, so I continued to find ways to add little quirks to my wardrobe. It became part of how I defined myself.

I breezed through my freshman and sophomore years and established myself as a student leader. I'd also discovered that I had a great sense of humor. I suppose because of the unhappiness that had surrounded me over the past few years, I'd had very little opportunity to express myself in a humorous way. But now I was finding that I had a quick wit that was gaining me a whole new level of respect from everyone. I had gone from being the "weird but cool girl" to the "*hilarious* and cool girl." I was loving life.

I initially made this discovery through my position on the school newspaper staff. I wrote a monthly column which looked at everyday high school life and how absolutely ridiculous it was. No one in the building was safe from my biting, yet humorous, analysis. I managed to criticize everything from school food to the principal's wardrobe, without ever really offending anyone.

I compared and contrasted teachers in different departments. (Why do history teachers have bad breath and English teachers only eat organic food?) I was able to do this in a way that actually flattered the subjects of my criticism. I actually had teachers asking me when they were going to get their names in my column. My column became the most anticipated monthly event at Sweetwater High. As our football team never won a game, I became a rallying point for the whole school. I was making my goal of being a high-school rock star come true.

I allowed this newly discovered humor to pour over into every other area of my life. It became my way to try and find even the smallest point of humor in all that I experienced. I had morphed into the "class clown" of every single class. I was always seeking opportunities to entertain others. My teachers had no problem with this. Maybe it was because I managed to be funny in an intelligent way. In history I would make relevant jokes about historical figures. In literature I would make literary jokes. And so on, although I never really found a way to make math funny.

As I started my junior year, I was absolutely on top of the world. I had gone from being the shy, nerdy, bookworm with no friends in middle school, to the outgoing, interesting, intellect who was everyone's friend in high school. Having successfully pulled off this transformation in myself, I felt capable of anything.

My first class of the day of my eleventh grade year was U.S. History. I always enjoyed social studies classes the most, because they provided the most material for possible jokes. I walked into this class with the greatest anticipation, ready to make my mark here for a third straight year.

I dropped my books on the desk that was front and center. This was always my favorite place to sit because it allowed everyone in the room to see me. Before I could take my seat, I heard my name.

"Noble Thorvald?"

I looked up to see a woman's head covered in long, thick auburn hair sticking through the door. She used a small hand to push a pair of horn-rimmed glasses up the bridge of her nose. I looked at her with raised eyebrows. She repeated, "Noble Thorvald?"

"Yeah."

"Can you come here, please?"

I strolled over to the door where she stood. I greeted her with a smile. "Hi." I extended my hand toward her. "You must be Ms. Chandler."

She took my hand lightly and gave it a quick yank. "Yes, I am. And, obviously you're Noble Thorvald."

"I am." I smiled again, feeling quite proud that my reputation had preceded me.

"Well . . ." She crossed her arms across her chest and leaned against the doorjamb. "I want to get a few things straight before we start today."

My smile faded and I knitted my brow. "Okay." I was unaccustomed to this sort of first day welcome.

"I know you're smart, and you're funny, and eeeeevvvrybodyyyy loves you." She waved her arms around to emphasize this last part. "But I just want you to know one thing about me." She once again took up her leaning position in the doorway.

"Sure." My face still reflected my confusion.

"I'm not easily impressed." She raised her eyebrows and pushed her glasses up and just kept looking at me.

I nodded at her. It seemed she was finished so I turned to walk away.

"And one more thing."

I turned back around to face her. "Yes?"

She used her index finger to summon me toward her. I took a step closer. She motioned more enthusiastically with her index finger and said, "Closer." I took another step. "No, no. Closer." I stepped so close that we were not even two feet apart. I was starting to get nervous.

She leaned her face toward mine and came within several inches of me. I withdrew slightly. Without warning, she opened her mouth and expelled a huge burst of warm breath right into my face. I closed my eyes and just stood trying to understand what was happening.

When I opened my eyes she was back against the wall, arms crossed again. She was biting her lip and I could tell the corners of her lips were slightly turned up. She pushed her glasses up, "Not *all* history teachers have bad breath."

I turned to go back to my seat. Despite my confusion about the situation, I found myself smiling. I took my seat and glanced back toward Ms. Chandler. I expected to find her still looking at me. But to my surprise—and I think to my disappointment—she had turned her attention to other students as they were entering the room. I shook my head and absolutely couldn't erase the huge smile from my face.

From that moment on, I made a point of doing my very best in

Ms. Chandler's class. I made a point not to be disruptive or steal her spotlight. I only spoke when she called on me, and I curbed my outbursts of humor. I was determined to impress her.

A couple of months into the semester, I had almost accepted the fact that I would never impress her. She rarely ever even seemed aware of my presence. I was disheartened to the point of deciding I would just be myself whether she liked it or not. Then one day, as I was passing her desk to leave the room she said, "Noble. Can you come by and see me for a few minutes this afternoon after school?"

I stopped in front of the desk. "Sure."

"Great." She pushed away from her desk, but before she could stand I asked, "You wanna tell me why?"

As she stood she shook her head, "No." and moved toward the doorway. She looked over her shoulder. "I'll tell you this afternoon. Just be patient." She smiled a closed lip smile and disappeared into the hallway.

I didn't move. Why did this woman insist on getting under my skin? It felt like she was determined to push my buttons. Well, I was determined not to let her.

As I strolled out of the room and brushed past her, I gave her a quick wave and said, "Later then." I walked away very casually.

The rest of the day dragged by. I looked at my watch at least every two minutes. I racked my brain, trying to figure out what she could possibly want. I knew I couldn't be in trouble. I doubted she wanted to apologize to me for being rude. Every possibility I came up with, I shot it right back down. Meanwhile, time seemed to have stopped completely.

Finally, the 3:20 bell rang and I practically ran to her room. I slowed as I approached, caught my breath, and entered using my casual stroll. She was sitting behind her desk looking through a stack of papers. She looked up when I entered. "Noble. Hi. You got here quick."

"Did I? I must've just been close, or something."

I was suddenly very nervous and I shifted from one foot to the other. She pushed away from her desk and motioned to a chair that was close by. "Have a seat. I hope you have a little while. I have a couple of things I'd like to discuss with you."

I sat down. "Sure. I have plenty of time."

"Good." She removed her glasses. It was the first time I'd seen her without them. Also the first time I'd noticed that her eyes were an interesting honey color. I couldn't stop staring at them. Then she rubbed them and broke my concentration. I looked down at my hands.

"I'm sure you're curious about why I asked you to stop by."

"No. No. Not Really."

She made a quick, laughing, hmmpf sound. "Actually, I *know* you're curious about why I asked you to stop by." She paused. "It's your nature to be curious." Another pause. "Am I right?"

I raised my head to face her, smiling and nodding. "Truthfully, it's all I've thought about all day."

She laughed again. "I knew that."

We laughed together for a few moments, until I finally asked, "So are you just going to keep me in suspense forever?"

"No. Sorry. I was wondering if you might be willing to do a couple of things for me."

"Depends on what they are."

"Well. First. I'm supposed to choose a student to write an essay for this, ummm…" She picked up a pamphlet from her desk and waved it around. "This 'American Heritage' contest thing. I thought with your writing ability and your grasp of American history, you would be a good choice." She tossed the pamphlet toward me. "I know you'd do a great job. Could be good for a scholarship or something."

147

I turned the pamphlet over in my hand. "Sure. Sounds good."

"And, you may not know this, but I'm the Junior Class sponsor."

"Nope. I didn't know that. Good to know."

She smiled. "I have to recruit some juniors to be on the prom committee."

I creased my brow and frowned. "I do not envy you that. Good luck with it though."

"Ha ha. Someone told me you thought you were funny." Then she sighed. "I just thought with your natural leadership abilities you would love to have the opportunity to serve on your class's prom committee." She sighed again and scrunched her nose. "People like you. I thought if you did it, other people would join." She relaxed her face. "I kind of need you. And it would enhance a college application."

I couldn't believe my good fortune. Suddenly, I was back in a position of power. She *needed* me. I put my elbows on her desk and leaned in. "What's in it for me?"

"Duh. I just told you the college application thing."

"Oh, no. Not nearly good enough. I already have a pretty solid college application. They might look at that committee, see how lame it is, and *deduct* points." I laughed at my own joke.

"Ah. Again with the funny." She threw a pencil at me and I ducked just in time to avoid having my eye poked out. I began to laugh hysterically.

I gasped for air. "I'm still not convinced. Remember you *need* me." The laughter continued.

"I'll take you out for a drink."

This silenced me. "A *drink* drink?"

"Coffee, whatever. We'll see."

"You got a deal."

"Great. Now get outta here before I poke your eye out for

148

real."

I began to walk away, still laughing just a little.

"And thanks, Noble. I'll get the committee information to you soon. I owe you one."

Without looking back I said, "Yes you do." And I practically floated out of the building.

My relationship with Ms. Chandler changed after that day. We chatted often about how things were going for each of us. I felt more comfortable expressing myself in her class. I assembled a prom committee for her and we began having regular after-school meetings to discuss prom plans. All in all, she and I were slowly getting to know one another, and I started thinking of her more as a friend than simply a teacher.

On a Friday in February, Sweetwater High was hosting the first round of state basketball playoffs. Unlike the football team, our girl's basketball team frequently made trips to the state playoffs and had, just two years earlier, won the state championship. It was always bound to be a huge event for the entire community.

As starting point guard for the team, the moment was especially exciting for me. The entire season had been a whirlwind of success and excitement for the team, and for me as an individual. I led the team in steals and assists and held in there as third-leading scorer. It was yet another thing which brought me that much-desired notoriety in school and in the community.

Throughout the season, I'd asked Ms. Chandler to come out and watch. She always insisted that she wasn't a sports fan and had no desire to sit through a game of any kind. I accepted that, and eventually left her alone about it.

On this game day, as school ended, I made my way to my locker and was getting prepared for my pre-game routine. I pulled things from the locker, allowing them to fall to the floor as I sorted through my bag, trying to determine what needed to stay and what needed to go with me.

"Hey, Noble. There you are. I was hoping to catch you before you got busy getting ready for your game."

I looked up from my locker mess to see Ms. Chandler approaching quickly. "Hey. What's up?"

She knelt down and started picking up some of my spilled locker contents. "What's this mess?" She stood with a handful of loose paper and held it out to me. "How do you manage to be so smart and so disorganized all at the same time?"

I took the papers with a smile. "Skill." I raised my eyebrows at her. "What brings you to the math hall?"

"I told you—I was looking for you."

"Well . . . here I am."

"Wanted to let you know I'll be at the game today."

"Really? That's great. I think you'll like it. It's exciting even if you don't understand."

"I certainly hope so. It could very well be both my first and last game." She paused. "I really wanted to ask you a question."

"Okay, ask."

"Do you have plans after the game?"

"Well, no, not really. Sometimes some of us will go out and hang out afterward, but nothing specific. Why?"

"It's just that you've helped me so much with all this prom stuff that I thought it might be high time I settle up on the deal we made."

I laughed. "You mean the drink you owe me."

"Coffee. Or food. Or whatever."

I shoved loose items into my locker and gave it a quick slam. "Sure. That sounds great."

"Okay then. Good." She smiled and turned to leave. "Oh. And good luck." She punched a fist in the air. "Score a goal for me."

"Of course." I watched her walk away before turning myself to go in the other direction. Shaking my head I wondered, *What is up with her?*

Later, during halftime of the game, I looked into the stands and saw Ms. Chandler sitting with a group of teachers. She gave me a dorky, double thumbs-up, and I looked away quickly. I tried not to let myself get distracted, but I think it was too late. We ended up winning the game by a very narrow margin. However, I was horrible. I turned the ball over several times and only scored half as many points as I normally did. Fortunately, my teammates played better than I did, and we managed to pull it off.

Following a post-game reaming in the locker room from Coach Stinchcomb, I walked out on to the gym floor as discreetly as possible. Spectators still mingled and talked and waited for players. I saw Ms. Chandler near the exit talking with what appeared to be a parent. I started in her direction, ignoring people who spoke to me as I passed.

She was just saying goodbye to the mom as I reached her. The lady left through the exit. She nodded toward the woman as her back disappeared through the door. "Jack Harper's mom."

"Friend of yours?"

"No. She's just concerned about his history grade. I knew there was a reason I didn't come to these things." She punched me in the shoulder. "Great game sport."

"Now I *know* you don't know basketball. I played terrible."

She furrowed her brow. "Really? I thought you looked pretty darn good. Hmmmm."

"You would be wrong."

"Oh well. You won. Isn't that what's important?"

"That's what they say."

"Ok then. You ready to take off?"

"Sure. Where are we going?"

151

"I thought we could just go back to my apartment. We won't have to worry about running into anybody that way. Is that okay?"

"That's fine with me if it's okay with you."

"I don't have a problem with it if you don't."

"Then I guess we're both okay with it. Sounds like."

We both stood nodding at one another. Finally I said, "All right then. Why don't I just follow you?"

"Good idea. Let's go."

A few minutes later we were entering her second-floor, one-bedroom apartment. She flipped on the lights, tossed her bag in a chair and said, "Have a seat. What would you like?"

"What do you mean?"

She had moved into the kitchen that was separated from the living from by a low bar. "I can get you some food. I could make coffee." She opened the refrigerator and leaned in. "I do have beer if you're really interested." She stood up straight and looked back toward me.

"Ummm. A beer would be great."

She came back into the living room carrying two cans of Miller Lite. She handed one to me and sat down on the sofa beside me. Before popping her top, she pointed toward my can. "You know this has to be just between us."

"Oh. Yeah. Of course."

"I mean. I'm not in the habit of contributing to the delinquency of minors." She let out a heavy breath. "I just think of you more as a peer than as a student."

"Sure. It's no big deal."

My mind was reeling. I listened to the explosion of released air as she popped her top. I focused my attention on my can. What in God's name was I doing? Alcohol had wreaked such havoc on my life that I'd chosen to avoid it altogether. I always missed parties and other events where I knew there would be alcohol. I

152

just made excuses so I wouldn't have to explain to my friends that I was a weak wimp who was terrified of drinking.

"Everything okay?"

She was looking at me intensely. "Yes. Fine." I held up my can and popped the top. I took a quick sip and followed it with an "Ahhh."

She sat her can on the coffee table and reached for mine. "Here, give me that." She took it from my hand.

"Hey! What're you doing?"

As she entered the kitchen she said, "I'm going to make coffee." She held the can high before placing it on the bar. "This obviously makes you uncomfortable."

She began to busy herself making coffee. For a moment I couldn't think of anything to say. "What do you mean? I'm not uncomfortable."

As she poured water into the automatic coffee maker, she angled her body so that she could see me. "It's okay."

"But I want the beer."

"No you don't. And it really is okay. It's not a big deal at all."

I heard the noise of the coffee beginning to brew. Hot water sputtering and spewing into the coffee-laden filter. It sounded like it was choking, and I could relate. I couldn't get words to come from my mouth. My throat was closing up and I felt like *I* was choking.

Here was a woman I admired and enjoyed. I was mortified that she would think I was an immature wimp. I didn't want her to be reminded that I wasn't her equal. I should have just guzzled the beer like a veteran alchie. I shouldn't have let her see my hesitation and worry.

"How do you like your coffee?"

I snapped out of my frantic state of concern and realized that I had to keep my head and try and salvage the rest of this encounter.

"Oh, ummm, cream and sugar."

After preparing two large mugs of coffee, she came back and seated herself next to me once again. She held my mug toward me and I gently took it from her hand.

I looked into the light brown warmth, trying to compose my next sentence before blurting it out. "Listen. I, ummm . . ."

"Noble. Please stop worrying. It's fine with me if you don't want to drink." She huffed. "It's actually *better* for me if you don't. I just assumed you wanted to."

I didn't look up. I watched steam leaving the surface of my coffee. "It's just . . . my mother."

She didn't respond. We both sat silently for what seemed like forever. I finally decided that I needed to venture a peek at her—if for no other reason just to make sure she was still there.

She was still there, and she was just staring at me, concern in her eyes. "Your mother?"

"It's just that she kinda has a drinking problem. And, I don't know."

She leaned toward me and laid her hand on my arm. "Oh God, Noble. Why didn't you say so."

"I don't know. It's no big deal. I mean, It just makes me a little hesitant to drink, you know?"

"I do know. *Absolutely*, I know." She squeezed my arm before withdrawing her hand. "And I really respect that decision. To be honest, I'm not much of a drinker myself."

She lifted her mug to her lips and took a slow sip. I followed suit, and soon we were engaged in deep conversation. It was as if my verbalizing my mother's problem had opened the floodgates to my soul.

Her honey eyes studied me from across the steam, and I essentially told her the story of my life. She listened intently, making an occasional comforting or understanding noise. I cried just a little and I was sure that I also got a glimpse of tears behind her glasses.

Talking about my mother and my life was like unloading garbage at the dump. I felt like I was getting rid of junk that had been cluttering my head. I was liberating myself from an intolerable burden.

I learned a lot about Ms. Chandler that night, too. I learned that, when we weren't at school, she wanted to be called Liz. I learned that her father was also an alcoholic. I learned that she was twenty-eight years old, grew up in Massachusetts, and had graduated from Wellesley. She wound up in Georgia because she'd moved here with a boyfriend who ended up dumping her. She'd decided to stay, at least for a little while.

By the end of the evening, I felt much closer to her. I felt like I had a brand-new friend. A friend I could really count on and believe in. Most importantly, I felt lighter and freer than I had in a very long time.

When it got late enough to cause me concern, I let her know that I needed to get home. She walked me to the door. "Noble. I'm very glad you came over. I'm sorry if I made you feel uncomfortable at all."

"No. You didn't. Thank you for listening to me. I've never talked about that stuff. I guess I've always been ashamed. I just keep it to myself."

"Well, you're so confident and well-rounded. I would have never guessed that you had endured such struggles." She squeezed my shoulder. "Not that you have to keep it hidden. You should never be ashamed of things that you've overcome. I think it's something to be proud of."

"Well, that's easier said than done. But I'll try to keep it in mind."

"That's a start." She surprised me by wrapping her arms

around me and giving me a tight hug.

I wasn't really accustomed to such displays of affection, and this one made color rise to my cheeks. I weakly returned her hug and pulled away from her abruptly. "Thanks again. I'll see you Monday."

"Yes. I hope you have a wonderful weekend." She beamed at me as I backed out the door. Just before she closed it she said, "Be careful." She held her hand up and wiggled her fingers in a silly wave. Then the door closed.

***

Rachel and Chad had never made the phone call to have Daddy rescue them from life with Mama. They were determined to stay where they were. Daddy said it was because they had gotten used to being able to do whatever they wanted and the idea of having to follow rules didn't appeal to them at all. At any rate, I became accustomed to being estranged from three-fourths of my family.

While I worked diligently to create the life I had only dreamed of several years earlier, I just started to accept that my mother, my brother, and sister were not going to be a part of it. We had almost no contact, and I was getting used to it. I occasionally missed them and thought about them. I sometimes found myself wanting to see them. Touch them. See if they had changed as much as I had. But I didn't let myself dwell on these things.

When I thought about those things, my world was dark. The painful memories would take hold and I would just want to crawl away and hide. I tried to think about the things that brought me joy. I tried to think of the unlimited potential I had inside me. I tried to think of the beautiful possibilities that were my future. That's how I kept from getting dragged under the porch into the vacant indentation where warm, furry love had once slept. That's how I, instead, stayed out in the open, in the sun, where love was abundant.

I just stayed focused on being a part of my very busy, three-member family, and didn't spend a whole lot of time worrying about family connections. I worried more about getting the most out of my educational experience, and some how translating that into a fabulous life. The more time that passed, the less I thought about the family members I never saw.

Through the final months of my junior year, I continued to spend time with Ms. Chandler. We managed to pull off an extraordinary prom. I became a devoted fan of American history. And our friendship bloomed.

My father and step-mother had little time for me. What time they had available, they spent it on each other. I think they saw me as just another person living under their roof. Ms. Chandler filled a void in my life that they were not filling. I don't even think I realized I had the void, until she was there in it.

She was interested in my school work and often times would help me with it. She was also interested in my extracurricular things and asked all about them. We discussed everything—from politics to *Saturday Night Live* skits.

She took me to my *Governor's Honors* interviews. She accompanied me to my extraneous speaking competition. She saw me opening night as Puck in *A Midsummer Night's Dream*. My parents weren't at any of those events, but I knew I had genuine support right there with me. Ms. Chandler was quickly becoming the single most significant person in my life.

The school year ended and we went our separate ways for the summer. She went home to Massachusetts to spend time with her family. My summer consisted of a summer job and some academic programs. Other than that, I would spend the time anxiously anticipating my fourth and final year of high school.

I knew before my senior year started what my schedule had in

157

store. Schedules were sent out the week before school started. So I knew, before I even stepped foot into Sweetwater High as a senior, that I would once again be in Ms. Chandler's class. She would be teaching American Government this year—and I, of course, had signed up to take it. I was looking forward to spending another year in her classroom.

This year, however, I had her at the end of the day, sixth period. That would make for a long day, waiting to see her. On the other hand, what a nice way to end the day.

I quickly got into the habit of hanging around her room for ten or fifteen minutes at the end of every day, just to catch up. It was all the time I had before having to run off to some practice or meeting of some kind. Not too far into the semester, during one of these short after-school sessions, she asked, "So, what are your plans for college?"

"Well. I'm not quite sure. I have a few places I'm really interested in. I've been contacted by some schools about scholarships."

Before I could go further, she raised her eyebrows. "What kind of scholarships?"

"What do you mean 'what kind'?"

"Like athletic, academic, what?"

"Oh. *Oh.* Academic mostly. I'm not really interested in playing sports in college."

She reached across her desk and slapped my arm. "Oh my God. That's great." Her face lit up.

I rubbed the spot on my arm where she had landed her blow. "Then why did you hit me?"

"Well, you jerk. You didn't tell me this. This is the first I've heard about scholarships."

"I guess I just didn't think about telling you. You know, until I decide."

"Are you kidding me?" She hit me again. "Before you ask, that's because you're being so stupid."

"What? Stupid?" I was sincerely confused.

"I want to talk with you about it *before* you decide." She apparently noticed the still-present look of confusion on my face. "To *help* you decide." She nodded excitedly.

"Oh. Well, I have a guidance counselor for that, you know."

With a dumbfounded look, she reached across and hit me a third time. This time much harder.

"Ouch!" I rubbed. "Ouch, for real. That hurt. What's wrong with you?"

"You hurt my feelings. That's what's wrong with me."

"How did I hurt your feelings?"

"You suggested that a guidance counselor would be better than me at helping you decide about college." She paused and bit her upper lip. "Me, who knows you." Pause. "Me, who cares about you." Pause. "Me."

"I just didn't want to bother you. Jeez."

"I *want* to help you. It's a huge decision and I want to make sure that you think it through."

"Okay. That's great. Screw the guidance counselor then—who needs one. You help me." I reached across and hit her in the arm.

"That wasn't necessary."

"Oh, I think it was."

She grunted. "Well, we need to set up a time to get together and discuss this."

"It'll have to be a weekend. My weekdays are packed."

"Okay. I'll come up with a day and let you know."

"Okay. Sounds great. Now I gotta get to softball practice." I turned to walk away.

"Wait. Come here first."

I stepped back toward her desk. "What?"

159

She grabbed a ruler from her desk and swiftly swatted my butt with it. "Don't ever hit me again." She smiled.

I rubbed my bottom as I was leaving. "Shit. You're crazy."

"And don't you forget it," she called out after me.

We decided on a Saturday evening several weeks after the ruler-swat conversation. She asked me to come over for dinner. She said she would cook and all I had to do was bring myself and all of my college related material. She told me I should come ready to take notes.

The weeks that followed our decision to get together went by slowly. I was eagerly anticipating the night. I was practically counting the minutes.

On a particularly nice fall afternoon, I was sitting at a picnic table in the school courtyard, eating a peanut butter sandwich for lunch, and reading Sylvia Plath poems. Russell Johnson, the quarterback of our notoriously horrible football team—and almost illiterate—suddenly stood over my table. He slammed a plate stacked with pizza slices on the table and sat down beside it on the table top. "Mind if I sit here?"

I looked up at him without lifting my head from my book. "Actually, yes, I do mind."

"Aw, come on Noble. I just want to chat with you. I want to get to know the super-cool, super-smart Noble Thorvald." He shoved pizza in his mouth and chugged Coke right behind it.

"Those are the best adjectives you could come up with?"

Orange pizza sauce was caked in the corners of his mouth. "What?"

I finally raised my head. "Super cool. Super smart. That's the best you can do?"

"Yeah. Whatever. What's that you're reading."

I closed the book and kept my place marked by holding my finger inside. "Something that is way, way, *way* beyond your

160

sophomoric intellect."

"Ha. Shows what you know. I'm not a sophomore."

"Great. Would you please leave me alone now?"

He was chewing on another bite of pizza and before he could swallow he said, "Hey, you know what I heard?"

I caught a glimpse of chewed bread and cheese in his open mouth. "Oh please enlighten me."

"I heard you were a lesbo."

I tilted my head to one side. "Really? Wow. That's interesting." I closed my book, laid it on the table, and slid closer to him. "You know what *I* heard?"

He ran his tongue across his teeth, "What?"

I lowered my voice to a conspiratorial whisper, "I heard you got emasculated by a girl."

He made a face. "Emascu . . . what?"

I shot my hand toward him and placed a vice grip on his groin. I clamped down with all my strength.

"Ughhhhhhhh." He jumped up and fell backward away from the table, causing me to release my grip. "Holy Christ! You stupid bitch. What the hell was that?" He continued to lie on the ground moaning.

I threw my trash away, picked up my book, and as I passed him I said, "*That* was emasculate."

Immediately following this encounter, I started to notice small groups of students staring at me and whispering. They would turn away from me when I looked in their direction. Fortunately, no one else approached me with revelations about my sexuality, or anything else for that matter.

I chose to ignore these banal, ignorant groups of gossipmongers. I thought about addressing the issue in my newspaper column, but decided to let it die rather than fuel it. I really didn't want to care what people were saying about me, so I

161

just ignored it.

The day of my Saturday night dinner with Ms. Chandler finally arrived. I was very excited about it. I enjoyed her company more than anything else in my life. I felt like she had a genuine, unconditional love for me. I thought back on how much Socrates had meant to me for that very same reason.

I wasn't sure why Ms. Chandler and I were so close. I had really never attempted to analyze the relationship. However, Russell's comment about the rumor that was circulating about me made me look at my feelings for her under a new light. I knew that some of our interactions took on the appearance of flirtation. I couldn't, however, convince myself that there was any more to it than that we were simply a teacher and student who had built an incredible friendship.

I arrived at her door that evening carrying a folder full of college information and applications. I rang the bell and waited briefly before the door opened. I was greeted by the warm smell of sautéed garlic and onions, and a musical background provided by Sting and The Police. Her smile was a welcoming beacon. "Hey there." The smile widened. "I'm glad you're here." She grabbed my hand and pulled me through the door. "Dinner is practically ready. We'll eat first and discuss that after." She pointed at my bulging folder. "You can just put those things anywhere." She hurried off to the kitchen.

I laid the folder on an end-table beside the sofa. From across the kitchen bar she said, "I hope you like pasta and vegetables."

I gave her my best smile. "Absolutely. It smells delicious."

"I hope you don't mind, I'm having some wine." She slowly lifted a wine glass sloshing with burgundy. Her face was a question. Her uncertainty was hiding behind a curtain of steam that was rising from a boiling pot on the stove.

"No. That's fine."

The question on her face softened a little. "You're sure?"

"Of course. It's not like I can't stand the sight or anything." I shrugged. "It just causes me to pause when faced with drinking myself. I don't expect the world to stop just for me."

The question on her face now turned to relief. "Good. I was concerned."

"Well, don't be. I might even have a glass myself." Her eyebrows went up and her head tilted. "Later, I mean. Maybe."

"You are welcome to have some, but don't feel like that's what I expect."

"I don't. I know you would never do that to me. You know. Pressure me."

"Of course I wouldn't. Ever." She went back to finishing the meal.

As we ate dinner, we talked about college in general. She told me the things she thought I should be looking for, things I should avoid, all of the things I should consider when making the decision.

"Noble, you've never really told me. What is it you want to do." Her face became very serious. "What do you want to be when you grow up?"

I put my fork down, took a sip from my water glass, and stared up at the ceiling. I sat this way for several moments, gathering my thoughts. I finally spoke. "I want to be famous." I moved my eyes to her.

She stopped chewing and crinkled her brow. She finally drank from her wine glass and swallowed. "Really? You want to be famous?" She nodded several times. "For what? Like how do you plan to gain this fame?"

"I'm not quite sure. I just know that I want my name to be a household name. I want people to know who I am." I stopped for a moment. "And to love me."

163

"Well, I for one am certain that if people know you, they will love you. But are you sure? It just doesn't seem to fit what I know about you."

"I want to be significant."

She sat her glass down a little too hard and her mouth fell open. "Oh Jesus, Noble. You *are* significant. You don't have to be famous to be significant." She leaned back in her chair. "Is that seriously what you're going to base a career choice on? Because that kinda breaks my heart."

"Why? Why does that break your heart?"

"Because you're amazing. No matter what you do with your life, I *know* you will be great at it, and I *know* you'll make a huge impact." She put her head in her hands for a moment and then looked back up at me. Her honey eyes pierced right into my blue ones. "Your significance is determined by how you live your life. Not by how many people know your name. You will always be significant." Her hand came across the table and came to rest on top of mine. "Please know that, Noble. Please, please, please, always know that." She squeezed my hand.

"Okay. So you're telling me that I *don't* want my name to be a household name." I smiled at her to try and ease the tension that had suddenly enveloped our conversation.

She returned the smile. "I have news for you." She withdrew her hand. "There are many households in which the word 'noble' will never be a household term." She let out a quick laugh. "And Thorvald? Come on. Who's gonna want that in their household?" She laughed again.

Despite her disrespect of the name that represented my Viking heritage, I had to laugh with her. "That was mean. I love my name. It comes from the Vikings."

"Well, if you want to be famous, you might want to give it back to them." She just kept on laughing at my expense. No matter

164

how hard I tried not to, I kept right on laughing with her.

After dinner, we moved into the living room and sat on the sofa with college information spread on the coffee table in front of us. She continued to drink wine while I decided to stick to my guns and just drink water. We went through all of my options and she gave me her opinion on each of them. By the time we finished, I had a list of three schools that interested me, met my needs, and had offered me scholarship money. I would apply, then go from there.

I gathered the paperwork from the table and prepared to put it back in my file folder when Ms. Chandler asked, "We talk about everything. But sometimes I wonder why you never talk to me about guys."

I looked up from my task. "Guys?"

"Yeah. You know. Dating. You never talk about dating."

"Maybe that's because I don't really date."

"Yeah, I know that. But why?"

With my attention once again focused on my college materials, I shrugged and answered, "Just not interested, I guess."

"That's unbelievable. A teenager not interested in dating. Almost impossible."

I shut my folder firmly, annoyed by her line of questioning. "What can I say? I'm not a typical teen."

"Oh come on. There's gotta be someone who turns you on."

I shoved myself deep into the sofa. "What do you want from me?" I crossed my arms across my chest. "Is there something you're trying to say?"

A look of shock touched her features. "No. I'm just making conversation."

"Do you wanna know if I even like boys? You wanna know if girls do it for me? Is that what this is?"

Her look of shock transformed into a look of confusion. "No.

165

That's not what I was thinking at all."

I settled myself deeper into the sofa, arms still crossed. I lifted my chin in a show of annoyance.

"What's up your ass? I was just talking. You don't have to get mean."

Silence settled over us. I wasn't sure how to respond. I felt my arms and my jaw relaxing. "I'm sorry. It's just something that came up this week."

"What came up?"

"Apparently there is a rumor circulating that I'm a dyke. I figured you were feeling me out to see if it's true."

"God, no. I haven't even heard that. Besides, if I wanted to know I'd come right out and ask."

"Okay. Sorry then. I just wasn't thinking. I'm a little touchy about it."

"Why so touchy?" She turned her body and leaned her back against the arm of the sofa. "Is there any truth to it?"

I chewed my upper lip, refusing to respond. She continued. "It's okay if there is. I'm just asking. Just curiosity."

"The truth is, I don't really know. I mean I don't know if I like girls or not. I've just never really thought about it."

"That's okay, too. You don't have to know that stuff yet. You have your whole life to figure out sexuality. Believe me, there's no reason to rush." She laughed lightly.

My hands were twisting in my lap and I couldn't take my eyes off of them. A tightness grew in my stomach and I was afraid I might be sick. I made the quick decision to press forward. "I know that I like you." I paused and kept my eyes down. "I can't really explain it. But I *really* like you, and it makes me nervous."

I still didn't look up. I just waited for a response that never came. My hands continued to twist and my stomach continued to tighten. I felt heat rising in my face and I knew eventually I would have to look at her.

I felt movement beside me on the sofa and before I could raise my head, her hands were on mine. She clamped hers shut, holding mine still. "Noble, I think you're very confused about your feelings toward me."

I finally looked at her. I couldn't speak, so I just used my facial expression to ask her to explain.

"You needed someone. You needed someone to be interested in you. Someone to talk to you and listen to you. Someone to support you and care about you." Her hands tightened around mine. "I just happen to be someone who fit that description." Now she began to gently rub my hands. "I think you've confused your feelings of gratitude and friendship for something else."

I watched her hands on mine. Her touch was soft and loving. "God, do I feel stupid."

"No. Don't feel stupid. It's understandable. I love you. I mean I *really* love you. You are very special to me. You are just plain special."

I spewed a burst of breath. "Right. I don't feel special at the moment. I feel ridiculous."

One of her hands moved to my face and she lifted my chin. Our eyes met. "You are not ridiculous. I am important to you, and special to you, and necessary for you. I would be upset if I weren't. But I'm sure you're not in love with me. We are just incredibly close. And we have a good thing."

I tried to lower my face again but her hand forced me to continue the eye contact. "I'm sure you're right." I tried to smile. "So maybe I'm not a lesbian. That's a relief."

She returned my smile. "You'll fall in love someday. You will find the love of your life. Might be a man, might be a woman. Doesn't matter. What matters is that you find the person who makes your world complete. And I'm certain you will." She lowered her hand.

"I'm not so sure I will find that."

"Psh. That's crazy. Of course you will."

"I'm a mess. I'm not sure I would want to saddle anyone with all of my baggage."

"There's someone out there who would love to have it."

"I'm really afraid that I will always just be looking for someone to give me the care and nurturing that I didn't always get when I was younger. Someone to do for me what my mother should have done."

"You need to stop that. You'll find the one."

I laughed. "Yeah, but as soon as I ask them to bathe me, tuck me in, and read me a bedtime story, they'll run for the hills."

"Noble, everyone has family history. Baggage. Most people get over it. You will, too."

"Hope so. But look at what I thought about you."

"Well, I'm flattered. And you're going to be fine."

***

My senior year flew by in a whirlwind. The rumors about my sexuality eventually lost steam. Karen Truitt's teen pregnancy took the gossip limelight away from me. Ms. Chandler and I remained close, but I was always a little nervous around her after that night. The year ended with me as both Valedictorian and Star Student of my class. My college plans were laid and I was ready to embark on yet another adventure.

***

Graduation night brought out most of my relatives. Daddy, Dee, and Mamateen were all there to see my moment in the sun. I chose not to invite Mama, but I did send invitations to Rachel and Chad. Chad didn't make it, but Rachel came. She drove her clunker Buick the hundred miles from Winder, just to see me graduate. During my speech, I saw her face amongst all the others,

168

beaming with incredible pride. That sight made it difficult for me to hold back the tears.

After the ceremony, Rache and I sat alone on the front porch steps of Daddy's house. She sat close to me and draped her arm around my shoulders. She filled me in on the path her life had taken. She didn't graduate from high school but dropped out her junior year instead. She worked her way up to shift manager at the Dairy Queen and was engaged to a guy she had been dating for about a year. They planned to get married some time this year. She told me Mama was still drinking and keeping her mother and sister busy getting her out of trouble. Chad had started drinking heavily, too, and was jumping from job to job with very little direction. He had also dropped out of high school.

After about an hour of conversation, she squeezed my shoulder. "I am so proud of you, Noble. I can't believe how far you've come."

"Thanks."

"Seriously. I never would have thought you would accomplish all of this."

"Thanks."

She pulled me toward her and held me close. "I'm sorry if I didn't do right by you. I mean, I was a kid, too. But, I feel like I should have taken care of you."

I felt her tears against my cheek. Her grip on me didn't loosen at all. "You did all you knew how to do. It's okay. I made it through."

I felt her body shudder with a sob. "But you were so little. And we left you all alone."

I pushed myself away from her and looked her directly in the face. Two sets of identical blue eyes searching one another. Tears flowing from both. "Rache, I'm okay now. That's in the past. Let's not think about it."

169

She held my face in both hands. "But just look at how awesome you turned out."

"Yes. That's right. I'm just fine. I'm awesome."

"I am *so* proud, Noble. God, I'm proud of you."

Chapter 13
September 1986-May 1988

I chose to attend Mars Hill College, a small, private, liberal arts college in the Blue Ridge Mountains of North Carolina. As my father had made it clear that he was financially unable to pay for college at all, the biggest factor that went into the decision was money. Mars Hill offered me a Presidential Scholarship. This particular scholarship paid for my tuition, room and board, books, and even paid me a small monthly stipend for living expenses.

In addition to the money, Mars Hill was located in a quiet, serene mountain setting that seemed ideal for focusing on maintaining the GPA necessary to keep the scholarship. There would be no party distractions. No fraternities or sororities. No college-town bar scene. Mars Hill provided a serious academic environment. It's what I felt I wanted, as well as needed.

I began as a business major and became quickly ensconced in academia. I made friends with others who were also serious students bent on success. With the beautiful natural setting of the campus, I got back to my love of nature that had been so central to my life in my early years.

Two months into my college career, I was comfortable and

171

settling into a productive routine. This routine consisted primarily of academic pursuits. My social life consisted of all-night Monopoly and Trivial Pursuit tournaments in the student center, and weekend hiking and canoeing trips. It was a simple but very happy time for me.

Every on-campus student had a mailbox assigned to them in the campus post office which shared a building with the dining hall. Part of my routine was to check my box for mail everyday as I entered the building to have lunch. Also part of my routine was the fact that I always found my box empty. I didn't expect mail, it was just a comfortable part of my day to check.

On one bright but cold November Tuesday, my routine got sideswiped. I punched my combination into my mailbox, swung the little medal door open, and found a lone white envelope lying in the bottom. I stared at it for a few moments to ensure that it didn't dissipate into a blurry fog. It remained the same. I reached in, pulled it out slowly, and read the writing on the front. It was addressed to me in a careful, block-lettered hand. The return address didn't include a name, but the address was one that I didn't recognize in Atlanta.

The presence of the letter sent me into a tailspin, and the safety of my routine was quickly forgotten. Lunch was pushed to a back burner. I left the building and dropped myself onto a bench right outside the door. I couldn't take my eyes off the envelope. My mind was working a hundred miles a minute in an attempt to figure out who the letter had come from.

After prolonged hesitation, I slowly ripped the envelope flap open. I pulled out a carefully folded yellow sheet of legal paper. Both sides of the page were covered in an elegant hand-written script in blue ink. I couldn't help myself. Before I began reading the letter I skipped to the bottom to see who had signed it. At the bottom of the page, the letter was signed, "All My Love, Mama."

For several minutes I could only stare at the signature in disbelief. Then it occurred to me—I hadn't heard from her in years. I didn't know anything about her. Suddenly, I couldn't read the letter fast enough. I read it and reread it three more times before I could actually digest what it said.

Basically, Mama had, once again, gone through rehab and was doing very well. She was living in Atlanta and working as a hostess in a nice restaurant. She contacted my father in an attempt to get in touch with me. All he would give her was my address. I assumed that was his way of letting me maintain as much control over the situation as possible.

Apparently she had heard about my accomplishments and wanted me back in her life. I kept going back to one particular paragraph in the letter and reading it again and again. The words on the paper made my heart swell. I was getting a glimpse of the old Mama. The paragraph read, "I heard all about your honors and awards in high school. And I know you're in college on a wonderful scholarship. I am so very proud of you. I always knew my little genius would grow up to be something special. And what makes it more amazing is that you did it with no help at all from me. I know that all I did was make it harder for you. I'm so sorry for that, Pooh Bear. That just makes me even more proud of you. You did everything on your own and you did it all for yourself. You are just something else."

She went on to say she would love to hear from me. She wanted to hear all about all of my accomplishments. She included her phone number and wanted me to call her, collect, any time I felt like I might want to talk to her. I was blown away. My Mama was back. I just couldn't decide if that was a good thing or not.

I went through the rest of my day robotically following my comforting routine. I tried to keep my focus on the tasks at hand, but my mind just couldn't leave the letter. The words from the

173

lined yellow pages just kept floating around inside my head. The phone number she had printed in the letter was repeated in my brain so often that it became permanently engraved in my memory.

After dinner in the dining hall that evening, I laid on my bed in my dorm room reciting the number quietly. I wanted to call it. I longed to hear my mother's voice. It was a distinct voice, but it had been so long since I had heard it, that the memory of it was a wavering mirage. I was afraid to hear that voice. Afraid I would not be able to handle the emotions it might evoke. I simply recited the number. Over and over. Trying to decide what to do with it next.

After an hour of this behavior, I left my room, went down the hallway, and entered the four-foot by six-foot space known as the phone room. The cubicle contained a small bench and a pay phone attached to the wall. I lifted the receiver of the phone and slowly dialed a zero followed by the newly memorized number.

After several clicks on the line someone answered, "Operator."

"Collect call, please."

"Who can I say is calling."

"Oh. Ummm. Noble."

"Noble?"

"Yes. Please. Noble. Please."

"One moment."

The line clicked and went silent as the operator made the connection. My mouth felt like it was full of sand and I feared I wouldn't be able to speak. I felt warm liquid crawling up my throat, and I struggled not to vomit. I couldn't remember the last time I felt this nervous.

The line suddenly clicked again. "Pooh! Pooh! Is this my precious Pooh Bear?"

My mother's voice washed over me like a bath of Epsom salt.

I felt the aches and pains of years without a mother wash away with it. I tried to open my mouth to speak, but the dryness caused it to stick. I quickly tried to conjure up a mouthful of saliva and was finally able to say, "Yes. Yes, Mama. This is your Pooh Bear." A huge smile cracked my face.

"Oh my God, Baby. How are you doing?"

I was afraid I would cry, but instead I wanted to laugh. I just wanted to roll on the floor and laugh and laugh. "Mama. I'm really good, Mama. How are you?"

"Oh Baby, Baby. I've heard all about what you're doing and I know you're doing good. Hell, you're doing great. And, I'm doing A-Okay myself."

I could hear the smile in her voice, and it warmed me up. The dark, concrete phone room had become light and warm. "Good, Mama. And you sound really good. I was glad to hear from you. I've missed you. And it sounds like I can be proud of you, too."

"Oh, I'll tell you what, I'm trying Pooh. I'm really trying."

"I know Mama. That makes me happy."

"Baby, listen. I know where you are, and I know you're real busy. But, I am just dying to see you. I mean to tell you, I am literally dying here." She laughed her deep laugh. Oh, what a beautiful sound. "I want to try to come up and visit. What do you think of that?"

I felt the hair on my arms stand up and my feet tingled like they had fallen asleep. Since Daddy and Dee dropped me off two months ago, I hadn't had any visitors. The prospect of Mama visiting me both excited and scared me.

I so wanted to see her and let her wrap me up in her long, slender arms. However, I couldn't forget about all that she had done to me. Mars Hill had become *my* place. My safe haven from the horror that was my history. I didn't want Mama to come here and soil that. I didn't want *my* place to be tainted by her ghost.

175

"I would love that, Mama." The words were out of my mouth before I could talk myself out of it. I knew that deep down, my desire to see her outweighed my fear of what she might do to my haven.

"Hip, hip hooray! That makes me so happy, Babygirl. I'll come up and spend the weekend. We'll have a big ol' time."

"That'll be nice." I felt my smile broadening. Other kids had their parents visit on occasion. Now was my chance.

"Let's plan it!"

We decided that she would drive up the following Friday and spend the weekend. She would get a hotel room and I would stay with her. She said that planning the weekend activities would be up to me. She was up for anything I wanted to do. She said not to worry about anything, that the sky was the limit. I had a week-and-a-half to come up with ways for us to spend our time together, and for me to get myself mentally prepared for what that would mean.

On the day of her planned arrival, I trudged my way through the day scarcely hearing a word any of my professors said. My final class ended at two o'clock, and she said she would be here at 2:15. She didn't want to waste any time. I would meet her in the student center.

Dr. Morris dismissed my Western Civilizations class at exactly 1:58. I grabbed my belongings, shoved them in my backpack, and high-tailed it across the front circle, through the courtyard, and straight into the student center. At 2:03, there was no sign of Mama.

I sat my bag on the floor, caught my breath, and sat down in a chair facing the door to wait for her. I checked my watch about every two minutes. At one point I was sure the second hand jumped backwards. I looked down to check for the fourth time, 2:12, when I was startled by a familiar voice. "Pooh Bear!"

I raised my head and jumped from my seat simultaneously. I

saw her running toward me, arms spread wide, giant shapeless purse flapping against her hip. "Just look at you. All grown up."

Before I could respond, her arms were around me and she was squeezing me hard enough to make it difficult to breathe. I wiggled a little to give myself a bit more room. "Mama." That was all I managed to say.

She grabbed me by the shoulders and pushed me out to arms' length. "Now let me just get a good look at you."

I stood quietly while she studied me. "My oh my. You've hardly changed." She poked me in the stomach. "Just a bigger body is all." She ruffled my hair. "Same crazy blonde hair. You got that spiky hairdo. Guess all those cowlicks that gave me hell when you were a kid are finally coming in handy."

She held my shoulders again. Gently shaking her head, she looked me directly in the face. "Same gorgeous blue eyes. Same perfect smile." The corners of her own smile practically touched her ears. "You are just the most beautiful thing I've ever seen." She pulled me toward her and went right back to squeezing the life out of me.

When she finally released me, I took a moment to study her. Her light brown hair was flecked with streaks of gray. Wrinkles were grouped at the corners of her eyes and grew deeper with her smile. Tiny lines radiated from her lips and gave her mouth the appearance of being constantly puckered. Her eyes were still the same sparkling blue-gray, and her scent was still Yves Saint Laurent's Opium.

"Hey. I brought you something." She opened her large purse and rifled through it. She pulled a small package from within. It was about the size of a deck of cards, wrapped in bright orange paper. She wiggled her eyebrows and held it out to me. "I know the paper is a bit loud, but I couldn't find any in turquoise."

At first, I wasn't sure what she meant, but decided not to

pursue it. It was as I was tearing away the paper that I realized she was referring to the colors of my beloved Dolphins. I stopped tearing the paper for a moment. "Mama, I really don't keep up with the Dolphins much anymore. I've kind of gotten over my football obsession."

Her face broke into an exaggerated frown. "Uh oh."

"What?"

"Well, I didn't really know that. But, just go ahead and open your gift."

I just nodded and went back to tearing away the orange paper. As the paper was pulled back, a small, clear, plastic case was revealed. Two tiny screws kept the case shut tightly around its contents. Through the plastic case I saw a picture of a very young Larry Csonka. It was a faded football card. Larry was wearing the orange of Syracuse University rather than the orange of Miami. I turned the card over to read the back through the plastic. It was Larry's 1968 rookie card. The picture was taken before he had even officially become a Dolphin.

"Baby, I had no idea that you weren't interested anymore in . . ."

I cut her off. "No, Mama—it's perfect." Tears were starting to fill my eyes. "The most thoughtful thing anyone ever gave me." I kept my eyes focused on Larry's serious face. I didn't want her to see that I was about to cry.

"Well I was at a flea market and this guy had a booth with sports memorabilia. I just started looking and came across that. I just knew I had to get it for you."

"It's really perfect." I sniffed a little and tried to force the tears back. I finally looked up at her. "I don't think anyone else would even remember about him. He was my hero." I laughed. "My best friend really. Silly, but he was really important to me." I took a deep breath, still fighting the tears. "Thank you for knowing that,

178

Mama." The dam burst and the tears came flowing.

"Oh, goodness gracious Pooh. Don't cry." She once again wrapped her arms around me. We just hugged for several minutes, not saying a word to each other. I sniffed and wiped my eyes, trying to gain control of the tears.

We eventually separated. She gave me the most motherly look I'd seen in years, and the tears almost broke through again. Just before they did, she asked, "Would you like to show me around? Then we'll go check in the hotel."

I looked at her and returned her smile. I couldn't get enough. I wanted to consume her. I wanted to climb into her pocket and curl up against her. I wanted to feel her warmth, hear her heartbeat next to mine, smell her skin. I hadn't realized how much I'd missed having a mother. I'd forgotten how wonderful and loving she was. I'd forced myself to remember her as a monster. That was probably just my way of making it easier to be away from her. Now, I remembered our songs, our baths, our heart-to-heart talks. I remembered that she was a great mother. I remembered who she was originally, before she lost herself to her addiction.

I reached out and took her by the hand. "Yes. I would love that."

We spent the weekend getting reacquainted. I filled her in on everything that had taken place in my life in her absence. She listened with great interest and pride. She frequently made noises of appreciation and excitement. It was apparent that she missed me and still cared very deeply about what was going on in my life.

During that weekend, I showed her my dorm room and classrooms and everything else on campus. We ate out and went bowling. We went to a movie and had ice cream. On Sunday, before she had to drive back to Atlanta, we decided to go for a hike on one of the amazing local mountain trails.

We walked along a path that followed a slow-moving creek.

There was a damp chill in the air. The trees had lost their leaves and the bare branches waved heavily in the cool air. As we walked, we talked about Rachel and Chad. We talked about Daddy and Dee. We talked about future plans together. We reached a bench in a clearing facing the creek and decided to sit for awhile.

We sat silently for a moment, watching the creek roll sleepily past us. I broke the silence. "Mama? Can I ask you a question?"

"Of course you can, Baby. I'll do my best to answer anything you ask."

"I was just wondering something." I paused.

"Okay." She urged me on.

"Why do you keep drinking?"

I was watching the current in the water. She didn't respond. I looked at her to find her also staring blankly at the brown water. "I mean, I was just wondering why. Like, when you aren't drinking you seem so happy. And you're just this completely different person." I looked back toward the creek and followed a bobbing stick as it made its way downstream.

"I just guess I don't understand what makes you do it again. Why do you give up being this wonderful and happy person just to take a few drinks?" I looked back up at her. This time she was looking at me.

She reached over and grabbed my hand. "That's a great question, Pooh. Wow! That's a really good question." She shook her head. "It doesn't make much sense, does it."

"No. Not at all. I just don't get it, Mama." I took my hand from hers and picked at a splinter of wood on the bench. "I've always wondered if it had something to do with me. Like maybe I wasn't good enough for you and you replaced me with alcohol."

"God, no, Baby. No!" She grabbed my hand again.

"Or that maybe I broke your heart and all you can do to make it better is to get drunk."

180

She squeezed my hand. "Absolutely not, Babygirl. Absolutely not."

She looked at me for a long time before going on. "My problem has nothing to do with anyone else. My drinking is my own fault. Don't you *ever* feel guilty for that." Her face sagged into a look of complete despair. "You are a perfect child. Always have been. Don't ever think you had anything to do with my problems. *Ever.* Do you hear me?"

I nodded. "I guess so. But then why, Mama? Why?"

She took her hands back and now held her head in them. "Lord, Girl, if I could answer that question I'd be a bazillionaire." She heaved a heavy sigh. "I'll give you my best answer. I'll try."

Now she drew in a deep breath as she formulated her words. "I don't want to drink. I hate it. But there's this desire. This . . ." She waved a hand trying to find the right word. "This obsession. And no matter what I do, I just can't make it go away."

"That makes no sense to me."

"Have you ever heard of 'fighting kudzu'?"

"No. I don't think so."

"Well, you know what kudzu is?"

"Sure." I knew from eighth grade Georgia History that kudzu was a plant that was brought here from Japan to prevent erosion. The climate in the southern United States was apparently ideal for this plant, so it took off and grew like wildfire. Now, all over the South, you would see houses, barns, trees, telephone poles, anything in its path, get covered and consumed by the fast-growing plant.

"Well, you probably know then that kudzu is next to impossible to get rid of. People try spraying it, pulling it, even burning it. It almost always comes back."

I nodded. I remembered something along those lines as well.

She continued. "My Daddy used to say that trying to change

things that were not in your control was like fighting kudzu."

I still just continued to nod.

"You can't get rid of it. You can't change it. You're fighting kudzu."

"Yeah. I understand that part."

"Well, for me, fighting my alcoholism is like fighting kudzu. I get it under control sometimes, but it just comes back."

"But isn't it in your control? I mean it's not like you're trying to change the weather. It's your own behavior. And you *do* have control over that."

"Not in my mind. To me, asking me to never drink again would be like me telling you to never have a stomachache again."

Shaking my head dramatically I said, "That can't possibly be right."

"I'm sorry Pooh. But that's my best explanation."

We sat quietly for a few minutes. I stood from the bench. "We should probably get back."

"Yes." She stood. "We should."

We walked side-by-side and she draped her long arm around my shoulder. "Just don't ever think it's you. It's my own weakness. If I were a stronger person, maybe I could get rid of my kudzu. But it's me. For sure. Never you."

She gave me a little nudge and a wink and moved her arm from my shoulder letting her hand fall to mine. She entwined her fingers with mine and started swinging her arm along with mine. We walked the entire way in silence, swinging our arms in rhythm with our steps.

Before leaving, she vowed to stay in close touch. We planned future visits and activities. At her car, she hugged me tightly, then kissed me over and over all over my face. "Be good, sweet girl."

I couldn't stop smiling. The dampness of her sweet kisses on my face made me want to float away. "Always."

182

"Of course." She beamed. "My perfect daughter."

She got in the car and rolled the window down before pulling off. She blew a kiss and waved. "Until next time."

I waved at the tail lights as she drove away and quietly said, "Until next time."

***

As promised, we kept in close touch. We wrote each other regularly. I went to visit her in Atlanta when I was home for holidays. She even came up to visit m. one more time in the spring. Our relationship was growing and we were once again becoming very close.

I completed my first year of college as a success in every way imaginable. I was happy. Not only was I rekindling my relationship with my mother, but I also felt I had finally found my place. As my freshman year was ending, I realized that the last thing on earth I wanted to do was go back home, even if it was just for a couple of months in the summer. I looked for ways to stay and spend my summer close to the campus that had taken on more of a feeling of home to me.

I discovered the means to remain through the Girl Scouts of America. I applied for and received a summer job as a camp counselor at a nearby Girl Scout camp. I spent that summer hiking, canoeing, swimming, singing, and advising young girls. It was also during that summer that I began to document my daily life in a journal. I found that writing helped me to keep my head clear. It made it easier for me to keep my worries and fears at bay. It brought back to me memories of the enjoyment I experienced in high school while writing for the school paper.

My first college summer was a turning point in my college career. I'd chosen business as a major because I thought it would offer me the most potential for a financially secure future. After my summer of enjoying the natural world and putting my thoughts and

183

feelings on paper, I knew I wanted to do something that would bring me joy, not simply financial success.

When I returned to school in the fall, I spoke with my advisor about my desire to pursue a career that involved writing. There was still, however, the pull to go in a direction that would offer opportunities for a successful future. Her first suggestion was journalism. Again, I remembered how I enjoyed my newspaper job in high school. Journalism sounded like a winner to me. Before the end of the day, I had officially changed my major through the registrar's office. Business was already a distant memory. I walked across campus with a little bit of a hop in my step.

I continued to stay in close touch with Mama. She called me every other day, and she wrote me at least once a week. She always included at least ten dollars with each letter. I loved getting her phone calls and letters. I also enjoyed writing her back. It was a wonderful relationship.

Students got the entire week of Thanksgiving off for the holiday. The Friday before the break, I left campus at around three o'clock to make the four-hour journey home. The 1973 green VW Beetle that my father had bought for me when I turned sixteen had seen better days. However, it had always been reliable and I loved it with an undying passion.

I planned to spend the Sunday before Thanksgiving with Mama. She was going to cook dinner for the two of us and we would have our own celebration. Thanksgiving Day I would be with Daddy and his family at Mamateen's house. Thanksgiving was always a big spread and a big family deal with Mamateen. I was really looking forward to the holiday.

My day with Mama was perfect. We went shopping in downtown Atlanta. She loved to buy cheap designer knockoffs from street vendors. She pranced around in a fake mink coat and a beret. We laughed at all of the junk we bought. We went back to her apartment and made Thanksgiving dinner from boxes and cans. We listened to the radio and sang and danced around the kitchen. It was definitely perfect.

We briefly got in an argument over a song on the radio by Falco. I told her the name of the song was "Rock Me Amadeus," but she insisted it was vulgar and he was singing "Fuck Me Amadeus." She eventually admitted that she simply preferred singing it her way. So, I let her have it, and perfection returned.

I decided to spend the night with her. After dinner we went to the movies to see *Fatal Attraction*. It had been out a couple of months and we both wanted to see it before it left the theaters. We decided that it gave us the creeps badly enough that I slept in the room with her. As I was drifting off, listening to her breathing beside me, I felt content in knowing that we had just had the best day ever.

The next morning we went to eat breakfast at I-Hop. I was making my way through a short stack of buttermilk pancakes dripping in syrup, and Mama was eating toast and drinking coffee. "Pooh Bear, I have to tell you, I just had the best time ever yesterday."

I swallowed a sweet bite. "Me too, Mama. It was awesome."

"I have a great idea."

I felt my happiness begin to dissolve. There was still too much unknown with Mama for those words to generate positive anticipation.

"What?"

"I think you should just stay and spend the whole week with me."

"I don't know, Mama."

"Well, Chad's not going to come over. He's out of town with friends. Rachel is going to be with her new husband's family. I just thought you might stay." I didn't respond. "Otherwise, well, you know. I'll be alone on Thanksgiving."

"But Mama."

"I know, Baby. I know you have plans with your dad's family."

"Yeah."

"But that's such a big family. And with me, well, it's just me."

I wanted to spend that day with Mamateen. Her house at Thanksgiving was one of my favorite memories and I always looked forward to revisiting it. "But . . ."

"They probably wouldn't even miss you. And I would give you my full attention. It would just be you and me."

"Mama. I really like going to Mamateen's. I like the big family. It's always fun. I don't want to miss it."

I could see the tears slowly taking form in her eyes. "You're right, Baby. You need to do that. I'll just go serve food at the homeless shelter or something." She wiped at her eyes. "It's not a big deal. I won't really be alone."

"Mama, we planned that yesterday was our celebration. Thursday is my celebration with Daddy." I put my fork down. My appetite had disappeared. "That's what we planned."

"I know, Baby. It's okay. I know." She smiled but I still saw the tears in the corners of her eyes.

Despite her continued insistence that she would be fine, the worry began to eat away at me. As I drove away from her that afternoon, I watched her waving goodbye in my rearview mirror. As I watched her shrinking, waving figure, I had my doubts about how she would fare alone. A rock sat in the pit of my stomach as I turned the corner and she disappeared from view.

The rest of the week eased by me very slowly. I found myself thinking about Mama almost continuously. I couldn't stop worrying about her. Thanksgiving Day turned out to be a frigid and blustery day. Snow flurries swirled in the gusty winds. The day

186

was huddled under a low, gray blanket of clouds.

Despite the chill outdoors, Mamateen's house was warm with fireplace heat, bodies clad in sweaters, and aromatic steam rising from covered dishes of food. The dinner and the holiday were bright reminders of the warmth of family. However, even while I was enjoying my turkey and dressing, I was worrying about my mother.

After dinner I snuck into Mamateen's bedroom where there was a phone on her nightstand. I picked up the phone and dialed Mama's number. I thought I would at least wish her a wonderful day. The phone rang ten times and still there was no answer. I placed the receiver quietly back on the cradle. I continued to look at the receiver, contemplating trying again. Then I remembered what she had said about the homeless shelter. I assumed she would be there spooning food on plates for those who had nowhere to go to celebrate the day. My mind was momentarily eased and I shuffled back to the front of the house where the family party was still going strong.

There were cousins on the sun porch playing cards and board games. Mamateen, Dee, and various aunts were sitting around a cleared table, drinking coffee, discussing the secrets of how to create the perfect dressing. Daddy and several uncles were in the den watching the Lions game on television.

I continued through the kitchen, out the door and onto the front porch. I sat in a rocking chair. A gust of freezing wind struck me in the face. My carefully styled spikes of hair blew backward and my eyes stung and began to water.

I pulled the sleeves of my moth-eaten, mustard, wool sweater over my hands and covered my face with my hands. The smell of old wool, damp from the cold air, filled my lungs. It was a comforting smell. I forgot the chill in the air, and my mind wandered again to Mama. I hoped she was okay. I was sure she was, but I couldn't shake the feeling that something wasn't right.

The screen door opened behind me and then squeaked shut. I removed my hands from my face and looked up to see Mamateen standing in front of the door. "Noble, what in the world are you doing out here?"

"Just thinking."

She slowly seated herself in a matching rocking chair. A tiny groan came out of her as she settled herself in the chair. "What are you thinking about?"

"Just my mama."

"What about her?"

I looked into Mamateen's eyes. The clearest blue, sliding deeper and deeper into folds of age marked skin. "I'm not sure. I'm just worried about her."

"Noble, when are you ever going to stop worrying about her? She's an adult. Let her worry about herself."

"I can't help it. She's alone today and that scares me."

"What are you scared of?"

"That she'll be so depressed she'll drink again."

"If she's gonna drink, she's gonna drink. Doesn't matter if she's alone or not. There's nothing you could do to stop her."

"I guess you're right. But I'm still worried."

A sharp gust of wind cut across our exposed faces. "Holy Christ!" Mamateen made a big show of shivering dramatically. "I'll tell you what I'm worried about. You out here in this cold." The wind kicked up again. "Whew! It's colder than a witch's titty out here."

I couldn't help but laugh at my grandmother's silly analogy. "Get inside before you catch your death."

I followed her through the door and asked, "Wouldn't it be cool if you really could catch your death?"

Just inside the door she stopped abruptly forcing me to run

into her large rear-end. I took a step back. "What do you mean 'wouldn't it be cool . . .'?"

"I mean like people who want to die could just catch their death. You know. Instead of like having to kill themselves. It would be easier, I guess."

She put her hands on her hips. "Noble Lee Thorvald. Don't ever let me hear you talking about easier ways to die. That's just not something that should even be on your young mind."

"Sorry. I was just thinking."

"Do you want to be dead? Ever?"

"Well, I guess sometimes. I've thought about it. I think everybody does."

"I sure as hell don't." She pointed at me. "And neither should you. You need to just push that crap right on out of your head."

"Okay."

Her tense body relaxed slightly. "Noble, I know you kids have had a rough life. But you have so much more ahead of you to look forward to. Everybody has hard times now and again. Nothing is ever bad enough to wish you were dead. Never. You understand?"

"Yeah. I understand."

"Promise me that if you're ever thinking about that kind of thing again, you'll call me. Right away. No matter day or night. Promise?"

"Yeah. Yeah, I promise."

She pulled me into her and wrapped me in her loose folds of skin. "Let's go get some dessert."

I tried to call Mama a total of twelve times over the next three days. She never answered. I was so worried I was having a hard time focusing on anything else. Chad lived less than a mile from her. She saw him regularly. She gave me his phone number, but I chose to have little contact with him. I never called him, but I had seen him twice, briefly, while visiting her.

189

For the first time ever, I dialed his number into the phone. It rang several times before being answered by a machine. "You've reached Chad and Ken. Sorry we're not available. Leave a message and we'll call ya back."

There was a beep. "Chad, this is Noble. I've been trying to get in touch with Mama but she's not answering. Can you please check on her and call me? I'm very, very worried." I said thanks and left my number. I remembered that he was out of town until Sunday evening.

I headed back to Mars Hill drowning in a pool of uncertainty. I could only hope and pray that I would soon hear from either Mama or Chad. I felt a knot of dread growing inside me.

Late Sunday night I was curled up in a blanket sitting on my bed. The heat in the old dorms was substandard and the cold nights seeped their way inside. I was organizing my school work for the next day's classes when there was a knock on my door. Through the door I heard the voice of Samantha, the Residence Assistant. "Hey Noble. You have a phone call."

"Okay. Thanks. I'm coming." I jumped up and ran down the hallway in my pajamas and sock feet. I ran into the phone room and grabbed the dangling phone receiver. "Hello?"

"Hey there, baby sister!" It was Chad.

"Hey Chad. I guess you got my message."

"Yeah. Listen. We drove by Mama's and the place was pitch black. She's either sleeping or not there."

"You didn't go in?"

"Didn't see any need in it. Worst case scenario, she's passed out drunk. There's nothing I can do."

I heard the slur of his words and knew that he too would soon be passed out drunk. "Chad I wish you would just go look."

"Listen, kiddo. Don't worry. I'm sure she's fine. If we haven't heard from her by tomorrow, I'll go check on her when I get home

190

from work."

"Well, okay, I guess. Thanks for calling."

"No problem. And just relax. This is what she does sometimes. She always turns up. She's fine."

"Okay. Call me tomorrow."

"Will do, little Sis. Good night kisses all over your face." He laughed.

"Yeah, thanks for that. Good night."

I trudged back down the hall feeling not the slightest bit better. Chad had this happy-go-lucky, devil-may-care attitude all the time. Regardless of the situation, he always seemed jovial. That's how he had been his entire life. I often wondered why I had to be the one who inherited the Type-A worry gene that constantly gnawed at my insides.

The next day brought with it a bright blue sky dotted with high floating puffy clouds. There was a bit of a nip in the air, but the bitter cold of the past few days had passed. Even though there was still concern for Mama in the back of my mind, the beautiful day, combined with my reentry into my routine, put a tune in my head that I couldn't help but hum as I crossed campus on my way to class.

My spirits continued to lift throughout the day. I immersed myself right back into my studies. I caught up with friends. I began to plan for the upcoming end of the semester. All in all, I felt my worries scattering. Chad was probably right. Everything would be back to normal very soon. I let myself get worked into a worry frenzy for nothing. I decided just to enjoy myself and push my worries aside.

Dinner hour came and went with no phone call or phone message written on my door. I sat at my desk working on an essay for my English class. I was sure Chad or Mama would call me soon to update me. The hours passed with no phone call, and the worry crept back into my bones. It was so distracting that I finally had to give up on the essay.

It was after eleven and I couldn't take it any more. I was digging through my backpack in search of Chad's phone number when there was a knock on the door. It was Samantha. "Phone call, Noble."

"Thanks." I flew past Samantha and sprinted to the phone room. I grabbed the receiver. "Hello?"

"Noble?" It was Daddy's voice. The ball of dread that had grown in the pit of my stomach started climbing slowly up my throat. I felt dizzy so I closed my eyes and leaned my head against the wall.

"Yes."

"Noble. This is Daddy."

"Yes."

"How are you, Baby?"

"Good. What is it?" I wanted him to get to the point.

"Baby, are you alone right now?"

"Daddy! Please!" The room spun. I braced myself against the wall.

"Rachel called me a little while ago so I could call you."

"Daddy?" Tremors jolted through me. "Daddy?" My knees buckled. I slowly slid down the wall.

"Sweetheart, I'm sorry. It's your mama. She's . . . umm."

"Oh God, Daddy. Oh God, Daddy." My legs completely gave way. I hit the floor. The phone no longer reached to my mouth. "Oh, oh, oh, please God, no." Sobs distorted the words.

"She's dead, baby. God, I'm so sorry."

I screamed. I slammed the phone receiver against the wall over and over and then threw it. I heard Daddy's voice in the distance. Phone dangling, speaking with Daddy's voice. I screamed. I punched. I kicked. I screamed. I was driven by panic. I

192

flailed on the floor. In a frenzy. I couldn't control my movements. Grief grew from my core. I threw my head back against the wall and moaned. I did it again. And again. Darkness started taking hold of me.

The phone room door flew open and Samantha stood there in her long gown. Several other dorm mates stood behind her. "Noble! Noble! Stop! That's enough." She grabbed my head and cradled it safely in her arms.

My energy finally abandoned me. The flailing was replaced by hysterical sobbing. Wendy Tatum had grabbed the phone and was now talking on it. Samantha held me, shushing me, rocking me.

Kelly Donovan, my roommate, was drawn to the phone by the commotion. She pushed past the crowd that had gathered outside the door and fell to the floor beside me. Samantha still held me tight and Kelly started rubbing my back.

As my sobs grew quieter, I heard Kelly's voice. "What in the world happened? What's wrong with her?"

Wendy still stood beside the phone. Her head was in her hands. "Her mother died." The words came out quietly. I heard a collective sigh and various "oh no's and "my God's." "Her dad and step-mom are on their way." Wendy never raised her head.

"Noble? Noble, do you hear me?" Kelly lifted my face so that she was looking into my eyes. I nodded at her. "You're okay, Sweetie. You're okay. We're going to get you back to the room."

She stood and grabbed me under one arm. Samantha took me under the other arm. Together they lifted me to my feet. The crowd walked with us as we made our way back to my room. Wendy was now walking alongside. "Her dad said it would be four or five hours before they get here."

Samantha looked at the group. "Anybody have any alcohol? Something to relax her?"

She was met by a bunch of wide-eyed stares. As Residence

Assistant, it was her job to enforce dorm rules. Someone answered, "Not on campus."

"Oh, bullshit." The RA let go of me for a moment. "This is one time when I couldn't care less about the rules. Will somebody get her something, please?"

There was a short hesitation. "I have vodka." A freshman named Debbie ran off down the hall sliding bunny slippers along the slick hallway.

Soon I was lying in my bed with ten fellow Mars Hill students hovering over me, all trying to figure out the best way to comfort me. The sobbing and crying had stopped and I'd reached a point of numbness. Objects swam in and out of focus. I was convinced that I was in the middle of a bizarre and cruel dream.

I vaguely recall Debbie entering the room and Samantha taking a large, clear bottle from her. Kelly handed her a huge coffee mug and she poured into it from the bottle. Someone lifted my head as Samantha said, "Here Noble, you need to drink this." She lifted the mug to my lips and I took a quick sip. Immediately my throat was on fire and I gagged and coughed. The vodka spewed right back out, spraying Samantha's face.

"She's gonna have to drink that quick. She can't sip on it." Debbie spoke from the back of the group.

Samantha nodded. "Noble, you're gonna just have to slam this back. All in one gulp. Don't sip at it."

All I could manage was to shake my head. I knew I didn't want to put any more of the fiery drink in my mouth.

"Come on now. Just do it. It'll help you relax. You need it. Real quick. Here we go." She raised the mug to my lips again.

This time I just opened my throat and threw my head back. I felt the burn roll down the back of my throat and hit my stomach. I coughed once as Samantha pulled the mug away. "Good job."

Instantly, warmth radiated from my center outward and to the ends of my limbs. A vibrating sensation filled my chest and head. Everything felt heavy and my body seemed to just sink into the bed. Whoever had been holding my head, gently laid it on my pillow. My eyes were too heavy to open. I heard and felt movement all around me. Soon the room was quiet and I saw the lights dim from behind my eyelids. I felt a hand on my shoulder and managed to open my eyes long enough to see Kelly sitting on the edge of my bed.

"You're going to be fine. Just rest and someone will let you know when your dad is here." She gave my shoulder a firm rub and then left me alone.

The bed seemed to be sucking me in and I found it impossible to move any part of my body. Warmth was flowing through me, forcing my muscles to relax and my mind to clear. As I drifted away to sleep, I thought I might be getting a glimpse of why Mama had such a hard time giving up the comfort of alcohol.

Several hours later I was awakened by a gentle shaking. I slowly opened my eyes to find Daddy sitting on the edge of the bed. Dee was standing beside him. They told me they were going to take me home for a few days. We talked very little as Dee helped me throw together a bag of necessities. I was shoving jeans and sweaters in a duffel bag.

Dee had her head in the closet. "You'll need something to wear to the funeral." She was rifling through my hanging clothes. I straightened from my bending position and just stared at her without words. "Do you have a black dress?"

The garments hanging in my closet consisted of a pair of British Army pants that I'd bought at an army surplus store, three men's blazers I'd purchased at a thrift store, and my winter navy pea coat. There wasn't a dress of any kind any where to be seen in any of my belongings. There never had been. I briefly wondered if Dee knew me at all.

195

"No. No black dress." I went back to shoving items in my duffel.

"Well, we'll have to get you one."

My dad looked at his watch. "We really need to hit the road. We have a long drive."

I shouldered my duffel. "I'm ready." I walked out the door with Daddy right behind me. Dee was still looking in my closet as if she expected some funeral-appropriate attire to suddenly materialize. Daddy turned back toward her. "Come on, Dee. Let's go."

She sighed and closed the closet. "I'm coming."

It was early morning but still dark. I climbed into the back seat of the car. I used my bag as a pillow and stretched out on the seat.

As Daddy entered the highway he glanced in the rearview mirror trying to see my face. "How are you doing, Sweetie? You hanging in there?"

"Yeah. Sure."

"Do you need anything? Hungry? Something to drink?"

The least appealing thing I could think of at the moment was putting anything into my stomach. "No, thanks. I'm good."

Quiet descended over us. I heard the thumping of the tires on the pavement. The rhythm was relaxing, but the vibration caused my nose to itch, making it impossible to get too comfortable. I sat up. "Daddy?"

"Yeah?" Once again he glanced at the mirror.

"Can you tell me what happened? I mean, how did it happen?"

He sighed. "Nobody knows what happened. They're doing an autopsy."

"Where was she? And, you know, was she alone or what?"

"She was in her apartment. Chad went over to check on her. Couldn't get her to answer the door. He used his key and went in and he, ummm, he found her there."

196

I grabbed my hair and pulled at it. "Oh God. What did he find?" I felt sweat pooling at the base of my spine and my head was spinning.

"She was lying there. On the floor, I think. No clothes. She had some minor cuts and bruises, but no, you know, apparent injuries or anything like that."

I leaned back in the seat and let my head fall backward. I used my hands to press on my forehead as hard as I could. "Christ. What happened?"

Dee turned to face me. "Noble, sweetheart, you don't really need to know all of this."

I sat up quickly. My head throbbed. "Oh yes I do! I desperately need to know all this." Lights blurred and flew past the windows. Hot air from the car's heater washed over me. I felt like I was rocketing through space, completely disconnected from anything else.

I banged on the car door. "Pull over! Pull over! Now, Daddy! Pull over!"

He swerved into the emergency lane and screeched to a halt. I barely managed to get the door open and lean out before I was vomiting. It splattered the pavement and bits of it flew back onto my face. My belly kept heaving until I thought I was going to vomit up everything inside of me, leaving only an empty bag of skin.

Dee was grabbing napkins from the glove compartment and trying to exit the car to help. My body was racked by uncontrollable convulsing that caused me to fall from the car and land on my shoulder on the pavement. My puke was at my face, but I couldn't manage to stop heaving and get off the ground.

Daddy and Dee were both at my side simultaneously. My convulsions had turned to shivers and my teeth were chattering. "Dave, we need to get her off this cold ground."

197

"I know that, Dee." Daddy grabbed me under the arms and lifted me. "That's what I'm trying to do."

Meanwhile she was wiping at my face with the napkins. "Noble, baby, are you okay?"

I coughed and nodded. They sat me back down in the car. Dee squatted down and looked me directly in the face. "Are you finished? Are you gonna be sick anymore?"

I shook my head and caught my breath. "No. Think I'm done."

"Okay. Well, here. You keep these." She handed me the napkins. "We'll stop first chance we get." She shut the door and climbed back into the front. Daddy was already behind the wheel.

"Dave, we need to stop at the next exit. Clean her up and get her some water."

"My thoughts exactly." He put the car in gear and pulled back out into traffic.

We stopped at a McDonald's where Dee went with me to the bathroom and helped me wash my face. There was a little dried vomit in the side of my hair where I'd been lying in the pool on the pavement. We cleaned it out as best we could. When we returned to the car, Daddy had a sack of Egg McMuffins and drinks. My drink was water and I drank it aggressively. My throat was raw and burning. Daddy held the sack toward me. "Hungry?"

I turned up my nose at the greasy bag. "No. Thanks."

Soon after, I managed to fall asleep in the back seat and sleep for the remainder of the trip. When Dee woke me, we were pulling into the driveway of our house. Daddy's hair was mussed, he had a stubbly face, and his eyes were red-rimmed.

He opened the back door and reached for my bag. I felt sorry for him. He obviously had not had any sleep in a long time. I grabbed my bag. "I got it, Daddy."

His jaws were drawn downward. He closed his eyes briefly and nodded. I grabbed my bag and followed him into the house. As

198

I made my way down the hallway to my room, Dee said, "Noble, you should jump in the shower. We all need to rest for awhile."

She didn't have to tell me that I needed to take a shower. I couldn't wait to stand under a warm, cleansing stream of water. I walked straight through my room into the bathroom, shedding clothes as I went.

Rather than standing in the shower, I sat in the tub. I drew my knees into my chest and wrapped my arms around them. My head rested on the tops of my knees. Steaming water hit me in the back of the head and ran down my body. I tried to relax and let the grief and the guilt be cleansed from my spirit and follow the water down the drain.

I sat that way, without moving, until my skin was shriveled and the water had grown tepid. Still, I didn't move. I attempted to disconnect my thoughts from the situation. I mindlessly hummed *True Colors*. A sharp knock at the door roused me from my Cyndi Lauper disconnect. "Noble? You okay in there?" It was Dee.

I raised my head. "Yeah. I'm about to get out."

"Okay. Well, I have something for you when you finish in there."

I was now pushing myself slowly up to a standing position. "All right. Be right there."

I heard her walk away from the door. I turned the water off and swiped at myself with a towel. Still dripping, I wrapped the towel around me and left the foggy bathroom. I threw on a T-shirt and gym shorts and went to the kitchen. Daddy had already showered and shaved and was sitting at the kitchen table in sweat pants, drinking a cup of coffee. He looked up at me. "How ya feeling?"

"Better." I sat down across from him. "Where's Dee? She said she had something for me."

"Bedroom I think. She'll be right back."

"Okay."

As if on cue, Dee padded into the kitchen in her slippers. She sat a white pill on the table in front of me. "I want you to take that." She crossed to the cabinet, pulled out a plastic cup and filled it with water. She placed that in front of me as well. "Here ya go."

I was holding the small pill between thumb and forefinger. "What is this?"

"It's just something to help you relax. And sleep."

"Ahh. Very cool." I popped the pill in my mouth and swallowed it with the water.

She poured herself a cup of coffee and sat down. "You need to go get in bed. Try to get a little more sleep." She took a sip from her mug. "We're going to do the same soon."

I nodded toward her mug. "And that's to help *you* sleep?"

She held it toward me. "Decaf."

"Oh. Right." I pushed the salt shaker back and forth between my hands. "So. What happens next?" Daddy looked at me with a question on his face. "I mean, what do we do now?"

"Well, after we get some rest, we'll call Rachel and see what's happening. Your grandmother had life insurance for her, so she's doing the funeral. They're taking her to Winder after the autopsy. That's where the funeral will be."

"Oh." Pins of light were flashing behind my eyelids. Autopsy. Funeral. Beads of sweat popped up on the end of my nose. Dee sat her mug down quickly. "Noble? You okay?"

"Not sure." My mouth was swollen with dryness. I didn't have the strength in my neck to keep my head up. Daddy shoved away from the table and grabbed me. "Come on. You need to get in the bed."

I had nothing to say. I just tried to help him move me to my room. I had no muscle. I was dead weight and just wanted to drape my body on the floor. I let Daddy drag me to my room and lay me

200

on my bed. I swirled in a heavy mist, calling Mama's name. Begging her to come back. *Come hold me. Please, Mama. Come back.*

When I awakened and emerged from my room several hours later, Daddy and Dee were, once again, sitting at the kitchen table. This time they were both dressed and chatting quietly with each other. When I entered the room, their chatting stopped.

I crossed to the refrigerator and poured myself a glass of water. "How are you feeling?" A pad of paper was sitting on the table in front of Daddy, and the phone was beside that.

I sat down with my water. "I'm not even sure anymore." I gulped the water down, quenching a terrible thirst. "I think I'm okay. But who knows how long that will last."

He patted my forearm. "It'll get better. I think you're just still in some kind of shock."

"Yeah. Probably."

Now Dee spoke. "It is shocking because it was unexpected. I think Rachel and Chad are really struggling with it, too."

It hadn't even occurred to me to consider what they must be feeling. "Have you talked to them?"

"I spoke with Rachel, but no one has talked to Chad since last night. He called Rachel shortly after he, ummm, found her. But now Rachel can't reach him. Nobody can."

"How's Rachel?"

"She seems to be holding up pretty well. She wants to talk to you as soon as you're ready."

"Okay." I took a deep breath in an attempt to prepare myself to hear the answer to what I was about to ask. "Do we know yet about the funeral and stuff?"

"They completed the autopsy earlier today." Daddy stopped and watched my face for signs of a breakdown. He must not have seen any, because he continued. "Her body is being transported to

Winder in the morning. Her mother has already started making arrangements. She and Rachel have already butted heads about some of the decisions. Not sure how that's all going to work out." He stopped again and studied me closely.

I was breathing as deeply as possible, trying not to let the words upset me. I gulped down the last of my water. "I told Rachel we would be there in the morning. You can help with some of those decisions, but you don't have to. It's up to you."

I closed my eyes and breathed in through my mouth. I wanted answers. Needed them. Just so afraid of what they might be. "Do they know why she died?"

He shook his head. "Autopsy results will be released in the next day or so."

"Was she . . . uhh . . . did, umm, someone hurt her?"

"No, Baby. It doesn't look like there was any kind of suspicious circumstances."

Relief flowed through me, but it was followed by a terrifying knowledge. I knew that if she wasn't harmed by someone else, that meant that she did this to herself. That, in turn, meant that we all contributed. We all sent her down the path to her own death.

My head began to swim. I put my face in my hands and pressed my thumbs deep into my temples. I felt tears squeezing out of my tightly shut eyes. A hand gently touched my back. "Let me make you something to eat, Noble. What would you like?"

I wiped my tears as I removed my hands from my face. I looked up at Dee. "I really don't feel like eating."

"You're going to have to eat sometime. There's nothing that you might want?"

"Not now. Maybe in a little while. Thanks."

Later that night, after managing to eat a sandwich and sleeping, I decided to call Rachel. She answered the phone before the first ring had even ended.

"Hello?"

"Hey, Rache."

"Noble, hey. I'm so glad you called. How are you?"

"I'm okay, I guess. I've been sick. And pretty upset. How about you?"

"I'm not bad. Busy. The phone has been ringing off the hook. I've been trying to help MeeMee and Aunt Louise pick out stuff for the funeral, and that's been a bitch."

"Oh, I'm sorry. I'll be there tomorrow and maybe I can help."

"Oh. It's okay. MeeMee just wants to make all the decisions. We've been arguing like crazy."

"Well, you sound good. Are you doing okay, you know about Mama?"

"Yeah. It was a shock, but once I got over the shock, I've been okay. How 'bout you?"

"I'm just sick. I can't believe it. I was just starting to get to know her. You know what I mean? Again, after not knowing her for years." I felt heat on my skin and tears rising. My voice began to quiver. I didn't want to cry anymore. I tried to control it. "I just wish I had done something. Wish I had spent Thanksgiving with her." I took a deep breath. "Or something."

"I felt that way at first, Noble. But, then I really thought about it. For years, Mama has been a big question mark. We never know what's coming next. Hospitals, jail, rehab, everything. You missed most of that. Me and MeeMee always had to be there for that crap." She paused. I could tell she was thinking about what to say next. "In all honesty, Noble, I'm kinda relieved that those days are over."

My struggle to contain my tears ended, they freely flowed down my cheeks. I didn't try to stop them, I didn't wipe them away. I let them flow, hoping they would take with them the toxins of my emotions. I cried silently for a long moment.

"Noble?"

"I can't even believe you said that, Rachel."

"I can't help it. She has caused us so much pain. And it only got worse with time. It made life chaotic. Unpredictable. Stressful."

"So you're glad she's dead? Just so your life is a little easier? Christ, Rache. She's a human being. She's our mother." The peanut butter sandwich I'd eaten earlier churned in my stomach and I was afraid it was coming back up. I swallowed and breathed and tried to keep myself together.

"I'm sorry. It's how I feel."

Anger burned in the back of my throat. My grip on the phone tightened. My hand throbbed from holding it. I wanted to have my hands on her. The sadness and anger mixed inside my head. I thought I would explode from the pressure.

"Rachel, I gotta go. I don't feel well."

"Okay. Guess I'll see you tomorrow."

"Yeah. Bye." I hung up and fell face down on the sofa. I started humming. Wasn't even sure of the tune. I just needed a distraction. I needed to calm down. Stop crying. I hummed. Letting the musical notes carry my spirit.

The next morning, Daddy drove me to Rachel's. He just dropped me off and said he and Dee would return for the funeral. Before he left, he made sure that I was okay. I promised him I was fine and I entered Rachel's house.

It was my first time at her home. She and her husband, Steve, had bought a cute starter home. Two bedrooms, two baths. Nice flower beds in the front and along the driveway. Bright green shutters. Steve was an auto mechanic and owned his own business. Rachel had done well to overcome some of the obstacles she had faced. I was proud to see that she was building a nice life for herself.

I entered through the kitchen door carrying a small suitcase. I heard Rachel's voice, and I followed it. I found her sitting in a chair in the living room, talking on the phone. She saw me and motioned for me to have a seat.

"I just think she would like the silver better. You know how she liked flashy things." She rolled her eyes at me as she listened. "But you already picked that God-awful dress, and that preacher who didn't even know her." She listened again. "MeeMee, we're gonna have to talk about his later. Noble's here." Listen. "Okay. Bye." She hung the phone up. "Oh, God. I'm so tired of her. She's just nuts."

She got up and came to me. She wrapped me in a firm hug. I was taller than her. That was strange for me. I just always thought of her as being bigger. I returned her hug weakly. We finally separated.

"Let me show you around. I'll show you where you can put your things."

She gave me a quick tour of the house. It was small but nice. We entered the final room, the second bedroom. "This is where you'll be sleeping." The room was furnished with a double bed and a small dresser.

"Okay. Thanks." I put my suitcase on the bed. She was standing in the doorway. A slight smile was tickling at her face. I couldn't understand. I didn't even remember the last time I had wanted to smile. But there she was, looking happy. "What? Why are you smiling?" I felt my anger rising anew.

"Nothing." She waved her hand around. "Just this room."

"What about it?"

"It's gonna be the baby's room." Her smile widened.

"Oh." I scanned the room. "That's nice."

She ran to me and grabbed me. "Noble. I'm pregnant! Three months." She hugged me. "Isn't that great?"

205

I was sure I was physically incapable of experiencing joy, and. I was having a difficult time understanding her ability to do so. "Sure. Yeah. Great." I nodded robotically. "Congratulations."

She pushed away from me. Frustration covered her face. "That's sincere."

I sat on the bed. "Sorry, Rachel. Guess I'm still grieving. Can't really enjoy happy stuff right now."

She rolled her eyes. "You're gonna have to get over it. You can't be sad about it forever."

"God, Rache. She's only been gone a day. I think I'm entitled to a little more than a day to be sad."

"That's fine. Be miserable."

"I'm sorry that, unlike you, I'm not happy that Mama's dead."

"I'm not happy." She turned to leave. "I just think it will be easier for everyone. Even her." She paused. "She was an unhappy person. I'm sure she's in a better place."

I threw myself back on the bed. "God. I hate when people say that. It's just something to make you feel better about death. She's not in a better place." I pushed up on my elbows. "She's dead, for Christ's sake."

"I have things to do. If you decide to stop being so gloomy, come find me." She stormed out.

I plopped back on the bed and lay staring at the ceiling. Maybe it was selfish of me to wish Mama were still alive. It didn't feel selfish. But Rachel was right, in a way. I thought about the conversation Mama and I had next to the creek. Now that she was gone from this world, her battle with the kudzu was over. Maybe this was the only way to beat it. Death was the only way she could defeat the kudzu.

After a few minutes, I eased into the kitchen. Rachel was sitting at the table, smoking a cigarette, and writing on a notepad. She looked up briefly, then went back to her list. "Should you be smoking if you're pregnant."

She released a breath full of smoke toward me. "I'm trying to quit."

"Your house is nice."

"Thanks," she said. She continued her writing.

"And, congratulations on the pregnancy. Sorry I wasn't very excited about it." She didn't say anything. "I'm just trying to figure out what I'm feeling. I'm just sort of confused."

She finally looked up. "I know. I do understand." She ground her cigarette butt in an ashtray. "I have really mixed feelings, too. It's just hard. For all of us."

"I know. I'm sorry."

A smile touched her lips. "It's okay, Pooh."

Her use of that name startled me. The sudden realization that I would never hear Mama's voice again, never hear her say my name, engulfed me. I felt the table spinning, and I held tightly to its edges to keep from falling out of my chair.

"Noble?"

"I'm fine. I'm fine." I breathed deeply. "I'm fine."

I continued to breathe and hold tightly to the table. In my head I repeated, *I'm fine, I'm fine, I'm fine.* Eventually the spinning stopped and I felt in control again. I opened my eyes.

Rachel was calmly watching me. "Okay now?"

"Yeah."

She rubbed and patted my hand. "You're gonna be fine." She took her hand away. "So. The funeral is day after tomorrow." She looked at her list. "I chose the casket. MeeMee chose a hideous dress that she literally would never have been caught dead in." She laughed a little. "Sorry, bad joke." She went on. "We still need music. It's a battle. MeeMee wants church hymns that Mama had probably never heard before. I just don't know." She sighed heavily. "Any ideas?"

Like a movie playing before my eyes, a vivid memory came crashing into my head. I was young, maybe six, just me and Mama in her sewing room. I was sitting on the floor, stringing buttons onto a thread. She was cutting fabric at a table, humming a tune. She suddenly stopped cutting. "God, that song is sweet but it makes me sad. Not sure why I'm humming it."

I continued working on my buttons, just letting her talk. "Ha. Of course I know why. It's absolutely beautiful. Sad or not." She shrugged toward me. "Roberta Flack." She went back to cutting, and now she sang the words. "The first time ever I saw your face, I thought the sun rose in your eyes. And the moon and stars were the gifts you gave to the dark."

"I like that song Mama." It was a pretty song.

"I know, Pooh Bear. It's beautiful." She smiled down at me on the floor. "I think I want that song to be played at my funeral." She nodded. "Yes. I definitely do." She went back to work and I went back to my buttons.

Remembering all that, I said, "'The First Time Ever I Saw Your Face,' by Roberta Flack."

Rachel looked at me. "What?"

"That's the music she wants. I'm sure of it. She told me."

"Really?"

"Yes. She and I talked about music all the time. She definitely wants that song at her funeral."

"Okay. I'll tell MeeMee. She'll put up a fight."

"No. We *will* have that song. I won't let her take that away from Mama."

***

People were bringing food to MeeMee's house and hanging around to pay their respects. Rachel, Steve, and I went over that evening to eat and to discuss the final details of the funeral. The music was the last of the details to be decided. Rachel graciously decided to let me be the one to tell MeeMee of my non-debatable musical choice.

I hadn't seen any of Mama's family in quite awhile. As we arrived, MeeMee and Aunt Louise both greeted me with half-hearted hugs. They both looked tired and old. Neither of their faces showed even the faintest memory of a smile.

The house was currently absent of any visitors. It was just the family. We all fixed ourselves plates of food from various containers that sat on the stove or in the refrigerator.

After everyone was seated and began to eat, Rachel decided not to waste any time getting to the matter of the music. "Noble says she knows what music Mama wanted."

MeeMee looked at me through eyes hidden beneath numerous folds of skin, and behind smudged glasses lenses. "Really, Noble? And what's that?"

I swallowed a piece of dry ham. I had to follow that with a quick swig of sweet tea to keep from choking. "Well, yeah. She did tell me what she wanted."

She simply raised her eyebrows, opening her eyes a little.

"She, um, told me she would like to have 'The First Time Ever I Saw Your Face.'"

"What's that? Is that some rock and roll song?"

"Well, it's really more of an R&B song. Very pretty."

She laid her fork down forcefully. "No. No rock and roll music. I don't even think the church pianist could play that." She shook her head back and forth so quickly her loose jaws flapped slightly. "No."

"Well, we could actually play the recorded Roberta Flack version on the sound system. That's the version she wanted anyway."

She slammed her palms on the table top causing silverware to jump. "No!" She was louder than I had ever heard her. "I said no rock and roll."

I glanced across the table at Rachel. The corners of her mouth were pulled down and her eyes wide, in an "I told you so" look.

I thought of Mama. She wasn't here to speak for herself, so by God I was going to do it for her. I tried to keep my voice even. "First, it's not rock and roll. Second, Mama liked it. Last time I checked this was *her* funeral."

"Well, Little Miss Sass, last time I checked, *I'm* paying for this funeral. So I think that entitles me to do what I want."

I put my fork down as calmly as possible. I took a moment to study my plate, take a deep breath, and put my words together. I raised my head and clasped my hands in front of me. "I can't believe that you are being such an incredibly selfish bitch." I saw Rachel's mouth go from the downward pull to an obvious smile-stifling pucker.

"You've already chosen to have the service in a Baptist church rather than a non-denominational chapel. You know how she felt about the Baptists. 'Judgmental hypocrites,' she called them." I took a breath and continued. "On top of that she's wearing a royal blue chiffon dress. She hated royal blue, chiffon, *and* dresses. She would have wanted to walk into the afterlife in comfort. Natural fibers."

Thinking of the things that were important to my mother caused my anger to boil. Clarity filled me. I pushed away from the table. "This is her last chance—her *very last* chance to enjoy the things that were important to her in this life." I stood and leaned on the table. Faces around the table were all surprise.

"Music. That's what she loved. Your dead daughter loved to listen to music." Warm tears seeped from the corners of my eyes. "Not Baptist hymns. Rock and roll, R&B, dance, new wave, punk. *Not* hymns."

I stood up straight. "She will have her music if it means I have

210

to walk to the front of the church, unannounced, with a boom box and a Roberta Flack tape." I pushed my chair under the table. "She will have her music."

I calmly left the kitchen and pushed through the front door. As the cold air hit my face, emotions flooded from me. The tears were now flowing freely. Anger was heating me from the inside. I ran to the center of the front yard.

Anger continued to simmer and rise and tear me apart. I was angry at MeeMee. Angry at Mama. Angry at God. Angry at the world. I would never listen to music with her again. I would never sing with her. Never hear her voice. Never touch her hand. Never see her smile. Never. Never. Never again.

I looked up toward the gray sky and let out a guttural, primal scream. She was gone. For good. When my scream ended, I fell back onto the damp grass and I cried.

I felt an arm around my shoulder and I looked over to see Rachel sitting on the grass beside me. "Way to go."

I sniffed and wiped my eyes. "What?"

"Way to stand up to her." She started to giggle. "You really told her." She laughed harder. "That was priceless."

I giggled a little with her, but I was still mired in my anger. "It felt good."

She sighed. "I bet."

"But it really is about what Mama would want. I'm so angry that this will be our last moment with her. This will be the last time we are actually in the presence of her physical body. I want it to be all about her."

"I know. I get it. But the thing is, funerals aren't really for the deceased. They're for the people who are left behind. Mama's gone. She's not in that body anymore." She leaned into me. "Your thoughts about her and memories are going to be the same, no matter how she's dressed, no matter what music is played."

"Yeah. But it's still important to me."

"I know. And you did great." She rubbed my back.

The following day, we had to spend time at the funeral home for the viewing. I didn't understand this concept. I spent my time circling the perimeter of the viewing room. I saw the big, shiny, silver casket located at the front of the room. Fluffy, satin fabric puckered at the top edge. Flowers were placed all around it. I knew my mother's body was inside. Visitors made their way up to her to take a final look. I had yet to gain the courage to see her. I didn't think I could handle seeing her lifeless body. I knew I would eventually have to say my goodbyes, but I wasn't ready yet.

People I had never seen before in my life came to wish me their condolences. Family, old friends, coworkers, her AA sponsor. They were all there, wrapping me up in their smelly, crepe-paper skin. Moaning about their deep sorrow. I was beginning to feel smothered by them. Age spots and bad breath, hairy ears and mothball suits closed in on me from every direction. I felt my throat closing up. I pulled at the collar of my starched black shirt. I couldn't breathe. The air was heavy with body odor and too much perfume. It stuck in my mouth and nose when I sucked it in.

I hurried to the family room where they kept cold drinks and chairs for the family to take a break. I grabbed a Coke and popped the top. I took a deep swig, but still had trouble swallowing. A back door led from this room to a narrow back alley. I ran through the back door, thinking that fresh air would open up my throat.

I ran right into a cloud of smoke. I coughed and hacked violently. Bending at the waist, I gasped for air.

"You okay?"

I straightened with one final cough. Rachel was leaning against the wall, lit cigarette in hand, smoke rolling from her nose.

"I'm okay." Cough. "Just couldn't breathe." I drank again from the Coke.

"Any sign of Chad?"

I gulped down more cold soda. "No. I don't think so. I haven't seen him."

She inhaled slowly from her cigarette. "I talked with Ken this morning. He said he has seen no sign of Chad since the day he found Mama."

I sat down on a low step outside the door and continued to drink. "What do you think?"

"I'm worried. I think he lost it. Who knows where he is. What he's doing. He's always been a pretty big mess himself." She inhaled again. "He's as bad as Mama ever was." The words came out in a blast of smoke.

"Maybe he just needed some time. To think or something."

"He should be here. It's not fair for him to run away from the responsibility."

I finished the last of my Coke. "Maybe that's not what he's running from. Maybe he's running from the pain."

"Still doesn't seem fair. We're all in pain."

Rather than respond, I starting bending my aluminum can in and out. Focusing all of my attention on the can.

"Have you looked at her?"

Still focused on the can. "No. Not yet. Haven't been able to. You?"

"Yeah." She exhaled smoke through her nose. "It doesn't look like her." She let out a short laugh. "Her hair, make-up, dress. Barely resembles herself."

I sat the can on the ground and stomped it. "Shit. I don't know if I can do it."

"You don't have to. Remember her the way you want."

"I don't want all these people around. These strangers are killing me with their sympathy. They don't know us. They don't know anything about us."

213

"It's just what's expected. It's what people do."

"I just want to be with her on my own. Say goodbye without people hovering."

"You'll get a chance if that's what you want."

I nodded and kicked my can away. "I wish you would stop smoking. Your baby can't be happy about that."

"I'm still trying." She threw the butt down and ground it under a black pump. "Mama smoked with all three of us."

"Yeah. Look how that turned out."

She came over and sat beside me on the stair. She gently laid her head on my shoulder. "I didn't tell you this, I just didn't know if the time was right."

I tilted my head so I could see her face. "What?"

"MeeMee got the autopsy results today."

"And?"

"Cause of death was massive organ failure due to chronic alcoholism."

"What about the blood? The injuries?"

"She had a missing tooth, swollen jaw, broken wrist, broken tibia."

"How did they explain that?"

"Maybe a fall. Maybe a fight. None of it was fatal. She was just physically a mess. Her body couldn't handle any kind of stress, I guess."

"That sucks."

"Not surprising."

"What do you mean?"

"Life in the fast lane. You know? You spend your life treating your body like shit, it eventually repays the favor."

"Said the heavy smoker." I couldn't help but laugh.

She pushed me sideways, causing me to lose my balance and fall off the step. We both laughed uncontrollably. I laughed so hard

I couldn't catch my breath. She snorted and we laughed harder. It felt nice just to enjoy a brief light moment with my sister. Even though we didn't always see eye-to-eye, I knew she was the only one here who could even begin to understand me.

I crawled back on the step and leaned over, laying my head in her lap. The laughter continued, but began to die. She took a deep breath and let out one final laugh. "Whew. That felt good."

I raised my head. "Yeah. It did."

"We should get back inside."

"Ugh. Do we have to?"

"Yes. I think we do. Come on." She stood and pulled me with her.

The evening passed and I still never went to look over the lip of the casket to see my mother. I was terrified of that sight. I watched others as they approached her, leaned over her, shed tears on the white satin, some reaching in to touch her. I watched their reactions. Some of them looked utterly pleased to see my mother looking her best on her funeral day. Others could stand only a brief glance before hastily leaving while dabbing at annoying tears. I didn't know if I'd be able to stand my own reaction.

As I was lying in bed that evening, willing myself to fall asleep, I thought about all of the things about Mama that I would miss. Memories of her crashed through me like an untamed river. My senses were on fire with her. I felt her, smelled her, saw her, heard her, and even tasted her salty skin when I kissed her cheek. Sleep was even further from my grasp.

I flipped on the bedside lamp and pulled my journal from the side pocket of my backpack. I wanted to write down some of the things I was feeling. I began to make a list: "Things I Desperately Miss About You Already."

Your deep voice flowing from you on a current of southern charm.
Laughter rolling hard from your thrown-back head.
Your comforting touch on my small face.
Your generous, loving spirit.
Your repertoire of old and new rock-and-roll sing-a-longs.
Loving blue eyes drinking me in.
Your guidance.
Your free spirit.
Your deep desire to understand the world.
Your desperation to find happiness.
You.

The words had been flying from my pen and I didn't notice that the paper was streaked with the stains of my tears. The page blurred and swam before me. I let the tears rain down. My words began to dissolve into each other. The pressure on my chest was incredible.

Oh God, Mama. What will I do? How will I survive? How would I make it without these things in my life? I understood that I hadn't seen her for so many years, so I should be used to life without her. But then, I always knew she was somewhere. I always knew if I really needed her, she was somewhere in the world. The comfort of knowing that was now gone.

Never. I couldn't wrap my mind around it. Never again. I would never again experience these things. She was gone forever now. So many things I would never have the chance to do again. So many things that I would never have the chance to do at all.

I fell back on my bed, holding the journal tightly to my chest. I cried until my head was full of liquid goo. I breathed heavily through my mouth. Images of her, of us, popped in and out of my head, until I finally drifted into a fitful sleep.

The next day began early back at the funeral home. Same scenario. People coming and going, whispering, hugging, laughing softly. Chad never showed up and we never heard from him. For all we knew, he too could be dead by now. Daddy and Mamateen showed up early, which I found very comforting. They both stayed close to me, Daddy holding my hand. Mamateen asked me frequently if I needed anything.

The time for the funeral drew nearer and my nerves began to vibrate with electricity. My hands shook visibly, and my knees buckled anytime I tried to stand for very long. I let go of my dad's hand and told him that I wanted to go outside for a little bit. He looked concerned, but I assured him I was fine and just needed a little time alone.

I returned to the alley where Rachel and I talked the evening before. The date was December 4, and the day was incredibly bright. The sun was low in the sky, and there was not a cloud to be seen. The air was dry, but briskly cold. There was a strong wind that carried with it a bite. I held my face into the wind and let it wash over me. The cold stung my eyes, but the breeze invigorated me. It was like a sweet caress from God. He was comforting me.

"Please don't tell me you're trying to catch your death." I looked at Mamateen through stinging, watery eyes.

"No. But it's a thought."

She stepped closer and stood behind me, her hand on my head. "Shouldn't even be a thought."

"Mamateen? Will I ever see her again?"

She rubbed my hair. "I say you have to believe you will."

"What do you mean, I have to believe it?"

"I think if people were to truly believe that losing a loved-one meant never seeing that person again, we'd all die of grief."

"I don't understand."

"Every major religion believes in some sort of afterlife. Even

217

back to the ancients, they believed in afterlife." She came around in front of me. "I don't know for sure if there is an afterlife of any kind. But I do know that the reason almost everyone around the world believes in it, is because it's comforting."

"Do you believe in afterlife?"

"Yes. Absolutely. The way I figure it, if there isn't one, I won't know until I'm dead, and by then it's moot." She shrugged. "And in the meantime, I find comfort in believing in Heaven." She paused for a moment. "You should do the same."

"I should?"

"Yes. Believe that your mama is in Heaven, and one day you're gonna see her there."

"When I die?"

"Yes. But not too soon." She took my hand. "Come on." She smiled. "Don't want you catching your death."

Back inside, the funeral director was herding people outside. As he did so, he quietly repeated, "We'd like for everyone to make your way to the church. We want the family to have some time before we close the casket and move her."

I knew this meant that if I were going to see her, it would have to be soon. The nerves kicked in again. I grabbed the back of a chair and held on, supporting myself. I bowed my head, eyes closed. "Dear God, please help me get through this. Give me the strength to say goodbye." Deep breaths. "And please, take her away safely. Keep her with you. Keep her safe until I see her face again." More deep breaths.

A heavy hand pressed into the small of my back. "Do you want me here with you?" Daddy. "I can wait outside. It's up to you."

I looked into his worried face. "I'll be fine." Rachel was standing behind him. MeeMee, Aunt Louise, Uncle Oliver, and their two sons, David and Mark, were at the casket. The rest of the room was empty.

"I'll just be back here if you need me."

I nodded. "Okay."

Rachel reached for my hand. "Ready."

"Yeah."

We slowly walked toward the front of the room, hand in hand. By the time we reached Mama, the others were leaving. I stopped just short of being able to see inside, and reached into the back pocket of my black pants. I pulled out a folded piece of paper and unfolded and flattened it. I studied the words. The stained and smeared words that fell under the heading: Things I Desperately Miss About You Already.

Rachel had stopped beside me. "What's that?"

"Something I want to give her. Things that I don't want her to ever forget."

She nodded and squeezed my hand, then led me to Mama's side. As I approached the side of the silver capsule, I was already looking where her face would be. Suddenly there was the familiar profile. The prominent nose and thin lips. I stepped closer and she came into full few. She looked like a wax dummy of herself. Her skin was solid, unmoving, not her normal color. Her hair was curled toward her face. She always wore it pushed back from her face. The blue chiffon pinched at her neck.

I inhaled sharply. "Mama." I felt Rachel's arm around my waist. "What have they done to you?" I instinctively reached my hand to her face. My touch was light at first. The skin cold and stiff. I was wary, hesitant to touch her. But before I knew what I was doing, I leaned my full weight on her casket and had her face cupped in both of my hands. My paper list now crumpled against her.

"Mama." I tried to lean in far enough to put my face against hers. Rachel pulled me back to keep me from knocking her over. I was drowning in my own tears. I just wanted to be close to her again. I wanted to crawl in and curl up against her.

Rachel pulled again. "We need to go."

"Wait." I straightened my crumpled paper. Wiped my tears, sniffled, took a breath.

"Mama. This is for you." I laid the paper on her chest. "It's what I miss." I lightly touched her face again. "It's what I love." I took my hand away. "Goodbye, Mama."

The two of us walked away, leaning on each other for support. Daddy met us halfway and supported us both. The attendants were closing the casket, readying it to be transported to the church. The top made a muted thud as it shut. I looked back over my shoulder. She was gone.

A wave of finality hit me hard in the chest, almost knocking me off my feet. I clutched at my father's arm. He held me around the waist, keeping me upright.

Thoughts of all of the missed opportunities weighted me down, stealing every ounce of my strength. All of the moments I would never get back. All of the things I should have said. All of the things I should have done. All of the things she needed from me and wanted for me. Those moments were gone forever. That knowledge pulled at my body and tore at my soul.

We rode to the church in a big, black limo. We were followed by everyone else in their own cars, headlights blazing on this sunny day. I stared out the window from the back seat. I watched other motorists respectfully pull off the road as we passed. I envied them all. They were out going about their normal day. Minimally bothered by the inconvenience of pulling over as a funeral procession passed.

The service went by in a blur. The pastor who spoke said absolutely nothing that made me feel better. Roberta Flack's voice over the sound system sent me into a weeping fit of anguish. But, for the most part, I was unmoved by the whole thing.

The service moved outside to the graveside. I sat on a folding chair that sat right at the edge of my mother's final resting place. Daddy's hands were on me throughout the entire thing. He held my hand. He put his arm around me. He held my elbow. He was always close.

More meaningless words were spoken, and then they were ready to lower her into the deep hole. I didn't want to see that part. I couldn't bear to watch my mother being lowered into the earth and covered by tons of dirt. I didn't want to see her pass into the eternal darkness of a six foot hole in the ground. When the service ended I wasted no time standing and leaving the gravesite. Daddy trotted to keep up. "You okay, Noble?"

"Yes. Just really ready to get outta here."

"Okay. Mamateen has the car. She'll take us back to Rachel's. We'll stay there as long as you want before we head home."

"I don't want to stay."

"You might want to just . . ."

I cut him off. "I don't want to stay. I want to get home. I want to get back to school."

"Noble, Mars Hill and all of your teachers are aware of the situation. You don't have to go back right away. You'll get incomplete grades and you can finish up when you go back after Christmas. They said that would be fine."

"No. I have finals. I need to get back."

"They'll let you take them late."

"No. I *need* to get back. For me. I need some sense of normalcy back in my life. I need my routine."

"Okay. If that's what you want, I'll get you back as soon as I can."

"It's definitely what I want."

I was ready to try to move on. I wanted to stop dwelling in this place of extreme grief and guilt. Rachel was upset that I didn't want to stay longer with her. Daddy and Dee didn't seem to mind that I was ready to leave home. I would be back in two weeks for the holiday. They happily drove me back to school the following day.

***

Immediately upon my return, everyone seemed shocked. No one knew how to approach me or what to say to me. As I buried myself back under the things that I loved, I finally felt a sense of peace and calm returning. As I regained this peace and started acting more like myself, people began to regain their comfort around me. Things slowly returned to normal.

I completed all of my classes including my final exams, and didn't have to receive a single incomplete grade. I spent the Christmas break at home with Daddy and Dee. I sulked and brooded and slept quite a bit during those two weeks. I worked hard not to think about Mama, but wasn't very successful.

I missed her more than I thought was possible. Her phone calls and letters had taken on a huge meaning in my life. They essentially were constant reminders that I wasn't alone. They often times had gotten me through difficulties. Now I was going to have to find a new place to get that comfort and reassurance.

I toiled through the remainder of the school year. Everyday it took tremendous amounts of exertion not to dwell on the loss of Mama. It took unimaginable energy not to feel sorry for myself. My drive to succeed became dubious. My grades faltered. I wanted to give up and fall apart. Somehow, I managed to find the strength to plod systematically through.

The times that I just wanted to fall and allow someone else to take on my responsibilities, I reminded myself of my upcoming summer-camp job. It was something I had so enjoyed the previous summer that I was looking toward it with the greatest anticipation.

I thought that some summer enjoyment and excitement might be what I needed to snap me out of my guilt-laden sadness.

I finished the year with only the barest of grips on my scholarship. With two more years of school remaining, I knew it was important for me to get my grades back up. I was clinging to the hope that the fall would bring with it a fresh start. I would put my tumultuous sophomore year behind me and move forward.

Chapter 14
Summer 1988

The aging cabins and thick pine trees of Camp Timberline were a welcoming sight. I parked my green VW in the hard-packed dirt parking lot. The cars of other counselors were already sitting in the dusty lot. I jumped out of the car and pulled a giant duffel bag out of the back seat.

I trotted to the director's cabin with the duffel thrown over my shoulder. I shoved through the screen door leading with the bag. The screen slammed shut behind me. I dropped the bag on the floor.

A stout woman of about thirty looked up from a desk. "Noble! Hi. Welcome back. Great to see you." She jumped up and came around the desk and wrapped me in a tight bear hug.

"Great to see you too, Melissa."

She released me and turned back to the desk. She picked up a binder and flipped through. "Let's see. You're going to be at Umiak with a new counselor named Taylor." She looked up at me. "Her camp name is Peach. She's already down at the site."

"Peach? That's a stupid name." Camp counselors were not allowed to use their real names with the campers, so each of us had a "camp name." Mine was Phoenix.

"She's from Georgia."

"Well, so am I, but . . ."

"So why Phoenix?"

"Long story. I'll tell you some other time." I picked up the bag and hefted it back onto my shoulder. "I'm in Umiak? That's aquatics?"

"Yes. Eleven year olds."

"Cool. I'm headed that way."

"Alright. Dining hall 5 p.m."

"Got it. Later."

I hurried down the path that led to my summer home. The camp was divided into four units. Each was given some ridiculous Native American-type name. Campers were assigned to units based on interests and age. I was going to have eleven year olds who were interested in water sports. Counselors bunked in small cabins, two to a cabin. Apparently I'd be sharing mine with another Georgia peach.

The cabins had wooden floors and support beams. The roof was a canvas tarp more like a tent than a cabin, and the sides were screen. No privacy. As I approached my cabin, I could see the silhouette of someone moving around inside beyond the screen.

I pushed the screen door open and a cherubic face topped by a bouncing blonde ponytail turned in my direction. A brilliantly white smile spread wide between two round, pink cheeks. "Hey there."

"Hi." I gave back a wary smile.

"You must be Noble." She put her hands on her hips and stood straighter. "Or should I say Phoenix?" She giggled.

"Yeah. And you must be Peach."

"That's me." She extended her hand. "Nice to meet ya."

I dropped my shoulder, allowing my duffel to drop to the

ground. I took her hand. "Nice to meet you, too."

She had already put sheets on one of the bunks and was placing neatly folded T-shirts in her footlocker. "I took this bunk, but if you want, I can switch."

"No, this one's fine." I kicked at my bag, sliding it across the floor to the other cot.

"Do you know Bear?"

I was unrolling my sleeping bag on my bunk. "Yeah. She was here last summer."

"Well, she's also here in Umiak. She's already in the other cabin unpacking."

I opened my footlocker and turned my bag upside down on top of it. The contents spilled loosely into the locker. "Great. She's cool."

Peach was standing still, just watching me. She smiled when I caught her looking. "Our lifeguard is coming from New Zealand." Her eyes widened. "Isn't that awesome?"

"Yeah. The internationals are always interesting." I let the lid of my locker slam shut. Stood up straight and dramatically slapped my hands together.

"All done?"

"That's it."

She giggled again and went back to placing her folded clothes in her own locker. "Her name is Kiwi." She was refolding a pair of shorts. "I mean, her name name is Cynthia, but her camp name is Kiwi." She put the shorts in with the other clothing and looked back up at me. Another giggle. "For obvious reasons."

I was now sitting on my cot leaning back against the wall, studying my perfectly perky cabin mate. "Obviously." I put my hands behind my head. "Apparently, when choosing a camp name, careful consideration should be given to the fruits of your homeland."

She looked at me quizzically. Then a light bulb turned on, and her mouth fell open wide. "Oh yeah, you mean because I'm Peach from Georgia, and she's Kiwi from New Zealand." She laughed.

I nodded. "Exactly." I crossed my legs out in front of me. "Of course, if we all did that, you and I would have the same name. Or maybe I could be Peanut."

Again she gave me the confused look with a tilted head. She reminded me of a dog I once had, Delilah. Whenever I would say Delilah's name, she tilted her head like that, and gave me that same look. This time there was no light bulb.

"I'm also from Georgia."

"Really?"

"Yep."

"Then why Phoenix." She let out a short laugh. "I mean I obviously thought you were from Arizona."

"Obviously. But that would be if I weren't creative enough to think of a camp name that has nothing to do with where I come from."

Her smile stayed plastered to her face. I gestured with my hands. "Not that I'm suggesting you and Kiwi aren't creative. I think I'm just *overly* creative." I moved my head from side to side. "I wanted my camp name to have significance."

"And the significance of Phoenix?"

"Rebirth. Rising from the ashes. A new beginning. That's what camp is to me. A phoenix from the flame."

She wore a dumbfounded look and nodded her head slowly. "Okay, then." She went back to her unpacking.

"Bear, well, she just kind of looks like a bear. Thick and hairy." I laughed. "I suppose we all have different reasons for picking our names."

No response. She just continued to unpack. I slid forward to the edge of my cot and put my feet on the floor. "Hey. I'm sorry if

I hurt your feelings."

She looked up at me. Her entire face was now pink. "You think I'm stupid."

"Oh. No. No, I don't really. I was just messing with you."

"Well, it isn't nice."

"I'm sorry. I really am. I was just being a pompous ass. I'm sorry."

She turned her eyes toward the floor and puckered her mouth. "It's okay. Forget it."

"I want us to be friends. I'm sorry I got us off to such a bad start."

She looked back toward me. The smile was back. "Okay. I want us to be friends, too."

Camp staff spent three days together getting camp ready for campers and getting to know each other as a staff. Umiak's staff consisted of me, Peach, Bear and Kiwi. Bear was a short, stocky recreation major from Appalachian State. She had a mane of thick, brown, curly hair. She was the leader of our unit. Kiwi was a rail-thin redhead with papery, white skin covered in tiny freckles. She had one of the most vulgar mouths I'd ever heard. She was working on curbing the language before the campers arrived. All in all I thought Umiak had a great staff. I was looking forward to a fun summer.

It was Sunday morning, and the campers were due to arrive that afternoon. Each unit leader had been given a list of names and relevant information on each of their campers. Before we were released back to our campsites to make last-minute preparations, Melissa, the camp director, asked all of the Umiak staff to stay behind for a brief conference.

In her office, she gave us information concerning a camper we would have in our unit. Her name was Heather Heron and she would be a special case for us. She was one of four siblings whose single mother had struggled financially to raise her large family alone. Eight months earlier, Heather's mother had been killed in a car accident, leaving her and her siblings parentless. She and her two sisters and brother had been separated and put into foster care. She was attending camp on a scholarship. Our instructions were to provide her with anything she needed that she didn't have. We were also to give her any extra care and attention that she might need.

The four Umiak staff members silently plodded through the woods to our site. Hearts were heavy with the burden of the young camper we would be taking into our care in just a few hours. No one quite knew what to say or how to respond.

As we entered our site, Bear asked, "Does anyone know which cabin we have Heather in?"

I spoke. "She's in cabin two. She's one of mine."

The campers lived in five cabins, four to a cabin. Peach and I were each assigned responsibility for two cabins. Bear, because of her overall responsibility to the unit, was not assigned any cabins. Kiwi, because of her additional responsibilities as the unit lifeguard, was only assigned one cabin. Heather was assigned to one of my two cabins. I would have primary responsibility for her.

"Okay. Well, just make sure we take good care of her." Bear shook her thick hair. "Poor thing. Tough life."

"I'll make sure she's okay." I already felt a connection to this girl I hadn't even met. Most of our campers came from affluent families who could afford to send their kids away for the summer. This one would not only have to struggle with her own issues, she would struggle with being an outsider.

Later that same day, the entire staff was set up at tables under huge banners, greeting campers as they arrived. The parking lot was a constant cloud of dust hanging over BMWs, Mercedes, Lexuses, Cadillacs, and other luxury vehicles. Parents milled around with their daughters, exploring camp, meeting staff.

I was standing at a table, sipping water from a plastic bottle, chatting with a parent who lived close to the Mars Hill campus. A roaring engine caught my attention in the parking lot. I looked over the shoulder of the woman I was talking with to see a dirty, noisy, old Ford pulling into the lot. The woman noticed I was no longer paying attention to her, so she excused herself and moved on.

I remained focused on the car. It sputtered after the ignition had been turned off. A large, middle-aged woman dressed in an enormous Atlanta Braves T-shirt and a pair of blue sweat pants emerged from the driver's side. She started for the tables without looking back at the car. It was several moments before the passenger door slowly opened.

A small girl with neatly combed, mousy brown hair hesitantly stepped from the car. She wore a solid pink T-shirt tucked carefully into pleated khaki shorts. She carried a small blue suitcase. She closed the car door and hurried to catch up with the woman.

Before these two reached the table, I knew who they were. I stepped away from my table to greet them. "Hi. Welcome to Camp Timberline. My name is Phoenix."

"Hey. This is Heather Heron. I'm her guardian, Pat Campbell." She put her hand on Heather's head. "She's here for camp."

"That's great." I knelt down to look Heather in the eyes. "It's great to have you, Heather."

Her face lit up with a beautiful smile. Her dark brown eyes were perfect accents to her olive skin. "Phoenix?" She giggled shyly. "That's a silly name."

I nodded in agreement. "Yes. It certainly is. We all have silly names."

"Hmmm. Why?"

"That's a darn good question. Maybe before you leave I'll

231

have an answer for you."

Ms. Campbell looked at her watch impatiently. "Do I need to do anything? Sign something?"

I stood. "Ah, no. Not really. I do have some paperwork to give you." I stepped back over to the table. "These are just basic rules and instructions." I handed her a stapled pack of papers. "Just covers phone calls, sending packages and other mail, pick-up instructions, that sort of thing."

She took the papers from my hand. "Alrighty then. I'm gonna get going."

She stooped down and gave Heather a kiss on the head. "You be good, now. Have fun and call if ya need something."

"Yes, Ma'am." Heather looked at her sweetly. "Thank you."

"You're welcome, dear. Bye now." She turned and strolled back to the car. Heather watched her the entire way. Watched her until the loud car was pulling away from the parking lot.

She turned back toward be. She smiled with her lips together, and her eyes squinted. "What now, Phoenix?"

I was amazed at her composure. "Well, you're actually in my unit. I'm going to be your counselor. So why don't I show you to your cabin?"

She stood up on her toes. "Oh, fun." The smile grew. "I've never stayed in a cabin. Cool."

I felt my own smile swallow my entire face. "Well, you are certainly in for a thrill. Follow me." I reached for her suitcase. "Let me get that."

"No, thank you. I've got it." She gave me the squinty-eyed smile again.

"Okay. Well, come on." I turned and headed down a nearby pathway. She was right on my heels. She began chattering immediately as we walked.

"So what are we going to do? Do I share my cabin? Who am I

232

sharing with? Will we swim? Will I get to build a fire? Where are you from? How many times have you been to camp? Do you ever get homesick?" And on and on. I struggled to keep up with her questions.

As she posed these questions, she skipped along at my side. We passed through a dip in the path that crossed a creek bed. She put the toe tip of her shoe down in a wet, muddy spot. She stopped immediately. "Uh oh."

I followed her eyes to her shoe. The white, fake leather sneaker had a smudge of mud across the toe. She licked her fingers and knelt down to rub at the mud stain. "Look what I did." Her face sagged into a frown. "Oh no."

I knelt down beside her. "It's fine. Just a little mud."

She looked at me, her eyebrows drawn tightly together over her large eyes. "These are my only shoes."

The worry hardened her soft features. I recognized her protectiveness. I remembered it in myself. I remembered in fifth grade when I dropped my new binder in a puddle after a rainstorm. I remembered crying because I didn't think I'd ever get another new binder. I remember the inexplicable desire to protect all of my meager belongings with my life.

I reached up and pushed a sweat dampened strand of hair out of her face. "Don't worry about it. I'll get it clean." I grabbed her hand and stood her up. "And if I don't, I'll get you some more shoes."

She tilted her head. "Really?"

"Absolutely. Now, just don't worry." We started off down the path again.

Once at the campsite, I showed Heather to her cabin and introduced her to two of her three cabin mates who'd already arrived. Both of them still had parents visiting with them. Heather said "Hi" politely and put her things on a bunk.

"Heather, come with me before you unpack and we'll take care of that shoe."

Her face lit up. "Okay." She ran for the cabin door. Before exiting, she turned back toward everyone. "Nice meeting y'all." She indicated the two girls. "I'll see y'all later. Bye." She hopped through the door letting it slam behind her.

She followed me to my cabin, where I took a cloth from my footlocker and led her to the bathrooms. The bathrooms were located in a concrete and cinderblock building. There were four toilet stalls, four shower stalls, and four sinks. Brown wooden benches lined the walls. I nodded toward a bench. "Have a seat there and let's see what we can do."

"Mmmkay." She plopped down on the bench and held both feet out.

I wet the cloth at the sink and squatted down at her feet. I gently dabbed at the mud on her shoe. I didn't want to scrub too hard. I didn't want to cause any more damage to shoes that she so obviously prized. I was able to turn the globs of caked mud into a small rust colored stain.

"I think that's as good as it gets."

She bit the inside of her cheek and nodded with her eyes closed. "That's much better." Her eyes opened. "That's fine. Thank you." She put her feet on the floor and hung her head. I knew she was still disappointed.

"Tell ya what, Heather. You're going to get a lot dirtier during camp. Camp is a dirty place. Let's leave it like this for now and, before you leave camp, we'll replace them with some nice, new, shiny, white shoes. How does that sound?"

She kept her head down. Eyes on the shoe. "They're fine. It'll be okay." She stood. "What do we do now?"

I could see a glimmer of her past excitement returning. "I've got to go back and make sure everyone has checked in. You can

234

head back to your cabin and get unpacked." I looked at my watch. "We're having our first meeting in a little more than an hour."

She jammed her hands into her pockets. "Sounds good." We both left the bathroom and went our separate ways.

A couple of hours later, everyone was checked in, all the parents were gone, and we had completed our first unit meeting. Introductions had been made. Rules and procedures had been covered. Questions had been answered.

Now our twenty campers and four counselors were marching in a line down a wooded path, making our way to the dining hall for dinner. I watched Heather throughout all of it. She was a pleasant and friendly girl. She appeared to have already made friends with her cabin mates. They laughed and talked and played together. It pleased me to see that she was going to fit in perfectly, and that she was enjoying herself.

I sat at the dinner table with my eight campers. Heather shared a cabin with Elise, Rebecca, and Claire. The four girls who shared cabin one were Joanne, Camille, Dana, and Brie. Throughout dinner they all chatted endlessly about themselves, their schools, and their families.

The girls had to couple themselves with a "buddy," who they'd be paired with for the entire summer. Heather was obviously leaning toward having Rebecca as her buddy. Rebecca was quiet and shy. Heather went out of her way to include her in the conversation and to compliment her continuously. The more I saw of this little person who had endured so much hardship, the more she amazed me.

Rebecca sat at the end of the table keeping her head bowed most of the time. Her eyes were lost behind fashionably thick-rimmed glasses. The lenses were also thick, causing her eyelashes to enlarge into flicking spider legs. She wore a khaki-colored ball cap. It was pulled low enough to obscure her eyes further. Heather sat beside her and touched her sweetly on the arm or shoulder every time she spoke to her.

Rebecca seemed a bit confused by the attention Heather was giving her. Each time Heather laid her hand on her, she looked at her with questioning bug-eyes. But she didn't seem bothered. As the meal progressed, she opened up and became more expressive.

Brie sat opposite Rebecca and was anything but a mirror image. Her platinum hair was still perfectly coifed, and her face was still showing signs of this morning's church makeup. I couldn't help but think that one day at camp would change her look drastically. She blathered on and on about her daddy's new sports car and how he was getting her one the very minute she turned sixteen.

She took a break from the sports-car talk to address Rebecca. "You know it's rude to wear a hat at the dinner table."

"Well, yeah I know. But this is camp."

Brie rolled her eyes in annoyance. "Still rude."

"I just don't want to take it off."

"Why not? Are you hiding something under there?" She leaned against Camille and they giggled together.

Heather answered for her. "Who cares? She wants to keep it on. What difference does it make?"

Brie sat back up. "Take a chill pill. I was just asking."

Rebecca quietly spoke. "I'm afraid of getting ticks in my hair. They live in the woods and I don't especially care for them."

Brie turned up her nose in disgust. "What? Ticks?" She turned toward me. "Should we be worried about the ticks?"

I shrugged and casually sipped from my Kool-Aid. "Well, sure, they're here. But no need to worry. We'll check you every night before we send you to bed."

She squinched her face tighter. "Ewwwww. Gross."

That night Bear, Peach, Kiwi, and I put the campers to bed and then met under our unit shelter. We were filling each other in on how the first day had gone, and were going over plans for tomorrow. Just as Kiwi began to brief us on her plans for swimming supervision, there came a high-pitched, terrified scream from one of the cabins.

I immediately knew it came from one of my cabins, cabin two. Instinctively I jumped off the picnic table I'd been sitting on and ran toward the cabin. The others were close behind me. Flashlights flickered on all over the campsite. Muted conversations were starting to grow out of the darkness.

I could see the light of several flashlights coming from within the cabin. I also saw four small silhouettes moving around in the limited light. I pushed hard through the screened door, breathing heavily. "What's going on in here?"

Rebecca was sitting up in her bed. Her glasses were gone, but the hat was still pushed low over her eyes. Heather sat beside her with her arm around her. Claire and Elise were each sitting straight up in their own beds. Flashlight beams streaked all over the cabin.

I had regained my normal breathing. "Is somebody gonna tell me what happened?"

Elise spoke. "We were sleeping. And Rebecca just started screaming."

"Rebecca?" I stepped closer to her. "What's wrong?"

Claire's flashlight beam struck her in the face and I could see the streaks of tears on her cheeks. "Someone was outside our cabin."

"No. There's no way." I sat on the edge of the bed. "We were all right outside. We would have seen if someone was over here." I pushed her hat back off her face. "I think you were just imagining things."

I could see her little body shaking. "I don't know."

I looked outside the cabin. The other counselors were making their way from cabin to cabin, calming the other campers. "I know there was no one there, Rebecca. I promise."

She slowly nodded her head. Heather pushed up onto her knees. "I have an idea."

We all looked at her. "We can scoot our two cots together. That way if she gets scared again, she can just wake me and I'll check it out." She beamed at Rebecca.

I looked from Heather to Rebecca. "How does that sound, Rebecca?"

She was nodding her head vigorously. "Yes. I like that idea."

"Okay. Well hang on." I pushed Rebecca's cot with the two girls still sitting on it. They laughed.

"Now, why are you still wearing that hat?"

"Ticks."

"The ticks can't get in here."

She cut her eyes to the side and chewed at her upper lip. "But, if it makes you feel better, whatever."

The four girls all crawled back into their own sleeping bags. Rebecca scooted as close to Heather as she could get. I looked around at all their faces, weary but a little concerned.

"So, are we all set now?"

Four little heads nodded in unison. "Okay then. Let me know if you need anything." I turned and left the cabin.

As I turned the corner, I heard quiet whispering coming from beyond the screens. I recognized the cadence as Heather's. I quietly halted, wanting to eavesdrop on the girls. The voice was so quiet, I had to lean toward the cabin and listen intently.

"Just fall asleep and get through the night. It'll be better tomorrow. Nightmares always disappear in the light." I smiled to myself at the young girl's wisdom.

A light flicked on in the cabin, and now I heard Rebecca's voice. "Then why don't we just leave this on?"

"Because we're supposed to keep our flashlights off. Besides, you'll use up your batteries." I heard movement. "You'll be fine. Just turn it off."

"Okay. Hope you're right." The light flicked off.

"I am. Good night, Rebecca."

"Night."

I remained outside the cabin for a few more moments. All was quiet. I slowly walked across the moonlit campsite, back to my own cabin.

The next day the girls had settled back in and the drama of the previous night was practically forgotten. Our first swim time was set for ten-thirty that morning. We had breakfast, did some camp chores, played a few games, and then got ready for swim time.

When we reached the designated swimming area in the lake, Kiwi posted herself on the lifeguard stand, the girls stripped down to their swim suits, and they all started plopping into the water one right after the other. Nineteen heads bobbed in the water. Nineteen children splashed, dove, and laughed. One child remained on the dock. Her arms were crossed over her chest and her knees were pressed together. She was staring at her own feet. A khaki ball cap was pulled low on her head.

I approached her. "Rebecca, why aren't you in the water."

"I don't really want to swim."

"Why not?"

"I'm not a great swimmer. I don't really like the water."

"What? Really?" I shook my head in disbelief. "You do realize you're in an *aquatics* unit." I paused. "That means we do a lot in the water. We swim. We sail. We canoe." I put my hands on my hips. "You get the picture?"

"Yeah. I know. But . . ."

"But what?"

"I'm sorta afraid of the water."

"Then why didn't you sign up for an equestrian unit? Or ecology? Or sports?"

"I'm afraid of horses. I'm really kind of afraid of all animals, so I didn't want ecology. Sports are dangerous. I'm scared I would get hurt."

"Wow. Are you pulling my leg?"

"What?"

I sat down on a wooden bench. "Are you seriously afraid of everything?"

She tilted her head and shrugged.

"Beck, you gotta get over that."

She looked up at me in surprise. "You called me Beck."

"Yeah, well, Rebecca's a bit cumbersome."

"I like it." She smiled.

"Good. Beck." I motioned for her to come over. "Come sit down with me." She timidly walked over and sat. "I'll call you Beck. But, I gotta tell ya . . ." I tilted her hat back away from her eyes. "Beck is a tough name. It's not the name of a scaredy cat."

She pulled her hat back down and kept her head bowed.

"If you wanna be called Beck, you're gonna have to toughen up."

Without lifting her head, she quietly said, "I'll try."

"Okay. Now get in the water." I stood. "Or I'll throw you in."

She looked up, eyes wide and unsure. "Okay."

I watched her make her way to the wooden ladder. She turned and slowly climbed backwards into the water. She held tightly to the dock and stayed very near the ladder. Her hat stayed pulled down tightly on her head. She stayed this way until Kiwi blew the whistle signaling the end of swim time. Rebecca made her way quickly to the ladder and was the first one out of the water.

This pattern continued for Rebecca through all camp activities. On our first day of sailing, I had to force her to get on the small

240

Sunfish, and she refused to take it out of waist-high water. She eventually avoided me at all cost. Apparently, the pressure I put on her to be involved was just one more thing that scared her.

She did, however, take a special liking to Kiwi and clung tightly to her for every activity. I think she believed that Kiwi would protect her from my forcefulness. Kiwi babied and coddled her. It was fine with me. I had done everything I knew to get this child to loosen up.

Heather, on the other hand, dove headfirst into everything. She immersed herself completely in all camp activities. She lit up with excitement and anticipation every time she was introduced to something new. She applied herself with total gusto. She became very adept at a variety of skills.

Everyday she was improving as a sailor. Her first day she tipped her small boat over several times and we spent more time flipping it back upright than she did actually sailing. After a couple of weeks, she would have her Sunfish flying across the smooth surface of the lake. She tacked back and forth with complete confidence and grace.

We were preparing for a late summer whitewater canoe trip. The campers were learning all paddle strokes so that they could maneuver through rapids. While most of the girls struggled to correctly perform a simple bow stroke, Heather excelled in the maneuvering of her boat. Nine of the ten boats would spin in circles. The girls in them would frequently remove their paddles from the water to change sides. Heather's boat was always under control. Rebecca would sit in the bow and never pick up her paddle, just hang on tightly to the gunwales. Her lifejacket rode up to her ears where it met the lower edge of her hat. Heather would both power and steer the boat from the stern, just by using J-strokes.

It amazed me that, before her arrival, we were worried that she

241

would have difficulty. What she was having was the time of her life. She had become an aquatics camp prodigy. All of the other girls looked up to her and sought her friendship and approval. She had a kind heart and proved to be a motivator to the others. Rebecca was the one exception. Rebecca was simply the nut that none of us could crack.

The fourth and final week of camp finally arrived. It was the week that we would be going on our overnight trip to canoe down the Nantahala River. The trip was our culminating event. We packed up our tents, sleeping bags, camp gear, canoes, and canoe gear. Everything was packed into two huge Econoline vans that pulled trailers loaded with canoes. Bear drove one van and I drove the other.

The girls were paired with their buddy. Each pair would share a two-man tent as well as a canoe. Bear and Kiwi would share a tent and a canoe. Peach and I would share. We pulled into the campsite just a little over an hour after leaving Camp Timberline. We all pitched in to unload the gear, and then each pair started setting up their own tents.

Our lunch was sandwiches, chips, and bananas that the dining hall staff packed for us prior to our departure. We would have to cook our own dinner over a campfire. By late afternoon, all of the tents were up and Bear built a blazing campfire. We sat and relaxed around the fire for a short time. The girls were all brimming with excitement. They sang, chatted, giggled, and chased each other around the campsite.

Heather focused most of her attention on the campfire. She poked and prodded at it, keeping it stoked. She wandered into the nearby woods, bringing sticks of dead wood to the fire circle and stacking them for later use. Rebecca sat on a log, staring into the orange flames flickering from the burning wood.

I strolled to the fire circle and seated myself next to Rebecca.

"What's up, Beck?"

She turned her bug eyes toward me. "You don't have to call me that."

"Why not?"

"I know you don't mean it." She shook her head. "I'm not a Beck."

"I don't think you should give up on it just yet."

"Well I do. Actually, I don't even think I can do this canoe thing tomorrow."

"What? That's ridiculous. You have to do it."

She faced the dirt ground and shook her head. "There's no way. I'm terrified of the calm water on the lake. The rapids are so much worse. I can't do it."

I placed my hand on her back. "Beck, you have to do it. We're all going to be on the river. What do you think we would do with you while we're gone?"

"I don't care. I'll just wait in the van."

"You can't. It's all day." I rubbed her back. "Tell you what. How 'bout if I let you go with me. In my canoe?"

"No offense, but no."

"What? Why?"

"Well. I'm a little scared of you, too."

"Hmmm. Well then, what about Kiwi?"

She looked up at me. I could see streaks on her cheeks left behind by tears. "Maybe."

"Well, you have to go. We can't leave you."

"Okay then, with Kiwi would be best."

I nodded and slapped her on the knee. "I'll take care of it." I left her sitting there.

Heather was still poking at the fire with a long stick. I walked over and stood beside her. "Hey. How's it going?"

She turned her soot-smudged face toward me. "Pretty good.

243

Fire's a good one. Ready for cookin'."

"Yep. Looks like it." I kicked at a loose log with my hiking boot. "Be careful over here. Don't want you getting burned."

"Sure."

"Hey. I have a question for ya."

"Okay."

"How would you like to go down the river tomorrow with Bear instead of Rebecca?"

She turned toward me quickly. "Why?"

"Rebecca wants to go with Kiwi."

"I don't really want to go with Bear. She's not much fun."

"Well . . ."

She poked me in the shoulder. "I'd rather go with you." She gave me that squinty-eyed smile.

"Oh." I laughed. "That's okay. That'll work. Peach can just go with Bear." I picked up a stick and threw it into the fire. "I'll just make sure everyone knows the new arrangements." I left her tending the fire.

As we prepared our campfire dinner, I told the other counselors about the new plan. Everyone was okay with it. Our dinner was ground beef and cut vegetables wrapped in foil. We tossed the foil packets on the hot coals of the fire to let them cook. A camp delicacy we like to call "silver turtles."

We ate our dinner and then tidied our site. The group sat in the dark around the campfire while the counselors took turns telling ghost stories. I could see in the girls' faces that they were slowly becoming more and more terrified. I feared that they would all be piled in my tent before the night was over.

We finally sent the girls to bed so they could get enough rest for the following day's trip. It took them some time to settle down. Lights were flicking on and off, ghostly noises and giggles were coming from within the tents, and soft whispers floated in the heavy air. We made our rounds from tent to tent, encouraging them to knock it off and go to sleep. Eventually the campsite was quiet, except for the rhythmic croaking of frogs and chirping of crickets. Everyone was snuggled in their sleeping bags, sleeping off pure exhaustion.

We were up very early the following morning. While Kiwi, Peach and the girls made breakfast, Bear and I shuttled the canoes to the drop-in point and left one of the vans at the pickup point. After breakfast we packed our gear into the remaining van and we joined our canoes at the river.

Before allowing the girls to board their canoes, we reviewed safety precautions and procedures with them. They donned life jackets and began piling into canoes with squeals of excitement. Heather and I were the first in the water. She took a position in the bow and I got into the stern. Bear and Peach were the last two in the water. The plan was for me to keep my boat in the front of the pack, and they would bring up the rear watching for stragglers.

The section of the river we'd be doing was for beginners. It contained four sets of rapids, none over class three. The majority of the river was simply smooth water with a hint of a slight current. We began on a wide section of the river and we floated along at a leisurely pace. The banks were lined with huge trees and thick underbrush. We heard birds singing and calling from all directions as well as small animals scurrying through the forest.

For the first few minutes, Heather and I paddled along quietly. The soft splash of water that came with each stroke was a comforting sound. I stopped paddling and let the current carry us. I simply used my paddle as a rudder to steer. Heather kept digging deep into the water and pulling hard.

"You don't have to paddle so hard. You'll wear yourself out. You can relax a while."

She turned sideways on her seat and looked back at me. "This is beautiful."

"Yeah. It really is."

"When will we get to the first rapids?"

"Not for about twenty minutes. It's a slow start, but it'll pick up once we reach that first set."

"I like it slow. It's very relaxing." She nodded her head forward onto her chest. "I could just doze off."

I laughed at her. "Well, don't do that. I want you to be alert when we get to the whitewater."

She sat up straight, eyes lit up. "Yay! Can't wait."

I heard distant laughter and yelling. I turned in my seat and caught sight of other members of our little caravan. The closest boat to us was a good seventy-five yards away. The others were all traveling in a fairly tight pack. "We definitely need to stop paddling. Try to let these others catch up."

"Okay." She was now facing forward again.

We were silent for a while and I was afraid boredom would set in for Heather. "So, Heather, tell me about yourself."

She turned again to face me. "Like what?"

"Tell me what you wanna be when you grow up."

She laughed. "Gosh. I don't even know."

"Well, what do you like. You know? What subjects in school do you like?"

"Oh, umm, I like social studies and math. English is fun. I love, love, *love* science." She laughed again.

"Well that's no help. Sounds like you like *every* subject."

"Yeah. I do." She smiled. "I guess when I grow up, I just want to be happy. I just want to be me. Whatever I do."

"Wow. That's great. That's a good goal."

"How 'bout you?"

"What do you mean?"

"Are you always gonna be a camp counselor?"

"No. Probably not. I want to be a writer."

"Oh, cool!" She turned further in her seat. "Like books and stories?"

"Probably for a newspaper or something."

She scrunched her face up. "Eww. That sounds boring."

I studied her for a moment and thought about what she'd said. I wanted to convince her that it was an exciting career choice, but couldn't think of a single convincing fact. Instead, I nodded at her and said, "Yeah. It does sound boring."

"Then why would you want to do it?"

I studied the water downstream. "We should get ready. Rapids are just around this bend."

She quickly turned around and got her paddle ready. I looked behind us to see that the others were still fairly distant. "Heather, once we get through these, let's pull over to the bank and wait for the others."

"Sure." She turned her head and looked at me with huge, dark eyes. "You ready?"

"Yep. You?"

She wiggled her legs rapidly. "Yes. Yes. Yes!"

We rounded a slight bend in the river and enormous rocks could be seen jutting out of the water. Several triangles of frothy water appeared between the rocks. "Remember Heather, we're aiming for a downstream V. Keep paddling and lean toward the rocks."

"Got it." She started paddling hard. I used my paddle to steer us into the most powerful water. We got sucked into the current and appeared to be just about to hit a large rock on our left. Heather pulled her paddle out of the water and I could tell she was about to panic. "Lean toward the rock! Don't worry."

Just as our bow was about to crash into the rock, I pulled hard on my paddle turning the bow sharply to the right. We shot down a

247

narrow tongue of water between the two large rocks and Heather got hit with a soaking splash. She screamed and then started laughing hard.

We reached calmer water and I was steering us toward the bank. Heather was still laughing. "Oh my gosh! That was so much fun."

"I know." I laughed with her. "It only gets better from here."

We tied to a tree and got out of the boat. We walked right along the edge of the water back upstream. We got just above the rocks and looked for the others in our party. They were already very close. I heard all three of the counselors yelling instructions at the girls. All the little faces looked petrified. Paddles were all hanging loosely in the water and mouths were hanging open.

"Watch what Kiwi does." Bear was still trying to get everyone ready. The boat containing Kiwi and Rebecca was first. Apparently the plan was for the others to follow the route taken by them. Rebecca sat in the bow of the boat. Her paddle was lying on the bottom of the boat and her hands were clenched in a death grip on the boat's sides. As she got closer, I saw that her eyes were closed. Even without help from Rebecca, Kiwi maneuvered expertly through the rocks. Rebecca screamed repeatedly until their boat was in calm waters.

Camille and Brie were coming up on the fast water. Their boat was perpendicular to the bank. They were floating along sideways and neither girl was paddling. Brie was in the stern. I cupped my hands around my mouth and shouted to her. "Brie, use your paddle. You need to straighten out." She looked at me then hesitantly stuck the tip of her paddle in the water. "Camille, paddle! Hard!"

Camille jumped into action. She started paddling hard, but the boat wasn't turning. "Brie, turn the boat! J stroke, J stroke, now."

Brie was like a deer in headlights. Her eyes were wide. Her paddle barely skimmed the surface of the water. She was making

248

no impact on the direction they were travelling. Now they were caught in the swift current, heading sideways toward the rocks.

"Oh, no." I heard the small voice behind me. I turned and saw Heather covering her mouth. "Heather, run back to the canoe and tell Kiwi to get ready to pull two out of the water." She took off. All I could do now was watch.

The side of the green canoe crashed hard into the rocks. It became wedged. The two girls screamed. I waded away from the bank and yelled to them. "Lean downstream!"

They couldn't hear me and they both leaned upstream. The rushing water was filling the canoe. It finally pushed free and continued to crash through the rocks. It was now full of water and turned completely over. The two girls were in the churning river.

I ran out until the water was waist high and then I jumped in and began swimming toward them. Full of water, the canoe weighed a ton. Camille's head bobbed upstream of the canoe. Brie, on the other hand, was downstream of the heavy boat. This put her in danger of getting crushed between it and the rocks.

I swam toward her as quickly as I could. My own life jacket was hindering me. Brie's body was being tossed down the river backward. She was facing upstream, watching the swamped canoe tumbling toward her. I got my head up high enough to yell to her. "Brie, turn around. Try to get away from the boat."

The noise of the turbulent water drowned out my calls. She continued her backward journey through the rapids and the canoe closed in on her. I rushed to get closer. Half-swimming, half-climbing over the rocks.

Her back bumped a rock and her feet came out of the water slightly. She stopped, no longer moving downstream. She was momentarily hung on the rock, her face showed relief and she appeared to be attempting to stand.

I staggered and lunged over the rocks. My legs were cut and

249

bleeding, but I didn't slow down. I tried yelling again. "Brie, don't stand! Turn around! Keep moving!" She couldn't hear.

She was raising herself out of the water when the canoe crashed into her. She raised a small leg in an attempt to push the canoe away. It was far too heavy and over-powered her quickly. It pushed her back into the water. She landed against the rock and the canoe was pushed against her by the forceful current. It crushed her chest and she began to scream.

I was close. I slipped and got caught in the current and had to work my way back upstream. Brie was holding her upper body out of the water by bracing her arms behind her. She was growing weary and her head was getting closer to going under.

The canoe was pounding against her as it shifted in the current. Her cries were getting smaller and smaller. I finally reached the boat. I grabbed the end of it and pulled myself closer. I was close enough now that she could see and hear me. "Hold on, Brie. Just hang in there." She couldn't respond. I could tell that she was having difficulty catching her breath. The pressure against her narrow chest was keeping her from being able to fill her lungs.

I positioned myself upstream of the boat, sat in the rushing water and wedged myself between a rock and the canoe. I placed my feet against the bow of the boat and pushed with my legs. Water was slamming into my back and I struggled to hold my position. I pushed with all my strength in an attempt to loosen the boat so that it would continue on downstream past Brie.

Brie could no longer hold herself up and her head went under. I pushed harder. With Brie's movement, the boat shifted slightly. I pushed in unison with its momentum. It was just enough to loosen the canoe. The bow turned downstream slowly and was finally caught in the rush. The current grabbed it and pulled it down the river beyond where Brie was trapped.

As soon as the boat moved, I lunged toward Brie and grabbed

the front of her life jacket. I yanked her head out of the water. She didn't seem to be breathing and I began to move toward the bank without loosening my grip on her.

I saw a pair of pale hands take her from behind. I heard a New Zealand accented voice. "I got her." At the same time I felt hands under my own arms. I turned to see Bear behind me. "You okay?"

I felt the adrenaline rush quickly out of my system and my body suddenly felt limp. Bear's hands held me firmly, and slowly guided me through the water toward land. Within several moments we were safely on the bank of the river. I sat down and put my head between my knees. I wanted to cry, but I didn't have the breath to do it.

I could still feel Bear's hands on me, gently rubbing the back of my life jacket. "You're okay. Just breathe."

I caught my breath and looked up. I saw Kiwi cradling Brie in her arms. Brie was crying hysterically. I started laughing. "She's okay?"

Bear answered. "Yes. She's fine. Just shaken up."

I worked on getting my breathing back to normal. I looked further down river. All of the canoes were pulled out of the water on a flat rock outcropping. The rest of the campers were seated on the rock and Peach was milling around them, talking to them, consoling them. At some point the rest of the boats had made it successfully through the rapids. I hadn't even noticed.

I looked into Bear's face. "Everyone's safe?"

"Yes. Brie was the only close call. We managed to talk everyone else through. No problems."

"Camille?"

"She's fine. She shot through the rapids like a pro, only no boat." She laughed. "I think she actually enjoyed it."

"Good. That's great."

Her face turned serious. "You did great. I'd go so far as to say you saved her life."

I put my head back down between my knees.

"No one else could have gotten to her in time. Thank goodness you acted so quickly."

I raised my head. "Instinct kicked in. Didn't even think."

"That's good. You think you're ready to move?" She jerked her head toward the rest of the group. "We're going to use this as a little rest stop. I'm going to talk to them again about safety and technique. Reminders. We still have a lot of river to cover."

"Good idea. I'm fine." I pushed up in an attempt to stand. My knees felt weak. It took a moment, but I finally got my feet under me.

She slapped me on the back. "Take your time. I'm gonna go ahead and check in with the others. When you get down there we'll get you a granola bar and some Gatorade. Get your energy back."

I gave her a solid smile. "Okay. Thanks. Be there in a sec."

She nodded and walked along the rugged bank to the rock where the group was gathered. Sitting close to where I was, Kiwi still held Brie's head in her lap. I went to them and plopped down beside them. Brie had stopped crying and was now filling Kiwi in on the details of her near-death experience. Her hands were moving animatedly, and her voice rose with excitement.

I gave her foot a shake. "Hey. How are ya?"

She sat up and looked at me with enormous, red-rimmed eyes. "I'm okay. How are you."

I smiled at her. "Never better. Glad you're okay."

"Yes. Oh my God! That was so intense!"

"It was pretty intense."

"I just knew I was dead."

"Nah. You did great."

She sat up straighter. "Did everybody see that?"

"I think they did."

"Holy crap! Wait till they hear how that felt." She looked down river where the other girls were all listening to Bear intently. "Shouldn't we get down there with them?"

Kiwi spoke up. "Well, I'm sure now that you're gonna be fine. Ready to get back at it, it seems."

I laughed with Kiwi. "Definitely. Now all she cares about is telling everybody about it. I guess that's a good thing."

"Yep. I'm fine. Let's get going." She stood.

The three of us made our way to the group. We were greeted with loud applause and whoops and hollers. Brie bowed dramatically. Kiwi and I looked at each other and shook our heads. She seemed to be fully recovered.

Bear had completed her lecture and everyone was taking a snack and bathroom break. While walking together, Kiwi and I had decided that we would complete the trip with Camille and Brie and put Heather and Rebecca back in a boat together. We thought the two girls who had had the accident would be shaken up enough to make it dangerous for them to continue the trip together. I told Kiwi that I would let Heather and Rebecca know about the change in plans.

Rebecca was sitting alone at the edge of the woods. I sat down next to her. "How are you?"

"I'm good. What about you? That was pretty cool how you saved Brie."

"I'm fine. Have you seen Heather?"

She used her head to indicate a path. "She's back there peeing."

"Oh, okay. Well, I need to talk to the two of you."

She looked worried and pulled her hat down lower so I couldn't see her distress. "About what?"

"Well, since Camille and Brie are a little nervous now, Kiwi and I are going to switch them out for you and Heather."

She kept her head down. "What do you mean?"

Heather emerged from the woods. Her face broke into a huge smile. "Way to go!" She held her hand up to me for a high-five.

I slapped my hand against hers. "Thanks."

"You're my hero," she said. I laughed. "I'm for real. That was awesome." She continued to smile.

"Well, thanks for your help." I slid over and made room for her. "Have a seat. I was just telling Rebecca something that concerns you, too."

"Okay." She sat. "What's up, chicken butt?" She giggled.

I giggled at her silliness. "Just telling Rebecca that we're going to put you and her back in a boat together. Camille will be with me and Brie's going with Kiwi."

"Cool beans." She looked at Rebecca. "Me and you, buddy." She raised her hand again for a high-five, but Rebecca didn't oblige. She slowly withdrew her hand. Rebecca continued to stare at the ground.

"Beck, you'll be fine. Heather's practically a pro."

"I can't do that."

"What? What do you mean, you 'can't'?"

"I can't go with Heather. I have to go with one of you adults."

"Rebecca, I don't think you understand." My voice steadily rose. "I'm not giving you a choice. You're gonna be with Heather."

She finally made eye contact with me. "Why can't Brie and Camille just go with Bear and Peach."

I stood and raised my voice all in one movement. "Why can't you just get a backbone?" The adrenaline which drove my actions earlier pumped back into me. I couldn't believe how selfish this child was being. "Why can't you take that stupid hat off?" I grabbed her hat by the brim and yanked it from her head.

Her mouth dropped open and her eyes glistened. "Why can't you stop being scared of everything, for crying out loud?" I threw the hat into the underbrush. She looked at me with fear in her eyes.

I couldn't stop myself. I was on a roll. "Camille and Brie had a terrifying accident today, and they're not as scared as you are." I turned toward the group and they were all watching me in complete silence.

"That hat won't protect you! Hiding from your life will not protect you!" I took a deep breath. "If you ever want to have pleasure in your life, joy, excitement, fun, for God's sake, you *have* to take an occasional risk!"

I looked at each and every face. I saw shock, fear, concern, and even support. I calmed myself and I took a step closer to Rebecca. I lowered my voice. "Now, *Beck*, you're going to get in that canoe with Heather, *Beck*. You're going to go down the river, *Beck*, and you are going to *BE* Beck." I bent and came closer to her face. "Do you understand?"

Tears rolled down her cheeks. She nodded her head vigorously.

"Why are you crying?"

She sniffed. "You're scaring me."

"There's a shock. Is there anything you're not scared of?"

She looked at Heather, who still wore a blank stare on her face. "I'm not afraid of Heather."

"Well, I guess that's something," I said quietly. I was turning to walk away when Heather lunged toward Rebecca and growled low and from her gut. Rebecca fell backward and screamed.

Heather smiled down at her. "Now are you scared of me?" She tickled Rebecca's sides and they both rolled on the ground laughing. I hid my smile and walked away.

Peach was the first person I reached. "That was a bit harsh, don't you think?"

I shrugged. "Maybe. But that kid is miserable. She needs to learn to let go and have fun. Even if it means I have to make her." I started in the direction of my canoe. As I passed Camille I said, "You're with me the rest of the trip." She jumped up and followed on my heels.

For the rest of the trip I was distracted. I kept our boat close to the pack so that Camille would not get bored. She carried on conversations with the others across the water. I remained in my own head. So many thoughts were climbing around inside me. My conversations with Heather. My frustration with Rebecca. Brie's close brush with death. It all had sent my brain into overdrive.

The sounds of gurgling water and laughing children and splashing paddles provided a background for my thoughts. As we floated down the river, they turned to my mother. I remembered her telling me to wear armor to protect myself from life. I remembered my football helmet. Rebecca was wearing her cap to protect herself from life. Mama eventually said you couldn't really do anything about it, just get ready.

She was right the second time. That's what I wanted Rebecca to see. Life came at you, and sometimes it would completely crush you. Just like the canoe had crushed Brie. Just like Mama's death had crushed me. Just like Heather's mama's death had surely crushed her. Those things would happen. There wasn't anything you could do to stop it. All you could do is brace yourself, and when it passed, try to get up and continue.

I thought of Mama's analogy of fighting kudzu. Maybe Rebecca's attempt to protect herself from everything was her own version of fighting kudzu. I concluded that everyone has their own version of fighting kudzu. We all have something that we want to stop, but we just can't. It just keeps coming back. I considered what it was in my own life that I fought, but just kept returning. I was stumped. I couldn't think of anything, even though I was sure it was there.

We got to the next set of rapids and Camille and I shot through first. She didn't seem the least bit afraid as we passed through the rocks. At the end, I steered us into an eddy behind a boulder, and we watched the others come through.

Heather and Rebecca were in the third boat. Rebecca came towards us with her eyes closed, gripping tightly to the boat. Heather maneuvered the craft perfectly and let out a war cry as she did. Everyone made it safely through the section and we went back to our leisurely float.

Rebecca was now laughing and talking with Heather. Her body had relaxed, the tension gone from her shoulders and white knuckles. She paddled along at a slow pace, digging into the water and pulling it backward with a new confidence.

At the third set of rapids, we followed the same order. Camille and I waiting at the bottom, while the other boats passed us by one at a time. As Rebecca and Heather approached the fast water, Rebecca was using her paddle to power the canoe. A smile was etched on her face. As they successfully passed, this time they both let out the war cry. I couldn't help but smile at the change.

I guided our boat alongside Rebecca. "Good job, Beck!"

She looked over at me and her smile faded. "Thanks." She turned away and began to paddle hard, causing their boat to surge well ahead of ours.

We finally shot the last set of rapids and found ourselves at the end of our ride. We all pulled our canoes to a sandy beach with a short path that led to a road. The effort it took to unload our gear and to get the canoes out of the water and loaded on the trailers was almost more than we could muster. The long day had finally taken its toll on everyone, and we were moving slowly.

We all changed into dry clothes that we had waiting for us in the vans. By the time we were all packed and settled in for the drive back to Camp Timberline, half of the girls had already dozed off. By the time we had been on the road for ten minutes, they were all snoozing. It was all I could do to keep my own eyes open for the drive. I rolled the window down and turned the radio up loud. I sang along as the wind whipped through my hair. I was happy. Very happy.

Back at camp we unloaded and stored everything, ate a cold dinner, took showers, and everyone hit the bunks. Umiak was silent as soon as everyone got in their cabins. No one had to be encouraged to go to bed. The girls were tired and content. The trip had been a wonderful experience for them all. Sleep came easily.

I lay in my own bunk, however, and tossed and turned. Despite my incredible exhaustion, sleep would not take me. I tried to erase everything from my mind. I created a blank slate in my head, but it didn't help. I just didn't want it to stay blank. I kept seeing the words, *Fighting Kudzu, Fighting Kudzu.* What was I fighting?

I felt the sting of tears in my eyes. I jumped from my bed and grabbed my flashlight. I crossed the campsite to the bathroom by the light of the moon, leaving my flashlight dark. I entered the cinder block building and leaned on a sink. I was fighting the tears that wanted to emerge. I was happy. I didn't want to cry.

I looked up at the mirror that was attached to the wall above the sink. I saw a round nose and round cheeks made pink by a day in the sun. I saw a thick mop of short, blonde hair sticking out in every direction. I saw dusty blue eyes, red around the edges, tired. I saw my own face, but somehow I didn't recognize it.

I bent over the sink and splashed cold water on my face. I looked back at the mirror. Nothing had changed except that now water droplets rolled down my face and dripped from my chin. *Who was I?* I wanted to know: *Who is Noble Thorvald?*

Memories flashed across the mirror. *Noble was a quirky five-year-old who played with imaginary football players. Noble was a shy, responsible fourth grader who took care of her mother and excelled in school. Noble was a boisterous, intellectual, unusual sixteen-year-old who used humor as a defense mechanism. Noble was a writer, a camp counselor. Noble sought fame and fortune. Noble was a loner who would never let herself get too close to anyone. Noble was a trendsetter who wanted to be remembered. Could this be Noble Thorvald?*

I could no longer contain the tears. They flowed from me. I continued to lean over the sink and the tears rained down on the white porcelain. In that instant, I finally understood my own kudzu. I was fighting myself. I was keeping my own identity at bay, suppressed by identities I had created for myself. I realized I didn't want to know who Noble really was, but she kept creeping back on me.

"Are you okay?"

The sudden intrusion caught me by surprise and I looked up quickly. Heather and Rebecca were standing in the doorway, both dressed in giant T-shirts down to their knees.

I wiped my eyes quickly, trying to keep my tears from the two girls. "I'm fine. What are you guys doing up?"

"Rebecca had to use the bathroom and I came with her."

Rebecca quickly added, "Not because I was afraid, but because you said we should go everywhere with a buddy."

I looked at the sink, avoiding their faces. "Okay. Well, that's good."

"Why are you crying?" Heather was now standing at my shoulder.

"Yeah. Why?" Rebecca still stood in the doorway.

"Oh. That. Just something in my eye. No big deal."

"Liar." Rebecca was now coming toward me. "I know tears. And you're crying." She sat on one of the benches.

Heather joined her. "Yeah. Spill it. What's wrong."

"Nothing you guys need to worry about."

Rebecca scooted forward and firmly said, "Tell us."

"Yeah. We want to help."

"It's really nothing you can help with."

"Well, then we can listen." Rebecca slid back against the wall.

I sighed. "It's really stupid."

Heather rolled her eyes.

I sat down between them. "I'm just trying to figure out who I am."

They giggled. "That's easy. You're Phoenix." Heather smiled at me.

"Ugh. That doesn't help. I'm really *not* Phoenix."

"Well. That's too bad, because Phoenix taught me a bunch of cool new stuff that I had never done before."

Rebecca added, "And Phoenix had the courage to save a girl's life today."

"Phoenix always takes good care of her campers."

"Phoenix is nice, but knows how to let people know she's in charge."

"Phoenix is funny."

Rebecca hesitated. "Phoenix taught me how to believe in myself. And trust people. And have fun."

My tears once again rolled in full force. These two young girls were touching me at my core. I had never felt this special before. And it felt nice.

Heather sighed. "Why are you crying again?"

"Because I wish I was Phoenix." I laughed. "She sounds pretty awesome."

In unison they said, "You *are* Phoenix."

We all laughed, and we grabbed each other in a three way hug. "Thanks guys. That really helped. You made me feel better." I gave them both a squeeze.

Rebecca wriggled free. "Good. 'Cause I really, really have to pee." She jumped up and scurried into one of the stalls.

Two days later, camp was cleaned, campers were packed, and everyone was waiting for parents to show up and take them home. The girls were all incredibly excited. They buzzed around main camp, squealing about what they would do first as soon as they got home. They shared all their memories of their four weeks at camp, getting themselves ready to share it all with their families.

I was feeling very melancholy about losing this group of campers. They had become special to me. I felt we had shared several special moments. To keep my sadness from dampening their palpable excitement, I stayed to myself. I busied myself at the checkout table, stacking and re-stacking pamphlets, checking and rechecking check lists. I felt a presence in front of me. I looked up from my busy work to see Rebecca standing before me.

"Hi." Her voice was quiet.

"Hi." I smiled. "All ready to get out of here?"

"Yeah." She fumbled with a container of pencils on the table. "I just wanted to say thanks. Before I leave."

"Oh? What for?"

She looked up at me. Her hair was a beautiful tangle of tight brown curls. Her big eyes were a lovely gray color, flashing under her long lashes. It occurred to me that I never really noticed what she looked like. All I had ever seen when I looked at her was the tan ball cap. Without it, her beauty was evident.

"Just for making me try stuff."

"Well, you are *certainly* welcome."

"I'm serious. I should have known better than to be afraid with you around."

I furrowed my brow and tilted my head. She continued. "You. Bear. Peach. Kiwi. You would never let any of us get hurt. I should have trusted you from the beginning."

I relaxed and leaned on the table. "Beck, I just wanted you to

261

know that you could do that stuff. I wanted you to have confidence in yourself. Trust yourself, as well as the people around you."

"I know. And I do." She shook her thick hair. "I'm starting to. I'll get there."

I reached over and tugged at one of her curls. "I'm proud of you."

She smiled. "Well, thanks. You know, for everything."

"You're welcome. And thank *you*, for teaching me a thing or two."

She giggled. "No problem." She came around the table and gave me a long hug.

"Me too, me too." I felt another set of skinny arms encircle me from behind.

I pushed out of their clutches and turned to see Heather's tan face beaming up at me. "I just wanted to get in on the hug."

"Of course." I lightly punched her on the shoulder.

We were interrupted by the sound of gravel crunching under tires. We all looked toward the parking lot to see the first of the luxury cars pulling in.

Several hours later, the campers were gone. I said brief goodbyes to them all as they trotted and skipped off with their parents. They were all far too excited to understand my sadness. They drove away amid clouds of dust and waves of excited energy. I waved goodbye to the backs of cars as I watched them roll out of my life.

I spent the following weeks, prior to my fall return to school, contemplating the path of my future. I considered what I had learned about myself at camp that summer. I realized, while I wanted to be special, while I wanted to leave a permanent impression on the world, while I wanted to be financially secure, I wasn't pursuing these goals in the best possible way. I was making career decisions without considering what I enjoyed and what I

262

was good at.

My summer at Camp Timberline opened my eyes to what those things were. I was an active person who was good at showing others how to do things. I was an open-minded person who was struck by the wonder and innocence of children. I was a student who always wanted to learn more. I was a young person who already had a world of experience to share.

I combined all of this, and made a discovery that seemed it should have always been obvious. I discovered what I felt was my calling in life. I went back to Mars Hill and immediately changed my major, again. I officially became an education major and began my passionate pursuit of a career as a teacher.

There were so many things that played in to this decision— most of them my own personal traits. But, in the end, I knew that I didn't simply desire to become a teacher in order to mold young minds. I knew that I wanted to be a teacher, not so much for what the kids could learn from me, but more for what I could learn from the kids. I knew in my heart that youth is defined as much by wisdom as anything else. I valued the knowledge that children possessed early in life, before it was stripped away and replaced by knowledge that is valued by society.

I gave up fighting my kudzu. I stopped wrestling with my identity. I discovered who I was and I accepted and embraced it. I was Noble Thorvald. I was a person who wanted to always know the joy of childhood. I was an adult who had lost my childhood to unnecessary worry and responsibility. I was an adult who wanted my childhood back, and who planned on never giving it away again. I was a lost soul who wanted to be found, and who wanted to help other children realize their worth, and eternally hang on to their youthful lust for life.

LaVergne, TN USA
19 May 2010
183262LV00002B/1/P